'Carroll's writing is astonishingly assured'

James Bradley, *Australian Book Review*

'by extending the characters' inner worlds out into the wider physical landscape the novel is told in a languid prose that flows with the speed of contemplation'

Perry Middlemiss, *Matilda* (online)

'Carroll's a rare beast in that he writes with great affection and understanding about life in the suburbs ... A lovely rites of passage novel that is oh so carefully crafted and captures the evanescence of time to perfection. Don't worry that it's a sequel; it works beautifully as a stand alone'

Jason Steger, *The Age*

'If, as they say, the past is another country, then Carroll is the ideal guide'

Paul Maley, *Sydney Morning Herald*

'an achievement of subtle force, a fictional performance that stands as one of the most uncommon and quietly arresting in Australia this year'

Peter Pierce, *Canberra Times*

'A must-read'

Australian Publisher & Bookseller

'Steven Carroll evokes adulthood with the eye of a child, curious and greedy for the future, whatever promises life may have broken'

Le Figaro

Praise for *The Art of the Engine Driver*:

'subtle, true and profoundly touching ... from the first lines of this very beautiful novel by Steven Carroll, an indefinable charm is at work'

Le Monde

'A veritable little gem ... a beautiful discovery'

Elle France

'*The Art of the Engine Driver* is a stunning work of masterful storytelling and sparing, assured prose'

Télérama

'Carroll has choreographed his story too well to be obvious. Resist the urge to flip to the end. It's the journey that rewards in this book, not the destination'

The Age

'a superb evocation of an almost-lost Australia, good or bad'

Matt Condon, *Sun-Herald*

'A brilliant novel'

Brigitte

'Deceptively simple, this novel has a quiet force that gathers dramatic dimensions as the party proceeds and as the Spirit of Progress, driven by Vic's teacher and hero, speeds towards them in the dark'

Debra Adelaide, *Sydney Morning Herald*

'An exquisitely crafted journey of Australian suburban life ... fresh and irresistible'

Miles Franklin Literary Award Judges, 2002

Steven Carroll was born in Melbourne. He was educated at La Trobe University and taught English in high schools before playing in bands in the 1970s. After leaving the music scene he began writing as a playwright and later became the theatre critic for the *Sunday Age*.

His first novel, *Remember Me, Jimmy James*, was published in 1992. This was followed by *Momoko* (1994), *The Love Song of Lucy McBride* (1998), and then *The Art of the Engine Driver* (2001) and *The Gift of Speed* (2004), shortlisted for the Miles Franklin Award in 2002 and 2005, respectively. *The Art of the Engine Driver* was also shortlisted in 2005 for the Prix Femina, France's prestigious literary award for the best foreign novel.

Steven Carroll lives in Melbourne with his partner and son.

Also by Steven Carroll:

Remember Me, Jimmy James

Momoko

The Love Song of Lucy McBride

The Art of the Engine Driver

The Gift of Speed

The Time We Have Taken

Steven Carroll

FOURTH ESTATE • *London, New York, Sydney* and *Auckland*

This project has been assisted by the Commonwealth Government through the Australia Council, its arts funding and advisory body

Fourth Estate
An imprint of HarperCollins*Publishers*

First published in Australia in 2007
by HarperCollins*Publishers* Australia Pty Limited
ABN 36 009 913 517
www.harpercollins.com.au

Copyright © Steven Carroll 2007

HarperCollins*Publishers*
25 Ryde Road, Pymble, Sydney, NSW 2073, Australia
31 View Road, Glenfield, Auckland 10, New Zealand
77–85 Fulham Palace Road, London, W6 8JB, United Kingdom
2 Bloor Street East, 20th floor, Toronto, Ontario M4W 1A8, Canada
10 East 53rd Street, New York NY 10022, USA

Carroll, Steven, 1949– .
  The time we have taken.
  ISBN 13: 978 0 7322 7836 6.
  ISBN 10: 0 7322 7836 8.
  1. Suburban life – Australia – Fiction.
  I. Title.
A823.3

Cover design by Darren Holt, HarperCollins Design Studio
Cover image: Getty Images
Author photograph: Ponch Hawkes
Typeset in 11.5/16 Hoefler Text by Kirby Jones
Printed and bound in Australia by Griffin Press.

70gsm Bulky Book Ivory used by HarperCollins*Publishers*, is a natural,
recyclable product made from wood grown in sustainable forests. The
manufacturing processes confrom to the environmental regulations in
the country of origin being Finland.

6 5 4   08 09 10

To the memory of William Francis Carroll (1917–1984)

and

to Jean Irene Carroll (nee Williams)
born 1921

contents

Part Three

Winter

Part Four

Spring

Part Five

Envoi

1970

Part One

Summer

I.

The Birth of an Idea

As Peter van Rijn steps onto his driveway and opens the door of his old Ford Anglia, he is conscious only of the enormous heat pouring down from the sky upon the houses, driveways and sprinkled lawns of the suburb. He doesn't know he is about to give birth to an idea. The car is still cool as he eases himself onto the worn leather seat and closes the driver's door. Ideas are far from his mind, sensations are all he registers. It is one of those mid-January days that hit early and hit hard, demanding the conservation of all effort — including the effort of thinking. And yet, for all this, by the time Peter van Rijn has entered the Old Wheat Road, where his television-and-wireless shop has stood for the last fifteen years, he will have given birth to an idea of such significance to the suburb that it will become the reference point for all official events in the coming year. And the unofficial. The still point around which the wheel of the four seasons will spin. Few events will take place without someone first referring to Peter van Rijn's brainchild, possibly the one truly inspired moment in his carefully ordered life.

He slowly backs onto the tarred road; although, now cool it will be soft and shimmering under a relentless sky by midday. The Anglia, meticulously tuned and polished, purrs up the street past George Bedser's, where the frail, solitary, retired frame of Bedser himself is stooped over his roses. There is a wave ready if Bedser should look up, but he doesn't. Peter van Rijn turns left at the top of his street, then right, glancing at the empty playing field of the primary school. When February begins in a couple of weeks, and the schools are back, the children of the suburb will once more assume sovereignty over the grounds, but not quite yet. As Peter passes the St Matthew's tennis courts, the caretaker slowly raking the russet surface, his mind is dwelling silently on the tasks of the day.

He is proud of his shop and has always been careful to do all he can to ensure that anybody who opens his door will feel good about entering. It is his first rule of shops, that a customer should feel good — better than they felt on the footpath — about being inside. He has always made sure that in winter he arrives early enough to warm the shop, and in summer early enough to put the fans to work. It is, he has always felt, a responsibility, and not just a civic one.

It was Peter van Rijn who, in the summer of 1956, first brought TV to the suburb. Peter van Rijn who displayed the latest televisions in his shop window so that shoppers and commuters might pause, summer or winter, and be pleasantly distracted as they watched the cartoon antics of a black-and-white mouse on a flickering screen. And he is now convinced that it was more than mere amusement that he offered shoppers and commuters back then when the suburb sat on the frontier of the city and those low, flat paddocks of tall grass and thistle marked the margins of Progress. His window, he liked to think, gave comfort, the way a well-lighted window in a warm shop does.

There are times even now, special events, when he sets the televisions up in the window once more. But rarely. And it is at this moment (barely aware of his hands on the wheel), as he is dwelling on the time they have all consumed, on the shop as it was then and the shop as it is now, on the suburb then and now, and all in such a way that it *feels* like history, real history, that a half-digested fact from a previous day's casual reading suddenly surfaces. A photograph in the local newspaper of a road junction, a few farm houses on a wide landscape, and — what caught his eye — the first wooden store to come to the community. And beneath that the date: 1870. It has since been rebuilt, a double-storey brick terrace, and is now occupied by the greengrocer, with a later date displayed upon it. The memory of the article rushes up to him with the speed of the T-intersection at the Old Wheat Road ahead of him. Scattered farms counted for nothing. Scattered farms don't even make a hamlet, or whatever it is that lies beneath a hamlet in levels of significance. But a shop, that was different. That is where things begin. A shop marks the arrival of Progress. A shop brings with it all the latest wonders the production process has to offer. A shop, is, in short, the flag of settlement. It was — this single, wooden general store (and his conviction is absolute) — the point at which the suburb could look back and say that is when we began. And, in a flash, before he even crosses the intersection and enters the Old Wheat Road, he knows that this is the year to pronounce the suburb one hundred years old. And if nobody else had noticed the significance of the date until now, it was because it took a shopkeeper to see it.

Somewhere between the tennis courts of St Matthew's Church and the Old Wheat Road, an idea had sprung from him like water from a garden sprinkler. This was, indeed, a year of great significance. And, instead of stopping at his shop early enough to set the fans in motion, Peter van Rijn continues straight on to the newly completed town hall almost a mile north of his shop, along one of the two major roads of the suburb.

The car park at this early hour — it is not yet eight — is virtually empty. But the mayor's car is in its appointed place, and Peter van Rijn strides across the car park towards the glass front doors of the town hall like a man with vital news that must be heard without a second's delay.

2.

Rita's Day Begins

Oh, God. He's at it again. She'll have to prod him. If it goes on much longer, she'll just have to give him a good jab. But even that will only buy her a few minutes of silence. Five minutes at most. If only he could hear himself, snorting and spluttering like one of those old engines he once drove. And as soon as the word 'engine' enters her thoughts, she can see and smell his old work clothes as if they were in the room. It's a good smell. Steam and soot. And something else, that sense of having been somewhere, of having travelled, and of having brought back with them the faintest scent of distant towns. His overalls, his shirt and that orange jumper she knitted for him (because he doesn't wear enough bright clothes), which he eventually wore to work (and that was the end of that), all drenched with the smell of engines and driving and night shifts that went on clear into the morning fill the room along with his snoring. And she knows she'll have to jab him or she'll get no peace or sleep.

And so she raises her arm and rolls to his side of the bed, only to find that the bed ends and if she doesn't watch it she'll fall out onto the floor. Has she rolled to the wrong side? No, she hasn't. She's rolled to his side. But he's not there. He must be. It was his snoring that woke her. Or did she give him a prod already, and fall back to sleep, and did he get up when she did? Whatever, he's not there and she's run out of bed.

Rita opens her eyes, looks around the dark room (either still night or early morning), and nods slowly to herself. He's not there, because he's not. Hasn't been for years. And she's run out of bed because it's not their old bed she's sleeping in. That went years ago too. It's her bed, neither small nor big. And the snoring she heard was the snoring that comes in dreams. He doesn't even have to be here any more to disturb her sleep and wake her.

She sits up, head back. Of all the things to miss. Of all the things to retrieve in dreams. She brings his snoring back. She ought to smile at that, but she hasn't got a smile in her. Nor a grin. He's this lost limb that she still thinks is there sometimes. And she checks her clock and is relieved to discover that it's almost morning and she doesn't have to try to sleep through the rest of the night. She's already done that. And slept well, till this snoring of Vic's woke her.

Now that it's gone, she is suddenly aware of the silence of the room, the silence of the house, and the whole suburb out there. Still sleeping. No cars, too early for the birds even. It's too early to get up, and too late to go back to sleep. And so she sits and decides to wait for the first glimmer of light to announce itself behind the thick curtains that shroud the room. Something tells her it's not right to get up and dress and breakfast in the dark when you don't have to, so she resolves to sit and watch and wait.

And it's as she resolves upon this course of action — or inaction — that she hears the first sound of the day. A distant car accelerates into the new morning, breaking the all-encompassing silence, and she knows that out there life is beginning to stir. And she can see it (if she closes her eyes), she can see it all from her room. Kitchens blinking into light, kettles billowing steam, the babble of radios, the opening and closing of doors, and the first footsteps of the morning resounding out there on the porches and driveways of the suburb as a new day revs into action.

The sound of just one car can do that. Make you feel like you're part of something. Remind you that there's something out there, after all. And as she ponders this, she watches with quiet wonder as the first beam of the day lights the edges of the bedroom window and the world comes back to her. Familiar, but new. And something lifts in her, lifts her heart, her chest, her whole body. She doesn't know what, but suddenly she's ridiculously happy. A shiver runs down her spine, and she's delirious at the thought of a warm cup of tea and one of those thick old crumpets she bought yesterday. Now she can't wait to get at the day. It's the wonder that's done that. She rests back for a moment to take it in. Where *does* it come from? And why doesn't it come all the time?

Yet even as she asks herself where all the wonder goes and why she doesn't feel it every morning, she knows the answer. You can't. You can't live with wonder in you all the time or you'd just burst.

And it is only as she swings out of bed that she remembers what day it is. Wednesday. And one look at the clock tells her that the horses of time are bolting, and that if she doesn't watch it she'll be late. They'll tell you, she says to herself, remembering the famous words of somebody or other as she heads for the bathroom, they'll tell you you've got all the time in the world, but the fact is you haven't got a minute to lose.

By the time Peter van Rijn is back in his shop after having informed the mayor of the significance of the year, the business of Rita's day is beginning. Carrying a shopping bag and fanning herself with the local newspaper, she strolls up the street that has been hers for just over fifteen years now. She came here as a young wife with a young husband and a young child in those distant days when the suburb marked the frontier of civilised life, a place so primitive she could never conceive of it as ever feeling like home. Now she is alone. Vic has gone north as he always said he would, Michael left the suburb as soon as he was old enough, and the house that was theirs became hers. And the street and the suburb that had always been beyond the pale, slowly, unobtrusively, became home.

The things she couldn't give Vic any more because he didn't want them (and in his heart he had moved on long before he left), the things she couldn't give Michael because her boy had outgrown her and all the things she offered, the things she couldn't give either of them any more (and which she had given away so freely then), she now put into the house. And the house took them in and together they grew. The French windows, the lace curtains, the brilliant white of the weatherboards, the garden lights that shone like so many full moons on summer nights, the new fence, the fancy European number on the letter box. These were the things she gave the house and that the house happily accepted. And knew she could safely give all such things to the house because the house wasn't going anywhere. They spoke of care, these things she gave it, and with the care came the anxiety, the dread almost, of wondering whatever might happen to the house should she ever leave it. And sometimes, because she knows she can't live forever, she even contemplates the fate of the house when she is gone and there is no one to care for it. Somehow, she had taken this inanimate object, and turned it into a living thing. One that lived for her, and responded to her inspired touches, and sparkled with delight when she brought the painters in or added something to it that wasn't there before, but which made all the difference. Michael, now living in the city with all his university types in the houses his parents fled from for this kind of suburb, is continually asking her why she stays. And she can't say. How could she? How could she say that to leave the house now would be a betrayal? To live in another, almost an infidelity. Silly to think of it like that, but think of it like that she does, as she closes the white metal gate and smiles upon the gleaming white splendour of her creation. The house she has always wanted (as a child, as a young wife) is now hers. The finest house in the street. The house of her dreams.

As she strolls up her street, she takes a quiet pride in contemplating the lesser constructions along the way, or pleasantly noting a garden here or a decorated window there that might provide her with some useful ideas. The street, once all mud or all dust and where dogs once howled like beasts from the Middle Ages, has mellowed into a pleasant walk; Rita's place — the one they all notice, even pause at, when the street passes, even if they don't much care for its fancy touches in the same way they've never cared for her fancy dresses.

Rita once demonstrated washing machines, ironing boards, blenders, ovens, anything that was new and that people were drawn to, but about which they felt uncertain. It was her job to show them the future in the form of the latest vacuum cleaners, the future contained in the present. There ready-to-hand, by those who knew how to use them. She assembled, demonstrated and disassembled the very instruments of Progress. Ready-to-hand became unready-to-hand when, say, a mix-master was broken down to its constituent parts, then, magically, ready-to-hand once more when swiftly reassembled. In this way she often amazed many a suburban and country audience. Like Peter van Rijn, she too brought Progress to the suburb, only she never thought of it like that at the time. She, who once commanded whole shop floors and country auditoriums crammed with women out for a little lunchtime entertainment as much as shopping.

But these days she's more than content to be looking after the Webster mansion. A year ago she answered a notice in the local paper and for the first time met Mrs Webster, who, more or less, stepped into her husband's office and slipped into his chair, not long after the fifty-seven-year-old Webster, known by the suburb simply as Webster the factory, drove at great speed out of this world and into local history. An unfortunate accident that left the suburb shaking its head at the pity of it all.

Rita likes houses. And they respond to her. The Webster mansion, over the last twelve months, has responded to her touches, like an armchair bears the imprint of a frequent sitter. It's a large old house, but easy to clean. Pleasant to be in, and, on days such as this, cool like an oasis.

As she turns into Mrs Webster's street, the drooping branches of the plane trees alive with invisible cicadas, she pulls a letter for Vic out of her dress pocket and slips it into the red post box, and, as she does, there is a faint sensation of touching him, as there always is. He may have gone north to that little fishing town that is no longer little, but he's still out there. And she knows where he is. And she can picture him there. Doing something. Right now. These are the things that matter. And the phrase 'stay in touch' means more to her these days than it ever did before. However fanciful it might seem, there is that faint sense of hands touching whenever she drops a letter in the post because she knows he will pick the letter up and his fingers will be pressed to the envelope where hers once rested. She calls that touch. And why not? In many ways she's never felt so intimate with him. It's not simply the shared envelopes, it is the words inside. She has said more to Vic in these letters over the years he has been gone than she ever did when they shared the house whose silences, in the end, were too great for both of them to bear.

At the Webster gate she scans that long winding driveway leading up to the pillared front door and the expansive gardens of this colonial estate and has the distinct feeling (which the young Michael did years before, although he never told her) of not so much stepping into another part of the suburb, as another country.

3.

Vic's Day Begins: the Rabbit, the Field and the Observer

Vic, in his bed, in his one-bedroom flat, a thousand miles to the north in the town he now calls home, is dreaming. His nose is in the air, that great hooter that Rita always said you could hang your hat on, and is blowing out air as if from the funnel of any of those great engines he drove for most of his life before coming here. His body is lying down in deep sleep in the sub-tropical warmth of this town to which he has come, but his mind, free to wander, is elsewhere.

There is a rabbit in the middle of an open field. The grass is winter green under the frost. This rabbit is standing on its hind legs, its nose to the air, its ears alert to the slightest noise, its eyes to the slightest movement. Its hole and the safety of its burrow is not far away, but, for the moment, this rabbit is at its most vulnerable. Food brings the rabbit up. All that lush winter grass under a coating of white frost. A long, thin, blue metal barrel is kept perfectly still and is aimed directly at the rabbit. Vic cannot see the hand that supports the barrel, nor the fingers poised round the trigger. He can see only the barrel, and the rabbit, at the end of an imaginary line that runs from sights to target.

But even in this perfect, still morning, the rabbit is alert to something. For whatever reason, it knows that something is present in this quiet field that ought not be present, and that the very stillness of the field and trees and sky is not a natural one in which creatures and grass mingle in harmonious ease. No, it is an unnatural stillness, one that contains tension, not harmony, the kind that comes before a disturbance. The rabbit knows all of this somewhere deep in its core, somehow knows that the barrel of a .22 rifle is pointed directly at it — even though the rabbit itself is not looking in that direction.

Its ears are working frantically. Its nose is twitching in the air. It smells danger and everything about the rabbit suggests it is about to flee, to fly back down into its hole where there is no danger. But it doesn't. Perhaps, in that same core that tells the animal it is in danger, it also realises that its moment of death is upon it and so it doesn't move. The moving and the not moving will not alter the structure of the picture — the rabbit, the field and the observer — its time has come and nothing will alter that. It is suddenly lifted from the ground. And, simultaneous to this, the quiet of the morning is shattered by an explosive cracking sound that reverberates all around the field like a cannon shot. As the rabbit is lifted and the silence is broken, field and sky respond, and all the potential for movement that was concealed behind leaves and branches and tufts of grass is released. Birds, all black, hundreds upon hundreds, burst from the trees bordering the field and take to the sky. Hundreds upon hundreds that swell into flocks of thousands take wing. And, within seconds, the clear sky is black. The pale, mid-winter sun is blotted out and darkness falls across the field. Pitch, country darkness. A darkness so dense no normal dawn could ever wash it away.

And in the middle of the field, under the black morning sky, the fourteen-year-old Vic (holding a dead rabbit by the hind legs with one hand, and a rifle with the other), stunned by the enormity of what he has unleashed, stands, stock still, staring up at the sky, wondering where on earth the sun could possibly have gone. Or if this darkness at the beginning of the day where there shouldn't be darkness is the new order of things. The black sky ripples with wings, from one end of the horizon to the other, and the trees bend in the disturbed air. And the boy, the centre of this disturbance, the cause of it, remains perfectly still in its midst. But he is no longer looking up at the sky. He is, through the wonder of dreams, peering forward into those years that he will live, where the Vic that he will become now lies, moving uneasily in sub-tropical slumbers.

That great hooter gushes air; sleep and the dream shudder to a halt, and Vic's eyes snap open, at first not knowing where on earth they are. A bedroom, yes. But which of the bedrooms, of the houses of his life, has he woken to? It is dark; everything is a mystery. And if this could be any of the bedrooms in any of the houses of his life, he could be any age. And he could be waking to any of his days, lived or unlived. He has no idea where he is. Is he alone in this place or in the company of others? Although his eyes are open, his mind is still back there in the dream and is slow to catch up. Then he recognises the sparsely furnished, simple bedroom of his flat and he knows that he is alone.

He was told that age would work like this. Not that he is old, but the years of drink, ignoring the pills that the doctors over the years have prescribed him and the years of being at war with himself, have taken their toll and he feels old, old beyond his years. And this is confirmed in people's eyes, for he can tell — if only by looking in the mirror himself — that he not only feels old, he looks old. He is tired now in a way that he was never tired before. The tiredness of the past, of youth, could be fixed with a good sleep. But now he wakes up as weary as he was when he went to bed. He is not surprised that he should be continually going back the way he does now day after day. What does surprise him is the clarity of it all. The clarity of his dreams, of his memories. And the things that his memory throws up, for no apparent reason, that he could have sworn he'd forgotten all about.

Vic lies back in his bed, darkness all around him, half a mind to walk back into that dreaming field, to the tiny hamlet where he grew up, as if he could open the back door of his flat and it would be there. He knows that field and all that lies around it. The sodden paddocks, the rusted wire and rotted wooden fences slowly sinking back into the soft earth, the deep footprints that cross the paddocks of his memory and lead back to the small wooden farm house a half mile from where the rabbit blithely skipped into the air as if breaking into a jig. He is familiar with all that is in the picture and all that is not. The intersection of dirt tracks that marks the centre of the hamlet, the three houses that cling to the tracks, the cricket ground that is no more than a cow paddock with a concrete pitch in the middle, the red-brick Swiss Family Hotel, and the faint path that leads off the road down into a deep gully where clear spring waters gurgle freely. It is all before him, the playground of his youth, the place to which his mother took him as a boy and in which they lived years that he knew, even at the time, were happy years. The dream gave him a clear picture of the field he has not seen since then but which he knows, even now, so well. Such are the wonders of dreams.

Vic is happy enough in this sub-tropical town to which he has come. It is compact, it is convenient, and all the things he requires to maintain this state of being happy enough — pub, shops, golf course, Services club, and people who are friendly without getting too friendly — are all here, a step or two away. Michael is grown. The boy, he is sure, will look after himself better than the old man ever did. And he and Rita are better off this way. It had to be done. The shooting through. It was rotted, the old life. They're better off. There's even a tenderness in the words they write to each other now, a tenderness that hadn't been there for years.

He imagines a chorus of 'Poor Vic' from all those who knew him in the old life. Among them, those who rot back there in that stuck-up town that calls itself a city, those who rot rather than shoot through because they are too weak to live. Poor sad Vic, they might say. Even poor silly Vic. But they can stick their poor sad Vics, and they can stick their sad, rotted comforts. He never looked for them. He never wanted them. But he got them anyway. They force them on you, their comforts, he muses, stretching out in bed. Because once they've got you wrapped up in all their comforts, they've got *you*. And you're not you any more, you're them. This is the other Vic, the one who went through the motions. This is the Vic he calls the 'they-Vic', the Vic that fell in between 'then-Vic' and 'now-Vic'.

The sky at the window is beginning to brighten and Vic watches night give way to day. Normally, the light is there when he opens his eyes because he is a good sleeper. But not lately. Lately, he is disturbed by dreams, the same kinds of dreams. Lately, he is always back there somewhere. He hasn't seen that field for forty years. It may still be there, may not. May be changed, may be miraculously the same. The dream got it right, though. He knew it, every detail. And it wasn't before him, or in front of him. He was simply in it. And it was as natural as being anywhere else. Being old, being young. Being here, or there. There was nothing so surprising about any of it. Fourteen one minute, old the next. And it was so easy it was frightening. Is this what comes with age? This ability to step in and out of the phases of your life as if the show's all over and all you're living through is a kind of summing up? Whatever, the years are with him, and all that they bring with them, wherever his wanderings around the town may take him.

This small one-bedroom flat has been his home since walking away from the old life. It's a modest 1920s number. Nothing fancy. Bare walls, bare linoleum floors. Sea green. A bed, a chair and a table here and there. No TV, only a small transistor radio in the lounge room, a reading lamp, books and newspapers. Clean, sparse. Sad to some, no doubt. Not a comfortable place, and that's why he likes it. These are the digs of someone who has returned to being what he always was — a single man. He is at his most content when his life is simple. A simple flat, a simple daily round, predictable from one day to the next. The comforts of the past, the being plural, the 'us', the 'we', the 'them' — it was never him. They can stick their comforts. He reclines on the pillow, the morning lights the edges of the chocolate-brown holland blind that covers the window. There are no curtains, no lace, no comforts of home, for the comforts of home belong to another Vic, the Vic who spent twenty years being them, not him.

He rises from bed and prepares for the day, and each day is a duplication of the other: shopping, checking the post, a pub lunch, a few beers, golf, a few beers, home and dinner, then the club, and a few beers, and a few beers more for good measure. Every day, they all tell each other up here, is a Sunday. There's no other Vic, going through the motions, up here, just the Vic that always was. Good-time Vic, who doesn't need to look ahead too far and make plans because every day is more or less the same. Every day plans itself, and all he has to do is step into it, as he is now preparing to do. Vic's day is about to begin.

4.

Mrs Webster at Work

Webster's noise, the noise that Webster brought to the suburb when he brought the factory, is all around her but she barely notices it any more. The scene is as familiar to her now as it was for Webster, for the chair in which she sits, the mezzanine office and the view out across the factory floor were all once the possession of Webster the factory.

In the ten years that have intervened since his departure, the world outside has transformed but little has changed inside the factory. The view from the mezzanine is still the same, and, although the machines have been replaced from time to time, and staff have come and gone, the sounds, routines and movements of the place — the whole production system — have virtually remained the same. If Webster were to be ushered through the suburb blindfolded, if he were to be left ignorant of the changes that had transformed the outside world and find himself back on the factory floor, he would assume that it had only been a matter of days, not years, since he had been gone. And a brief look at those objects the place produces — the recycled scraps, those isolated parts that are destined for the factories that turn them into the completed objects that are useful to people — would confirm this assumption. Nothing has changed, and this is the problem with the factory. It is a dying factory, and the sounds she hears are the dying falls of a once energetic beast now well into the old age of industrial obsolescence. Mrs Webster recognises all this. Once overloaded with orders, the contracts are now dwindling, the profits down, the precious goodwill draining from the place day by day. But she had sacked no one. Nor will she. It is a dying beast, Webster's factory, and she will let it die a natural death. And when this occurs, surely not many years from now, she will sell the carcass and whatever else is left, and whatever it is that Progress, by then, requires will stand on the same acre and a half of prime suburban land that Webster once ruled from.

She never took over the place to breathe new life into it, or to improve or extend it. It was never her intention, although she had seen clearly years before what had to be done. No, she wanted it to stay the same, to stay as Webster's factory in order for her to finally know just what constituted the mystery that Webster became.

For, if she stayed long enough, if she sat in Webster's chair, viewed the factory floor from Webster's window, kept the same books of profit and loss, and absorbed daily the noise that Webster brought to the suburb when the suburb was being born, then she would surely soon acquire the eyes and ears and fingertip sensations that were Webster's.

And with the eyes and the ears and the sensations would come nothing less than the mind of Webster himself. Webster the factory would live once more, and the centre the suburb thought it had lost would be retained just a few years longer. And when the mind of Webster revealed itself, so too would the mystery of his death.

In the days and weeks that followed his death, it was his absence (especially the physical absence, for Webster was a tall, robust man who filled space) that she felt in every corner of the house, in every corner of the gardens, his absence that cast its shadow over every rare smile that came along in the blur of days after he walked out of the house one warm summer's night while she slept, and drove into local history.

But, as she accustomed herself to his absence, as she adjusted to the cruel fact that the sheer energy of Webster had been extinguished overnight (and when she thought of Webster, she thought of the energy that she so missed), something else began to take hold of her mind until it grew to such an extent that there was only room for one thought — or rather, one question — in a mind that had always been capable of simultaneously balancing any number of fancies; namely, who was this man? The Webster she had lived with throughout the twenty years of their marriage — who drank only imported teas, whose marmalade was laced with marinated ginger and who kept his one infidelity parked under a tarpaulin in a distant corner of the garden — was familiar to her. But not the Webster who drove out into that summer's night ten years ago and never came back. She was familiar with the shape and bulk of Webster, the Webster that he presumably gave to everyone else, but she was denied that part of Webster that held ultimate sway over life and death, that part of Webster that could so easily have accelerated into life, but accelerated, by accident or design, into death. And whenever she contemplated this, she always thought of that distant corner of the garden where the garage was. And with that came the impulse to guard from public eyes everything that was Webster, one minute, and the impulse to tear down Webster the factory, brick by brick, the next.

And so, as the days of her mourning passed and the life of the suburb adjusted to the loss of its centre and eventually moved on, she was left with this one relentless thought — that she had never known him. That the years of their marriage had given her no more privileged access to the mind of Webster than the factory workers or the suburb had. And it was then, not long after his death, that she walked into the factory one morning, looked out across the factory floor, listened to the noise that he had brought to the suburb when the suburb was young and in need of noise, and set about the task of becoming Webster.

She rises from her desk as the factory floor goes quiet and the machinists and staff line up to clock off. As always, she will wait until the factory empties, because Webster always did. Out there, Rita will have completed cleaning the house. It is a large house, and this woman, who has lived in the suburb as long as she has but whom she had never met until she hired her, cleans the house in such a way that is worth every cent Mrs Webster pays her. For it is good, at the end of a day, to walk into a house that has not only been cleaned and polished but invested with something else indefinable that Mrs Webster can only call care. As the last of the giant pressing machines falls silent, she asks herself what Webster might have felt at this time of the working day, listening to the groans of his beast subsiding. Was it satisfaction or pride? Was he stirred by the sight and sound of something so elemental as production; bringing something into the world that wasn't there before he came along, so that the accidental lives of the machinists might find direction, that money and goods might change hands, and the world spin? Or was it the weariness of watching the same repetitive process day after day — and indifference towards all those he employed, who came and went year in year out, and who would, one day, come no more? And as she watches the factory floor drain itself of working life, she wonders if the indifference she too feels at this dead hour of the day might be the doorway into the secret chamber of Webster's mind. Then she dismisses it. Not Webster. She remembers the fire that stayed in his eyes till the last, the passion that he kept for this beast of production that he brought into being and for which he felt an almost paternalistic concern. She could never conceive of him deliberately walking away from the sheer dependency of the thing, any more than she could imagine him losing his passion for rousing the thing each day.

Long after the workers have clocked off, Mrs Webster makes her way to the reserved parking place at the rear of the factory and slips into the driver's seat of her husband's old Bentley. The Bentley that, over the years, became synonymous with Webster the factory, and that glided daily in black majesty from mansion to factory and back, and upon which the suburb gazed as if gazing upon royalty that had only just acquired — with the sheer weight of money — its title. Webster's chauffeur has moved on. She never hired another, and unlike Webster who viewed the world to and from work from the spacious rear seat, she views it from the wheel.

Now, with the mid-January sun low across the suburb, bathing the flour mills in a rich, orange glow, she asks herself again, as she turns the wheel homeward, what Webster felt at this hour of the day. But it has become more of a reflex than a serious endeavour. In her heart of hearts she knows she will never know, and has long since given up on finding out.

5.

A Formal Gathering on the Balcony

There they are. There they will always be. A formal gathering on the balcony. On the brink of the evening, in their gowns and hired suits. As Peter van Rijn is shutting his shop after a day of slow summer trade, and as Rita strolls home and Mrs Webster's Bentley turns into her street (the cicadas now silent), a young woman named Madeleine, a nurse at the main hospital just a short walk away from this inner-city block of flats, leans over the iron railing of her balcony, stares down into the communal garden below and draws in its many scents. They have summoned a taxi, currently floating through the soft light towards them. At first Michael is not told where they are going, or the nature of the occasion. Only that it is a ball. Madeleine then grins at her sister and her friends. The rest, she says, is a mystery. It is, it seems, a game they have all agreed to play. Then she buries her face once more into the summer scents below as the taxi horn sounds in the street.

But even when he learns the nature of the occasion, the evening will always remain a mystery because he forgets upon being told. It is an intoxicating evening (Michael has never been to anything so grandly named as a ball), and years from this night, when he tries to remember where they went, and why they all went there, he will not be able to. He will remember only a suburb somewhere he had never visited before (and quite possibly never seen since), the high white columns of the large public building to which the taxi took them, and open windows, music and wide lawns.

Perfume, what he will later identify as Madeleine's perfume, mingles with less significant scents inside the taxi. She is beside him, talking to her sister in the front seat, to the driver, to the whole cab. He is free to watch her: the red, black and white Bavarian dress that should look all wrong but doesn't, the light brown hair that falls across her shoulders, the fringe, the occasionally lifting eyebrow that tells you she is playing and doesn't really mean what she says, the small gold crucifix that hangs from her neck. This is only the second time they have seen each other, the second time they have 'gone out'. The first time they met (blind date), a week before, he had seen only the traces of a childhood infatuation in her face, shades of a young woman from his old street, shades of the unreachable, nineteen-year-old Patsy Bedser. Patsy Bedser, who, one day in 1958, drove her Morris Minor out the old street and back to Liverpool where she, like

Madeleine, came from; Patsy Bedser, whom he had fallen in love with at the age of twelve, whom he had never forgotten, but whom he could only ever hope to look at. And so that first meeting with Madeleine had awoken in him a nostalgia for someone else. He has not yet gathered much of this thing called 'the past', and nostalgia — he has been the nostalgic type for as long as he can remember — still comes easily, easier than it will when there is more of the past than there is of the future and looking back will cease to be pleasantly melancholic. And so, upon meeting Madeleine for the first time, he was — through the familiarity of her features, through the shades of resemblance she bore to someone else — able to go back and indulge emotions he never dared set free at the time. He could never, he told himself that first night, never love this Madeleine. She would only ever be a kind of gathering place for those legions of adolescent feelings that had assembled themselves inside him years before, legions of feelings that had never been set free, and that had lain in wait all these years for their moment to surface and breathe. And Madeleine was that moment. What did it matter that she was not the actual cause of these feelings, but had simply summoned them? The feeling was good, and he had been content, that first night, to be carried along by it.

But in the breezy, perfumed air of the taxi going God only knows where for God only knows what reason, he sees only Madeleine. The features, the shades of that other, earlier infatuation, have been completely wiped from her face. And it is like seeing her for the first time.

She is now that which she always was and that he was too blinded to see. It is a night of mysteries, but nothing will be more mysterious, now and after, than this revelation.

The river flows slowly down to the docks underneath them as they cross Princes Bridge. When they are over it, he looks back, as he always does when presented with a view of the city from the wrong side. It is a view that is always accompanied by the feeling that there has been a mistake. That he doesn't really belong here. And with that, uncertainty at being out of his territory, of not being in his city but someone else's.

Inside the taxi the talk is loud and constant, outside the parks have the quiet, officially clocked-off look that parks do after a long day. Soon they disappear, the city recedes, and a lost feeling descends upon him. The taxi, over which he has no control (and he doesn't like that feeling either), is speeding away from everything he knows into this other city, which he doesn't know. And when they leave the main road and enter a succession of unfamiliar suburbs he is filled with a fierce, illogical longing for his old street and the children's voices that he and his friends once had when they were young and the street was a world unto itself. He can hear them all clearly and distinguish the twilight voices of his old gang gathered together in summer shadow. Then it passes, and he is aware once more of being sped into the future. And as much as he once lived for speed (for the perfect ball and the kind of speed that would turn heads and be remembered forever after as the ball that Michael bowled), he is now wary, even a little frightened of it. It is a sufficiently distant Michael who bowled a worn cricket ball in the local nets, day after day, throughout his youth, to be a puzzle now. At the time it was all he needed to fill his days; now, as he sits in this speeding, noisy taxi, he is half wondering what he could possibly have been thinking back then, half entranced with this young woman he is, in essence, seeing for the first time.

Words are tossed back and forth about the cab, from the back seat to the front, and he watches Madeleine and concentrates on her. She is his fixed point. That lost feeling evaporates as he dwells on the sing-song, Liverpool voice, the raised eyebrow and the playful look in her eyes that reveals she doesn't really mean what she is saying, the playful look that also contains the promise that this night just might contain a few surprises and that at any second they might jolly well disappear down a rabbit hole in the road. And it is then that the playfulness leaves her eyes, and she stares at him with the kind of bold intimacy that Michael is not used to receiving, and he is both marvelling at the poise with which she delivers it and asking himself how she became so practised in the art of the intimate glance or if it just comes as naturally to her as her sing-song voice. And already the nagging question emerges: who else may have been the recipient of such glances? But, at this moment, the look, both innocent and experienced, is for him. Later in the year, and years later still, he will be able to read in it the affection of someone who has netted some rare species of innocent life, who is drawn to it, wants it, but, at the same time, doesn't quite know what to do with it.

*

Then he is alone. He is standing on the street, his wallet in hand, and as the taxi driver slowly, painfully, extracts coins from his coin dispenser, Michael goes over the sequence of events that left him here. The taxi pulled up at a fabulous white public building, all the more fabulous for being in a side street. A piece of antiquity dumped in the suburbs, its tall white columns gleaming under electric lamps. He was so enthralled by the sight of the building, its expansiveness, its many windows and wide lawns, that he didn't notice the others leave the taxi, or, indeed, disappear. He only remembers calling out, saying he would pay the taxi (a ridiculous gesture considering that, although in a few days he will become a first-year teacher, he is currently drawing no pay except for his meagre scholarship and is the poorest of them all). Whether it was to impress this Madeleine whom he has only this night discovered, or simply because he was the last one left standing by the cab, he doesn't know — but he pays. His eyes rarely leave the gleaming antique construction in front of him, and when the driver has finally extracted the coins, he doesn't even look to see what's there. The cab departs, and he stands, uncertainly eyeing the many rooms, the multi-coloured crowds that are at the mouth of the building or calling out from those many opened windows to their friends below. Already the place is bursting with life. Young life. Loud life. But, rather than relishing all that life and delighting in it as he usually would, he now sees it as an inconvenience, an impediment, for somewhere amongst all that loud, inconvenient life is

Madeleine. And the task of finding her will be made all the more difficult by the crowd.

Inside it is worse. Everywhere, all around him, everyone is dressed in what seem to Michael to be the most fantastic costumes. Medieval figures, like strolling players from another age, all deep burgundy, daffodil yellow and sky blue, pour in through the wide double doors; a whole Edwardian cricket team in harlequin peaked caps and creams, held up not by belts but psychedelic ties, rush headlong up the stairs as if fleeing a film set; and, at the top of the stairs looking down on the foyer, a line of bowler-hatted, dark-suited commuters, black umbrellas opened, stand well prepared for the eventuality of indoor rain. And they are all in groups and they all know each other. As he looks around the foyer he has the distinct sense of being carried along by events — as he is by the crowd — and he notes for the second time this evening his uneasiness with that feeling. And the music — there seem to be two, possibly three bands playing — floats from the windows and doors, upstairs and downstairs, and merges into an odd, disjointed jigsaw of sound. Pop songs and mellow tunes from his parents' youths mingling uncertainly in the all-accommodating summer air.

That is when he begins to push his way through it, all the inconvenient life that threatens to burst the building asunder. And, all of it, constantly migrating. He follows pop music into a vast ballroom. The floor is clogged. He has no sooner scanned one section of the room than it has altered. The task of spotting a young woman in a red, black and white Bavarian dress is all the more remote for the constantly shifting nature of the dance floor and he resolves to return when the music stops.

Back in the foyer he follows the crowd up the stairway (the line of bowler-hatted commuters having moved on), but as much as he scans the crowd around, above and below, he is, in his habitually fatalistic way, quickly coming to the conclusion that he will not find them. He follows the upstairs corridor, peeking into a smaller reception room (a Commedia dell'Arte clown sharing a joint with a young WG Grace leaning casually on his bat) and even comes across a small, sedate secondary dance floor — with a crooner at a grand piano — and eyes the dancers and diners, but she's not there. It is the same throughout the entire upper floor and, as he descends the stairway, he is convinced that he has lost her. Either they have found a small enclave in this vast, crazy place, and are enjoying themselves so much they have forgotten about him altogether (as indeed they had in the taxi), or they have gone outside to look for him while he is inside looking for them. It's hopeless. And the very ordinariness of his clothes (plain white shirt and academic corduroy trousers) only intensifies this feeling of being a stranger in a strange land. He should have waited outside. Instead of this, conceivably spending the whole night seeking each other out and never succeeding. He doesn't know the people he came with. He doesn't know Madeleine, for that matter. They could be having a grand old time somewhere in some back room without a thought for him, happy to pass the evening exactly where they are, oblivious of the fact that they now number one less than they did when they arrived.

With this gloomy speculation a settled certainty, Michael ambles out onto the wide lawns at the back of the building. Here, survivors of the dance floor are cooling themselves in the evening breeze and allowing the ringing in their ears to fade. It is quieter, less frantic on the lawns. He slows to a stroll, such is the effect of moonlight on lawn, half expecting some longed-for romantic scene when he will find Madeleine staring up at him. But no, there's been a dreadful mix-up and he may as well go home and phone her in the morning. He is now utterly convinced that they have either gone, or are part of some private function that he could spend the whole evening trying to find.

And it is then that he remembers observing Madeleine in the taxi, seeing her and her alone, no trace of other older, useless infatuations (from an adolescence that seems now to have been taken up entirely with infatuations), and remembers the thrill of knowing that he was with her, she was with him, and the glance that told him all this — the glance that invited him into the private life of Madeleine and that promised that the evening was theirs. But he'd let her slip from him. Now, it was just the way it had always been, Michael standing on some bare patch of lawn with the sound of parties old and new ringing in his ears and wondering why it is that things always turn out wrong. And it is at times such as these that curses seem real, and that he, Michael, has one placed upon him. That he was born into a house of fatalistic sensibilities and that's why things always go rotten, just when they looked so right.

Inside again he pauses, giving the dance floor a goodbye glance. As the band stops, the crowd parts, and there she is. Simple. There all the time. And the last ten minutes — or was it twenty? — becomes a trifle. A misunderstanding. One of those things. And once again they have the whole night before them.

She is leaning against a pillar at the back of the dance floor with a small group, but talking to an older-looking man beside her. Michael has no sense of crossing the floor but suddenly he is in front of her. He is aware of something childish in his voice, an immature urgency when he addresses her. He is not so much speaking as blurting words. And when Madeleine turns from the man with whom she has been immersed in conversation, he is convinced that, before a smile lights her face, something else — something disturbing — crosses her features. She begins to speak and he is still puzzling over what it might have been when he realises it was disappointment.

It was there for a moment only — in her eyes, her lips and the minute crease of her forehead — but a moment is all it takes. Love can be won and lost, lives come and go, everything that may matter in someone's life may be contained in a moment — just as whole worlds can turn or crumble in one. And, as he stands there staring at Madeleine, he is convinced that he has found her only to lose her. It is a conviction that is made all the more urgent by the equally sudden realisation that sometime between getting into the taxi, crossing the city, losing her and finally finding her again he fell in love.

What he has also realised, with absolute clarity (and time will not contradict the clarity of this realisation), is that he will be the only one of the two to fall in love. And it *will* be proved true, for, in the end, she will indeed return his love with the very best that she can offer — her gratitude. And she will not say this lightly when the time comes, towards the end of this year when spring arrives; she will say it with the sad sincerity of someone who, quite simply, cannot return another's love. It will always be entwined with the regret of never really having discovered what on earth to do with him, having netted him. And so she will set him free, offering her gratitude for the days they have had. She is Liverpool-born, Irish blood, and she will tell him as she sets him free that there is a saying that sailed across the Irish Sea with her ancestors: *We have known the days.* And when she gives him thanks for the days they have known, it will be with a strangely surprised look in her eyes, still deeply puzzled that they never found more. She will, in fact, not even say it. She will give him a poem to read one day, a poem that contains all of the things she longs to say, and which will do her talking for her — the way good poems should.

'Did I not tell you which table? No?'

Madeleine says this with such concern in her eyes that it obliterates the flicker of disappointment that was there a second before. And those eyes, which could be blue or green, depending on how you looked at them, far from signalling her disappointment at being dragged away from her conversation are signalling her concern. And he is suddenly exhilarated by this, for behind all such concern is care. She cares! The losing her is all worth it for the finding of her.

'No,' he says, distracted by his unexpected exhilaration.

'You poor thing. And you've been looking for us all this time?'

'Yes.'

'But you found us,' she grins.

It's infectious. He grins too. She takes his hand, and this man to whom she has been talking, this older man who has the relaxed look of someone used to the company of women (and who is, Michael notices, married), quietly slips away with the faintest of waves, which is acknowledged by Madeleine with the faintest of nods.

Michael wants to tell her how he looked everywhere for her, tell her how big the place is and how he'd pretty much given up on finding her. He wants to ask her who that man was, but he already knows it's none of his business. He knows this not only because she did not introduce them but also because she offers no explanation as to who he was. He is left to conclude that he is either someone of no great consequence — a work companion she fell into chatting with — or someone of consequence significant enough not to be introduced. Whatever, the exhilaration he just felt at her sudden concern is now diminished. Then, in a flash, it is gone altogether. The sulks are there instead. Probably all over his face. He feels younger than his years, like a child in a school playground who has found his best friend playing with someone else. He also feels, keenly, the year that separates them. Madeleine is a year older, and it shouldn't concern him (he hasn't even given it a thought until now) but it does. It will not be the first time that he will feel like a child in her presence. And, just as she will always be a year older, there is a part of him that already suspects he will always feel like a younger brother. It is as a child, a pathetically lost one, that he now speaks to her.

'I thought you must have gone, and there'd been some crazy mix-up. And that I'd *never* find you.'

As he says it, he curses the child that he seems to drag around with him wherever he goes, and who always shoots his gob off at precisely the wrong moment, embarrassing the all-too-fragile construction of this grown-up Michael (watching). Surely she is wondering what on earth she is doing here with a baby face, on the verge of embarrassing tears.

'You poor thing.'

He notes that she has already said this, and that she said it best the first time. The first time he was moved to the point of exhilaration, the second time he is unmoved. He is unmoved because, for all the concern in her eyes, her delivery is mechanical — a statement of concern delivered without concern. But it is not the feeling that this second use of the phrase is flat that bothers him — it is the possibility that she may have been just as flat and unmoved the first time and he didn't notice.

Then, her eyes glittering blue or green (he still can't decide), she brushes his cheek with her fingers, and kisses him on the temple. It is a miraculous act. A blessing. She has kissed the sulks away, and she knows she has.

Michael is not someone who dances with ease or enthusiasm. Once the world of rhythm and speed was all he lived for, the acquisition of speed, the perfect ball, the ball that would become known across his old suburb as the ball that Michael bowled. And when cricket no longer filled his days, he bought a guitar and its rhythms filled his room in the days that followed. But the rhythms of dancing do not come naturally to him. He tells her this and she says that all he has to do is just stand there. He does, and she dances all around him as if he were a sort of human maypole. She dances, he stands transfixed now by her abandon, having completely forgotten that earlier in the evening he lost her, found her, and discerned only a flicker of disappointment in her eyes when he did. He only knows that sometime between getting into the taxi and getting out he had become part of her world. And as she dances all around him, the Bavarian dress that should look all wrong, but doesn't, swirling as she spins, he is wondering if Madeleine will ever become Maddy (as her sister calls her) and if his part in her world will become a place.

They dance, they sit, they chat like — it would seem to an observer — two people who have known each other for years and who expect to know each other for years more. He relaxes, he expands, he grows in confidence and years. Fun, he thinks, they are having fun. And he is pleased that he can make her laugh, for observations tell him that all love begins with laughter, and if he can make her laugh then he just might be able to make her love.

Nobody sleeps that night. Nobody goes to bed. And when the early summer sun returns, dusting the foliage of the communal garden orange and yellow, they are all once more standing on the same balcony upon which they had assembled on that distant shore of the previous evening.

This was the night — in between losing her and finding her — that Michael fell in love with Madeleine. The night that he also realised he would be the only one to fall and would receive, in return, the best that she could offer.

6.

Mrs Webster at Home

Mrs Webster is standing in the wide dining room (rarely used in Webster's day) in this second week of February, a bright weekday morning sun igniting the trees outside and illuminating the whole room. She is reading a letter from the mayor's office. It is a puzzling letter (posted almost four weeks to the day after Peter van Rijn took his momentous drive and gave birth to an idea). A committee is being formed that will direct events in this the centenary year of the suburb, and she is invited to be part of it. Is the suburb really a hundred years old? The age of the suburb is not something she has ever pondered. And how can anybody know such a thing anyway? Where do you start? But it is an official letter, an official document with the Office of the Mayor stamped upon it. Somebody has apparently decided that the suburb is a hundred years old. The whole world moves in strange ways, why not the suburb? Ideas come and go, are casually thrown around official offices, and every now and then some of them are taken seriously enough to become fact. And this, it seems, is one. Although how this comes about, why some ideas stick and others don't, is a mystery to her and probably everyone else involved. All the same, she is both intrigued and amused by the idea and at being invited to join the committee. She rubs the edge of the envelope on her chin, contemplating whether to accept the invitation or not. And, in the end, the best answer she can come up with is 'Why not?'

She resolves to write back later that evening, but, for the moment, she is distracted by the house. New long flowing curtains have just been fitted and Rita is standing by the window closely examining the quality of the workman's job. When Mrs Webster advertised in the local paper the year before for domestic help, she expected to get a young girl but found herself with Rita instead. And at first she simply let her do the domestic work she was hired for, until a few months before when she asked Rita for her advice on how best to paint the kitchen and discovered that this woman had the gift of a designer's eye. Whereas Mrs Webster looks at a room (the house has never been changed) and sees only the room as it is and cannot conceive of it any differently, this woman sees possibilities. And her judgments are impeccable. So much so that when Rita suggests a particular type of material, a piece of furniture in such and such a corner, a colour that might lift a room, Mrs Webster finds herself saying 'Yes, yes' before Rita has even finished describing the full sweep of what she has in mind.

The curtains are a small part, a detail of the vast picture Rita secretly imagines, yet her eyes dwell on every detail of the stitching and folds, for, having been trained as a milliner, Rita knows a few things about stitches and materials.

'It's a new room.' Mrs Webster's eyes travel the dining room in wonder as if seeing it for the first time, reflecting that, if it had looked like this in the past, it might well have been used more often.

'Not yet.' Rita looks up from her inspection.

Mrs Webster smiles. Rita's confidence and sheer enthusiasm make her smile and she is not only glad this woman is in her house, but in her world. This woman cares for the house and the house responds.

Outside in the suburb, the schools are back and the streets possess a timeless quiet. As she drives through them to the factory, dreamy, she is aware that on days such as these she could, if she were not careful, spend the rest of her life being lulled by the leafy streets. It would, she reflects, be a kind of death, a big sleep, and death (in one way or another — the death of Webster, the death of the factory) has been on her mind too much. And not just lately, but for a long time. The sheer contentment of these leafy streets works on her, not like a balm, but like an anaesthetic. Then she is at the factory car park. She has changed gears, stopped at intersections, turned corners, slowed, accelerated and finally arrived — and yet she can't remember anything of the drive, only the deep, entrancing green of the leafy streets through which she has driven. And, as she walks to the factory, she is once again struck by the thought that, if she were not careful, she could well spend the rest of her life being lulled by these streets.

7.

Vic's Round

Breakfast is a simple matter for Vic. Always has been. A pot of strong, black tea — strong enough to stain the inside of his mug. It is coated, this mug, with years of drinking, like all the railway mugs he has ever possessed. A good coating, they all agreed, all the drivers and firemen from those days that are now gone, transformed ordinary tea into that vintage brew you could only drink in the cabin of an engine or by the side of the tracks upon which it sat. And, even now, Vic sees the giant hand of Paddy Ryan wrapped around, dwarfing, the tin mug from which he drank all his working life. This mug had only ever been rinsed, never cleaned. And Paddy said often enough that if anybody ever dared scrub the thing he'd wring the life out of them. And one look at Paddy's giant mitts and his eyes when he spoke convinced you that he meant exactly what he said. To stand on the footplate with Paddy Ryan was to stand in the studio of a grand master. Paddy Ryan was the Michelangelo of engine driving and he taught Vic all he knew. Well, almost. He never passed on the secrets, those defining touches that made Paddy Ryan Paddy Ryan. Those signatures that the great drivers left behind on the rails and that could be read, by those who knew how, as easily as reading a painter's signature on a canvas. It was up to Vic to find his own defining touches. Just as Paddy Ryan, the master of the smooth ride, had found his. It took a lifetime of labour to find those touches, and a lifetime of labour to keep them. Now, all gone: Paddy, the engines they drove, the defining touches that remain now only in the memories of others, or have long passed into railway mythology. All incomprehensibly gone. One minute you're twenty and it's all there before you, the next it's gone. And, like country stations in the night, in the blink of an eye.

A thousand miles away, Michael will, in a few hours, be strolling across magical college lawns that have never glittered so brightly, that unmistakable sensation that life is just beginning, *real* life, touching everything he looks upon, excitement in every step, in the same way that the young Vic would have strode to the first engines of his working life. Vic, mindful that his son will be doing something at this moment (and not that he worries about him, but Michael is always in his thoughts, as much for the things they did together as the things they didn't), throws back his tea, contemplates what the boy might be up to, finishes the sandwich and completes this railway breakfast with a Champion Ruby, rolled and ready on the table for when the sandwich is gone and the second mug of tea is poured. And, as the tea ripples down his throat and the air is filled with the blue smoke of the first cigarette of the morning, Vic could almost be driving again. The world could almost be wide again, like it always was when he drove, and he could almost pick up his bag, filled with his billy, his dinner, his swabs and soap, and walk straight out the door to work. He had it, and lost it. They all had it, and lost it — the best of their living. But at least they'd known it and known what it was to possess such a thing. One single pure activity, that's all it takes to turn a succession of days, months and years into a life. They may all be gone now, those days, but at least they had them. And with that he nods slowly to himself, drains the last of the tea and stands.

The flat is on a hill, and from his doorstep Vic has a full view of the town. From here, he can scan his world. The shimmering green of the banana trees in the garden below, the long, sweeping road that leads down into the town, the imposing white columns of the Twin Towns Services Club (where all evenings end), the shops to which he will now go, the post office, the pub at which he will lunch, and beyond it all (just visible), the wide green fairways of the golf course. His world is compact and complete. A duchy unto itself.

With his hat on (the summer sun is already powerful) and his thin legs supporting a paunch he never had when he was driving, he strolls easily down the hill, leading with his belly, into the town. Already, he can see the place changing. Or, rather, having change imposed upon it, this little duchy. New flats going up, new clubs. Apartments for southerners. Fancy shops for tourists. It was a sleepy fishing town even when he came here just a few years ago. A proper town, but not a nosy one, a town that let you be if that's what you wanted. But it's not sleepy any more. And he knows that soon they'll bugger up the place like they've buggered up everywhere else. But at least he can give thanks that he won't be around to see that. Progress, they all call it. And he snorts into brief laughter. He once drove a train called Progress, and he knows where that leads and how it ends.

And Vic knows he won't be around to witness the whole place being buggered up. These pills he takes, which are fighting a losing battle against the grog and the fags and all the damage of a lifetime, put things off. That's all. Vic knows it. He tells his doctor that he's not changing, as he's always told all the doctors of his life. And when his doctor, with detached simplicity, says it'll kill him, Vic replies, as he has for them all, that he couldn't care less. Neither of them ever attempts to kid the other, and they both know that Vic's day is coming. That it could be any day from now. In the suburb he occasionally wondered what sort of day it would be. But here he knows. The sun will shine. Bathers will go down to the sea, and the surf will be good. The best thing is not to give it too much thought. It'll all see itself through — these things always do — without Vic thinking too much about it.

Then he's thinking onions. And as he comes to the first of his routine stops at the front of the greengrocers, he can almost smell the onions he is about to buy, sizzling, as they will be that evening, in a rich butter sauce, the aroma of which will float from the kitchen and fill the entire flat. The anticipated scent in his nostrils, he steps into the shop and greets the round, middle-aged Polish proprietor who looks like she knows (along with her greens) a few things about sausages.

This world unto itself, this duchy for which he has taken out citizenship (having ditched the old self, the they-self, the old city and the old ways) is where his story will end. That's why he chose it. The sun will shine, the surf will be good and young bathers will go down to the sea.

8.

An Ordinary Morning

The college lawns, the moat, the brilliant blue sky itself, all sparkle just that bit more in this second week of term because there is someone out there after all. Somebody had come along. Instead of moving through the world as if it were someone else's property and he a mere visitor, and all the things that mattered happening to other people; instead of being a perpetual spectator, Michael is now *in* the world. As Vic's daily round of shops and pub and golf and club begins a thousand miles to the sub-tropical north where he has just finished his customary simple breakfast, Michael enters the deeply thrilling world of grown-up love.

There he is drifting across the green lawns while a popular love song floats out from an open college window. Love songs are everywhere now, and this one follows him over the moat and up the entire length of the gravel path that leads to the lecture theatres. And, in some ways, it is not so much the world that he is strolling through on this dazzling late-February morning, but an idealised view of it. A latter-day pastoral. He has known Madeleine for almost a month now and is still thrilling to the unfamiliar sensation that there really is someone out there for him. A way of feeling that had lain dormant inside him, unsummoned since adolescence, had come alive again, and this emotional renaissance, in transforming him, has also transformed the world he walks through.

But, above all, the word that occurs to him on this dazzling morning is the same one that will return to him years from now when he recalls it all and the rush of released emotions that came with it: ordinary. The wonder of the whole business is that he has discovered ordinariness. This is the way the rest of the world lives. A world of falling in love, making plans in plural and talking in terms of 'us' and 'we' beckoned. Someone had come along. And all the little ordinary things that everybody else took for granted had come along too. The 'us' and the 'we' still fell awkwardly from his lips, and, while part of him wanted the awkwardness to go away, part of him never wanted to lose it.

In front of the library, in the main square of the university, the various clubs and societies — Marxists, socialists, Christians, philosophical and sporting — have set up their stalls and are recruiting members, the colours of their flags and banners, the sounds and the milling crowds transforming the square into a kind of medieval market place. But, instead of selling goods, they're selling ideas. There is a large banner on a wall informing everyone that an anti-imperialist, anti-war march will leave from the university in two weeks from now. Prominent student political figures — most of whom Michael knows, as this is a new, small university — are standing out front of their stalls, like spruikers in a side-show, drumming up trade with a sort of melodramatic urgency, the words 'Vietnam', 'imperialist' and 'America' mingling with the popular music issuing from the public address system and the catch-cries of the stalls around them. One of these figures, in fact, nods knowingly at Michael. You, he seems to say, you uppity English students. Don't think those red socks you're wearing fool me.

The wordless exchange takes only a second, and Michael acknowledges some truth in the look, for he is only vaguely mindful of the activity around him (and, even then, it is the colour and movement that draws his eye). It is the personal world that absorbs him. There is an uplifting, unmistakable feeling of setting out this morning — and not just upon the year, but 'Life' itself. Since Madeleine had come along, Life had acquired a capital 'L', just as it did in the critical texts he studied. And now it is Life that is all around him, touching everything he looks upon and propelling every step he takes along the gravel path that will lead him to an appointment with his English tutor so that he can finish this broken degree of his (the teacher in charge of the school timetable having arranged Michael's classes to allow for it).

Days in which a completely ordinary gesture, denoting care or affection, a corny love song and a casual sentence become synonymous with a moment and are forever after the key that opens it up for recall. Nothing happens, and everything happens. An ordinary act transforms the familiar into the unfamiliar, and memories are born.

And this is what Madeleine will become. Not a story, but a string of memories and scenes. Not even a picture, but parts of a picture. Details of days that may have passed barely noticed at the time, but which lodge and stick and stay clear in Michael's mind through the years that come after when she is no longer there.

Later, that evening, he is walking beside her. She is carrying in her handbag his favourite book. A favourite book, Michael muses quietly, as if he were addressing Madeleine (which he is not, for he speaks better in his mind than he does in fact), is a very private object. Others may read this book, he continues in silent address, but not the way you do. A favourite book becomes yours when it enters your life. You are the one for whom it was written and, in being read by you, the book meets its other half and becomes effectively whole. It is, therefore, difficult to share a favourite book. There is risk. The act of sharing comes with an implied question. So, when the book passes from one hand to another, this act of sharing can be as fraught as a declaration of love. Sometimes they amount to the same thing.

Madeleine says she is famous for her long strides. She walks like a young woman going places, in the kind of short skirt that is the fashion of the day. Michael doesn't know how young women walked a hundred years ago, but he finds it difficult to imagine that they walked like Madeleine. Or Maddy. Her sister calls her Maddy. Her parents. Her friends.

Everybody does. Except Michael. So far, the abbreviated form of her name does not come naturally. Not as naturally as those long strides for which she maintains she is famous and which take her across an unattended service station and down into the student streets of an inner-city student suburb. The book is in her handbag, the strap of which hangs across her shoulder and swings back and forth as she walks. It is not a great book, not one that is even looked upon as being serious enough to belong to anybody's list of great books. Not anybody with judgment, that is. And, as a student, now teacher of literature, Michael is meant to have judgment. But he suspends it for this book. From the first to the subsequent readings of it (and they have been many), Michael has never asked himself if this is a good or even a great book. It is simply *his* book, and questions of its goodness or greatness do not arise. And the author, Mr W Somerset Maugham, is not one of those authors who is even studied, not the way authors of great renown are read and studied by students of literature such as Michael. The word 'entertainment' occurs to him as he follows Madeleine's long strides over the watery asphalt of the late-night petrol station, past the solid nineteenth-century building that houses the bank, to the lights and the crossing that will lead them to the shops and cafés and pizza houses of the main street. Mr Maugham, as his lecturers would call him, writes amusements and entertainments of a certain kind, 'gentleman's literature', and Michael is almost on the point of apologising for the book — as he always seems to do whenever he mentions it to anybody — when she speaks. She likes it, she says. It is not a great book, he quickly adds, and she shakes her head saying that it does not matter. She reads more than the students he knows and already he trusts her judgment more than theirs. What does it matter that no one thinks it a serious book? And she slows those long strides and stares at him candidly. An acknowledgment that the book was not really the point. And they both know what the point is, don't they? In giving her a favourite book, a question had been asked. She reaches into her bag, passes it back to him, and he places it in his coat pocket. She does it carefully, to show that she cares for the book. And, with this demonstration of care, the question he asked in giving it to her has been answered.

'Tell me about where you come from.'

'Liverpool. Well,' she corrects herself, 'a small town just out of Liverpool.'

She stops there. He waits.

'And?'

'There's nothing to tell. You wouldn't know it.'

'There's always something to tell.'

'The Beatles played at our local hall. My friends went. I missed it.'

'I wish I could say that.'

'It's got a nice park, and a lovely little station. But I don't miss it. Not much.'

'I'd like to see it.'

'Aren't you funny,' she says. It is one of her favourite expressions.

They stop outside a small café and contemplate the list of pizzas pasted to the inside of the window. Over the next few weeks, she and her sister will talk more to Michael about this place from which they come. And it will become apparent that although they say they don't miss it, they do. And the idea of this place from which Madeleine has come will enter his mind. It will enter, and it will stay there and a deeply private mythology will be born. The place from which she comes is being written in his mind, and over the following months he will unconsciously construct all the other moving and non-moving parts that constitute this place he has never seen but which one day he will, many years later, when the Liverpool of his mind and the real thing meet.

But, for now, a favourite book has been exchanged. A question has been asked, and an answer received. They stare into the pizza shop window, contemplating a cheap dinner for two. For Michael, part of that deeply thrilling world of the ordinary.

9.

The Story of Old Dresses

Rita returns home from the Webster house mid-afternoon, her transformation of Mrs Webster's dining room (new curtains, new carpet) now complete. It is too late to start something new and too early to put her feet up. It's a dead part of the afternoon; she can neither sit nor stand, and because of this oddly unsettling effect she finds herself pacing from room to room until she finishes up in the bedroom at the front of the house.

As she turns her head from side to side, looking about the room and wondering what on earth she's doing here, the wardrobe speaks. The wardrobe says, 'Open me.' So she does. And there they are. Her dresses. A lifetime of dresses. And, as she runs her fingers across them, they sway on their hangers as if dancing to the sweetness of long-silent melodies.

Then, one by one, she takes them from the wardrobe, these dresses of hers that were always just a bit too good for the street, and which she wore in spite of it. These

European dresses, like the fancy French windows at the front of the house, always spoke of other places, of the great world beyond the suburb, and so the street always took them as an insult. Well, stuff the street! Rita is not a woman who uses rough language, but she is not above telling the street to get stuffed when both sufficient cause and impulse come to her. Just as she is not above silently pronouncing the young girls of the suburb, with their mini-skirts and their tight blouses, tarts. As she takes the dresses from the wardrobe, those long-silent melodies, the songs that are forever attached to each of them, begin to echo in her ears and songs she thought she'd forgotten are retrieved by the dresses.

Somehow, and she can't remember doing this (not consciously), the dresses are arranged in order, consistent with the years in which they were worn. They are a story, chapters leading into each other. And it's a story that begins with the yellow-and-black summer affair, with the bright flowers and the one dark, bold strap, that she wore for the first time a thousand years ago to an engagement party at Bedser's at the bottom of the street. And suddenly, she's hearing one of those finger-clicking, jazzy numbers that always annoyed the hell out of Vic, about, what? Love, of course. They were all about love, which is probably why they annoyed the hell out of him. Only, in this song (which is now full and rich in her ears), love is a sort of figure. Not a person, not a man or woman — but a thing, all the same. And it's waiting, just around the corner. And Rita can't decide whether to be excited by it, or frightened, or sad. It's unsettling, that's what it is. Because she can't decide if this love thing waiting just around the corner is going to embrace her and caress her the way love should, or mug her. And the smooth-shaven, finger-snapping singer has a glint in his eyes like he knows something that only he and the song know, but his glinting pair of eyes are also telling her she's welcome to come and find out all the same. It could be fun and it could be scary. Then the orchestra takes over. And she remembers what it was to be mugged by love and Vic's that thing around the corner. Her mother is saying don't marry him, her sisters are saying don't marry him, everybody is saying don't marry him — and, of course, she marries him.

And as the song plays, round and round in her head, she's seized by the impulse to step back into that time when love mugged her and she took a chance. To step back into that time when love was a bit rough with the broad, because love knew no other way. And the dress says, yes, yes, you can. And she says, no, no, I can't. And she says it again and again. But the dress doesn't give up, and — in this dead patch of the afternoon while the suburb is dozing — she's peeling off the comfortable, loose summer frock she's wearing and taking a chance.

There's the faint whiff of moth balls and old times as she raises the thing above her head and begins to lower it. And her heart's going like mad and she doesn't know why because she's just trying on an old dress, but it is anyway, because there seems to be something urgent in the act that she wasn't aware of before she started. Something at stake, and she doesn't know what. But, somehow, having started, she can't bear to fail. And so, as she lowers it over her head (as she would have effortlessly and unselfconsciously fifteen years before), she is aware of every part of the process, the awkwardness of trying on an old dress. And although it takes a bit more time than it would once have done, soon enough she's in it. And she's not too sure about sitting down and standing up too fast, but she's back inside the skin of the young wife. And she pauses, examining the sensations that come with it. And with this skin come all the nights and the parties that she once wore it to and she's suddenly stepping into neighbours' houses long gone, with plates and beers. Then they all come back in a rush and a blur, a night or two in particular, such as Bedser's. Especially Bedser's. The engagement of that daughter of his, what was her name? And for a moment she's carefree and happy as she walks down their street in this new dress of hers under a summer sky glowing with a touch of eternity, as though the night itself would go on forever, and everybody standing under it. And she passes from happy to sad to just plain flat (as if she's just been run over by one of those great, snorting engines Vic drove) as she remembers that the night did end, and, like they all seemed to then, it ended badly. But did it always happen like that? Did they all start good and end badly? There must have been good ones in there. Must have been, only she's pressed to remember them just now. Or maybe it's just that the bad were so many, the shadow they cast so tall and wide, that they blot out the good. And the image that now prevails is that of a winter night, the table set, Rita and the boy that Michael was, waiting. And Vic not home. Not yet fallen in the back door in that way of his that always sounded like the briquettes had just been delivered.

And she's no sooner back in the skin of the young wife than she wants to be out of it again. She eyes herself in the wardrobe mirror, and, although she'd never let the street see her like this, she's happy enough with what her eyes tell her. Or is it what she tells them to tell her? Then she's pulling the dress off and happily reclaiming the garments of middle age.

There they are, from one end of the bed to the other, her dresses from all the years. And as she steps back, taking in the spectacle (which is also something of a history of recent fashion), she reads her story in the neatly arranged chapters of her dresses. And while it was good to know that she could slip back into the skin of the young wife, it wasn't really that good to be under old skin again. Even the skin of youth.

And as she's staring at them, reading chapter by chapter the story of her life, and the house and the whole suburb for that matter, she knows that the material of each dress is skin she has long since shed.

Slowly, she removes them from the hangers, her dresses, and folds them one on top of the other, year upon year upon year. And when she's arrived at the present she closes the wardrobe. The dresses fit neatly into a suitcase. Outside, the afternoon is quietly slipping towards twilight, and the sounds of children playing the last of the day's games and young families (the names of many she's not yet familiar with) rise from the street. In the morning she'll drop the suitcase off at the local opportunity shop in the Old Wheat Road. And perhaps, in time, a young wife will come along and slip into the skin that Rita once wore.

10.

Life Turns Another Page

Michael doesn't like pubs. He is not someone who is often to be seen in them. But this afternoon, while Rita is reading the story of her old dresses, he prefers the quiet of this public bar near the university and the hospital where Madeleine is now on duty to that of the constant hum and stale drowsy air of the university library. It is the final week of February and the plane trees and elms that line the wide street outside will soon be turning gold and crimson. Michael has only been teaching at his old school since term started, but the kindly maths master, who compiles the school timetable, has already arranged Michael's load so that he has two afternoons a week off to finish his degree. And so, and it almost feels a luxury, he has spent the afternoon reading. Traffic and trams move easily through sunshine and shadow. Life in *Middlemarch* turns another page. The public bar is quiet, except for a small group nearby.

The afternoon, in fact, has passed as though being played out to the time signature of another, less hurried, age. Slowness falls upon him. Nothing — neither his raising of the glass, the turning of a page, nor the motion of the bartender as he clears the counter — is hurried. Everything moves at a pace that would have been alien to the adolescent Michael whose measure of meaning was determined by the speed it took a cricket ball to pass from one end of a pitch to the other. Now, it is moments such as these and slowness that he is learning to value — whenever he feels it fall upon him — as much as he once valued speed.

And so it is with a sense of curious surprise that he finds himself looking up from the book and listening to the conversation of the small group of drinkers near him. A man is speaking. Not loudly, not with any great emotion. But there is something in the combination of the appearance of the man and what he is saying — in confidence to his friends — that has caught Michael's attention, lifted him from the fictional world he has inhabited most of this free afternoon, and back into this one. At first he doesn't know why his attention has been caught by strangers whose concerns mean nothing to him. But he is listening, and intently. And, as he ponders why this should be, he realises that the speaker is not a stranger and that he has seen him before, at the ball to which Madeleine had taken him — the older man to whom he was not introduced, either because he was someone of no consequence or somebody of consequence enough not to be introduced. It is now only four weeks since that ball, but already it has become the night upon which a before-and-after was established; the night that created the line between his life before Madeleine and his life after Madeleine.

He speaks quietly, this man, his audience a small group of younger men, some wearing the medical intern's uniform of the white dustcoat. But although he speaks quietly, even confidentially, he holds their attention completely, like a lecturer discoursing on a favourite subject. But it is not medicine or anything connected with it. Michael can see that. It is a bar-room performance, and Michael (who has paid no conscious attention to the address) can imagine that anecdote and innuendo are the key components of his act. And Michael can see, simply from his manner, that this man has delivered just such a talk on many occasions before. Michael is now thankful for never having been introduced. If he had, he would now almost certainly feel compelled to speak to him should they catch each other's eyes. And that would be unfortunate, for Michael knows, without even having met him, that he doesn't like this man.

And it is while Michael is giving thanks for this that the man turns his attention to those sitting beside him and, in so doing, turns in Michael's direction so that his words become clearer.

'Everyone,' he says, the hint of a smile behind his eyes, 'thinks she's as pure as a country field.'

He has the air of authority, this man. And whether he is speaking on the subject of women or grave and elevated themes, everybody listens with a sort of rapt belief. He has, Michael can clearly see, that kind of power over people. Madeleine spoke once of a man at the hospital, a resident genius (a vague reference, no names, but Michael, rightly or wrongly, immediately suspected who she was talking about). And she did not dwell on his looks or his manners or the incidentals of his life. No, she dwelt on his work, the importance of his research and the sheer wonder of what he did. She spoke briefly of him, but spoke almost in awe of somebody involved in one of life's mighty projects, a grand narrative currently lacking in her life, and which, by implication, she would never find with the likes of Michael.

'A country field.' He smiles once more. 'But not beyond ploughing.'

The small group strains forward, but he leaves it there, with a quiet nod. Then he rises, a tap on his wrist-watch indicating that playtime is over and the more serious matters of life and death await them.

And it is now, as they are leaving, that Michael and this man do, in fact, catch each other's eyes. It is momentary, but Michael is sure — as they exit — that there was recognition in the stare. Recognition, and something more. And, as they stroll across the wide street outside, Michael is left contemplating if that flash of recognition was real or imagined, and, if so, just what that something more might have been.

He turns the top corner of the page and life in *Middlemarch* snaps shut for the time. Even as he does, he hears the voice of Madeleine telling him not to do that, that the page feels it. Didn't he know? Her little ways and expressions have entered his day-to-day living — don't dog-ear the pages of books, TTFN at the bottom of a letter — and her very accent, for he constantly catches himself now slipping into her sing-song voice. And it is something that will never entirely leave him, so infectious is it.

There is a slight, almost autumn, chill in the air as he crosses the road and walks back into the university. He was, of course, this man, talking about anybody. Just anybody. And Michael shrugs the incident off — if that's what it is — as if shrugging off the sudden out-of-season chill settling over things. But it stays with him: the hint of a chill and the nagging image of Madeleine, cast as a latter-day Dorothea seeking the grand narratives of life in the works of someone else.

In his room, later in the afternoon, he sits at his desk, looking out over the street from his balcony window and waiting for the hour to roll round when he will rise from his chair and meet Madeleine. Twilight has almost fallen and she will currently be making herself ready for the evening. Or she will be ready and simply filling in time, chatting to her sister. It is the hour before meeting Madeleine. An hour, that in years to come, will be synonymous with this time of day, the clutter of his desk, the cheap plastic mug from which he occasionally sips and the thrill that infuses all the objects around him with a sense of moment.

He returns to his book. Life in *Middlemarch* turns another page, and once again he loses himself in the quiet rhythms of another time, another world. As he picks up the threads of the book, the threads of the afternoon return briefly (the easy words and easy smile of the practised raconteur surfacing again). Life turns another page. He forgets about it all. He is being silly. He is being worse than silly — he is being a child. He is, he knows, looking for things that aren't there.

II

The Search for a Key Term

I n the weeks that followed Peter van Rijn's momentous drive to work and his subsequent visit to the mayor's office, a committee was formed. The mayor, Harold Ford, Henry to his mates, who bears a striking resemblance to Mr Menzies (a resemblance he cultivates, and which, some suggest, alone gave him electoral success) had passed through five distinct phases during the ten minutes that Peter van Rijn had been in his office.

At first it was simple annoyance at having his morning ritual of strong tea and tobacco disturbed (and the mayor is a man who sits, stands and walks inside a constant tobacco cloud, the pipe rarely from his mouth) for no apparent reason other than some aimless chit-chat about local history. Once the annoyance subsided, he experienced a moment of indifferent dismissiveness, which soon turned to sceptical interest. By the five-minute mark, his tea was cooling, and the mayor was warming to the idea that Peter van Rijn had given birth to that morning and which he had brought directly to the mayor's attention. And, once he realised that there was something in this for all of them, he was a portrait of concentrated attention. Visions of fat government cheques and a whole suburb transformed into the very emblem of Progress passed across his mind; his suburb, his people, all brought together in mutual celebration, under the beaming gaze of the mayor whose vision had made it happen.

This, the mayor realised as both men stood and shook hands, was his doorway into local history. And not just a routine mention — a gold name on a board along with everyone else — but a shining place at the very centre of the suburb's story.

Now, in this last week of February, with the schools back and the suburb having shrugged off its summer slumbers, a committee is meeting. It is meeting, for the first time, in the dining room of the Webster mansion. Mrs Webster, a member of the committee and one of the first names on the mayor's lips, automatically offered the use of the dining room, which, in the days of Webster, rarely hosted a dinner.

It is a large room. Light and relaxing (made even lighter and more relaxing by Rita's changes). A place where the six committee members (the mayor, Mrs Webster, the vicar of St Matthew's, the newly appointed priest at St Patrick's, the local member of parliament and Peter van Rijn) can chat in an informal way; a place where the imagination might be set free, and where unusual, even inspired, ideas might be born.

The immediate task of the committee is to establish a name for the event itself. The word 'slogan' is never uttered, but everybody understands that this is what they're searching for. The suburb's history, it is tacitly taken for granted, is a grand and dignified matter. To think in terms of a slogan would be to cheapen it. They are not, after all, selling soap powder, but celebrating a hundred years of settlement.

The word that constantly recurs in the afternoon's discussion is 'Progress'. And, with it, terms such as production, prosperity and growth. But it is Progress that rolls so easily from the lips of the mayor, the ministers and the local member. Is not the suburb, they irresistibly conclude, the very picture of Progress: only twenty years ago a frontier community of stick houses and dirt tracks, now a wide, solid community of lawns and gardens and tree-lined streets? What was once a frontier outpost is now, indeed, the Toorak of the North that the estate agents of a hundred years ago had promised all their grandparents.

As they talk, Mrs Webster is distracted by her gardens, which are a mass of colour and leafy abundance. Progress. She hears the word thrown into the pot of conversation yet again, but it is thrown in such a way as to suggest that nobody really knows what it means. Rather, it is spoken like some article of faith. Or like a phrase that enters everyday conversation, and for a season becomes everybody's favourite phrase (a way for people such as the mayor or the local member to demonstrate that their thinking is up to the minute), without anybody ever really pausing to reflect on just what it might mean. And so it is no surprise when somebody suggests that Progress Suburb be the banner under which they organise the year's activities. A long discussion follows, but, for reasons that no one will remember afterwards, it is not adopted. Instead the mayor suggests that one of the main streets in the suburb be renamed Progress Avenue, and everyone agrees.

And so the search goes on for most of the afternoon, the sky clouds over, and one of those late-summer changes that brings with it a taste of the autumn to follow settles in. The day dulls, bringing an out-of-season chill (the same chill that settles on Michael as he walks from the pub to his room and the hour before meeting Madeleine), and just when it appears that everybody has been exhausted by the search, and are no longer capable of creative thought, Peter van Rijn — who has said little until now — quietly suggests Centenary Suburb. Simple, he says. But it tells everybody what they need to know, and is grand without being too grand. It has, he continues, a sense of history about it, a sense of debt as well as celebration. Although the mayor has never really liked van Rijn (he did, in fact, in an excess of youth, years before, throw a brick through the Dutchman's shop window, scrawling the word 'commie' on the footpath in front of the shop — something about which he has always kept mum), but for the second time in a matter of weeks he finds himself nodding in enthusiastic agreement with him. So too is the whole table. And, in a flash, it is agreed. They will become Centenary Suburb. The search is over. The meeting finishes and everybody agrees that this calls for a drink, and everybody (except Peter van Rijn himself, who is a teetotaller) raises glasses of the whisky Mrs Webster has passed around and toasts the occasion.

Centenary Suburb. It is hard for everyone to believe that it took all afternoon to think up two words. But they are the right two words, and when the vicar of St Matthew's suggests that good words, like good whisky, take time, there is general nodding all around the table.

And when they all leave the Webster mansion and step out into the street to go their separate ways, it is as though those two words have already transformed the suburb. The mayor is struck by a sense of its solidity and history that he has never appreciated before, and the two priests are discussing the farms that once existed where the houses and shops and garages of the suburb now stand, and Peter van Rijn is contemplating the frail wooden structure that first brought commerce to the community and thereby heralded the beginning of settlement. A shop, he reflects, brings with it the many gifts of production and the bonds of exchange. A shop does all that. It is the glue, the focal point of a group of people who have decided to settle in one place and call that place home. He gives no thought to the fact that others were there before them all and too called this place home; that earlier inhabitants, for millennia, walked the very ground that they have, just now, collectively decided to call Centenary Suburb. He simply does not think of it. When he thinks of the suburb before they all came to it he thinks only of open country and vacant land. As open and vacant as the blank page upon which their history will be written, for History begins with a blank page. As well as open country and vacant land. All of it untilled. Waiting only to be touched by the hands of History and Progress. Open country, moving irresistibly towards, yearning for that moment when the concentration of farms and houses is such that it can justify the existence of a shop and the history of the place can be said to have found its first chapter.

He strolls to his Anglia and drives to the shop to catch whatever there may be of the late-afternoon trade. The mayor returns to his office, more content from the labour that it took to dream up two words than the whole of the week's paperwork. The two priests part at St Patrick's, the vicar of St Matthew's continuing on to his parish, passing the grand old nineteenth-century building that once housed the Girls' Home and is now occupied by some government office or other. Mrs Webster sits alone in her dining room, absentmindedly taking in the stale whisky smells.

The day sparkles, as if in response to the birth that has just taken place in the committee room, to the phrase that will now define the year and the life of the suburb. The committee members go their separate ways, gazing at their world through the spectacles of the Key Term. All around them, all across the suburb, rich and profuse gardens of bright red, pink and yellow roses, geraniums and impatiens, hang over garden walls and fences; tennis courts and cricket fields echo with the gentle *pock-pock* of games past and present; the rattle of trains comes and goes; shop doors open and close; and each of the committee members takes it all into their lungs and limbs, this suburb of theirs, now transformed into a grand achievement by those two words.

A grand tale, they are now a grand tale, calling — right down through the generations — for recognition. To the mayor, now easing into his chair, to Peter van Rijn, currently rearranging his shop window, to the two priests now back in their manses, their world has changed and they now look upon the perfectly functioning organism of the suburb with a new-found wonder. The straight line of History has led, and was always leading, to this day, and they are all lucky enough to be alive, right now, to greet the moment.

Part Two

Autumn

12.

Introducing Pussy Cat and Bunny Rabbit

On evenings such as these, walking through a city park golden with autumn, he sees them as that rare thing — an old-fashioned couple in a radical age. Their old-worldliness is called innocence, and they take it with them wherever they go. At least that is the way he sees them on days such as these, when he can't even conceive of her having shared herself with anybody else the way she does with him. He is hers, she is his. They are theirs: a conservative couple, strolling hand in hand, through the wrong world. Not that Madeleine would ever accept this if he were to tell her (and he keeps this observation to himself), for she is always making gentle fun of the fuddy-duddy old man's shops he goes to for his fuddy-duddy old man's trousers. Can't he just wear jeans? Does it always have to be fuddy-duddy old corduroys? So, on evenings such as these, when he seeks ways to frame their innocence, he privately pictures them like this — of the Age, but *not* children of the Age. And as much as the children of the Age might find their innocence amusing (he is from time to time the source of jest and fun), they are, nonetheless, drawn to it. They are drawn to it as, perhaps, travellers might be, looking back one last time upon a town or place they will never inhabit again. And, on days such as these, Michael and Madeleine are that place, and the amused eyes of the Age that look back upon them linger just that bit longer than amusement requires.

It is still early in the evening. Michael and Madeleine are walking through a city park. There is another couple beside them. They, this other couple, are children of the Age. They are fellow students, living in the same student house they have shared with Michael and a painter called Mulligan since their early student years. Mulligan lives downstairs; Michael and the couple with whom he and Madeleine are currently strolling all live upstairs. Michael scrutinises them, these children of the Age. They read the same books, smoke the same cigarettes, take the same drugs and may even think the same thoughts for all Michael knows. And, like most children of the Age, they undress each other regularly, go to bed often, and copulate. In fact, they copulate very loudly. Michael knows this because their room, at the back of the house, is opposite his and he hears the sounds of their copulation often. In the household they are known as Bunny Rabbit and Pussy Cat. Mulligan, who seems to have no other name but Mulligan, christened them.

Bunny Rabbit's hair is long and dark, and he has the kind of droopy, dark moustache that musicians in bands wear. He puts his long, thin legs into flared, blue jeans and casually throws what Michael intuitively knows are expensive cotton shirts over his bony torso. Michael never knew what a Brooks Brothers shirt was until he met Bunny Rabbit. Didn't he know that Scott Fitzgerald wore Brooks Brothers shirts? No? Really? Well, now he would always know. Bunny Rabbit never consciously spoke down to Michael, and Michael never took offence. Bunny Rabbit spoke down to everyone. His father was, when it came to shirts, a sort of Gatsby. So when he goes home (rarely taking Pussy Cat, because Pussy Cat — like Michael — comes from the wrong side of life), he brings a shirt back with him because his father has a roomful.

Pussy Cat is what the Age calls beautiful. Long, dark brown hair, bright brown eyes that resemble a fox more than a cat. Magnificent eyes that are constantly living in the wild. Her light, cheesecloth blouses are smoked in incense and she has the constant aroma of some exotic elsewhere about her. Michael has never met an actress, but she looks like one. In fact, she bears a striking resemblance to the heroine of a popular film of *Romeo and Juliet* who leans over balconies with provocative innocence and has entranced a whole generation of young Romeos such as Bunny Rabbit. Pussy Cat has that kind of beauty. If he wasn't in love with Madeleine, Michael would fall in love with Pussy Cat, which would be a disaster because Pussy Cat only has eyes for her Bunny Rabbit. And Mulligan, too, for all his playful dismissiveness, concedes her beauty, even if it is couched in artistic terms such as bone structure and classical features. She is really Louise, Lou to everyone. He is Peter. Together they have adventures.

They are children of the Age for all this, but also for the way they look upon Michael and Madeleine, who are just about to leave their company at a fork in the path. Pussy Cat and Bunny Rabbit bid them farewell with amusement in their eyes.

'Can't wait to get at it?' says Bunny Rabbit, with a twinkle.

Dark shadows fall across the golden lawn, the invisible evening life of the park — hunting, gathering, sleeping, fighting and copulating — goes on all around them. The four of them are standing still, Madeleine staring down at the cinder path, Michael up at the trees that are humming with the sound of this secret life. He does not need to look at his friend to know what is in his eyes. And, while he idly scans the trees, he is asking himself why it is that his friend, and these children of the Age in general, should be so preoccupied with those who are not of the Age. On other days, his friends and their comments might bother him, but on days such as these when he sees himself and Madeleine as an old-fashioned couple out of joint with their time, actors on the wrong stage and in the wrong play and bringing with them the sensibilities of another age altogether, he is strangely unconcerned. Even superior. For, this sensibility that they bring with them, this innocence that does not yet copulate, they savour and explore in the same way that the children of the Age explore each other's bodies. And, at such times, he would have them no other way. At such times, this unfashionable conservatism of theirs is a gift. It is an occasion — and one that will not come again — to discover and explore a way of being that the Age itself has discarded. Their gift is this chance to explore a lost sensibility, one that will only ever live on in isolated cases such as Michael and Madeleine. The Age has dispensed with it, and, having dispensed with it, can never have it back. If Pussy Cat and Bunny Rabbit embody an age of release, Michael and Madeleine speak of an age of restraint.

And perhaps this is what moves Michael's friends to play with them, the way the sophisticated inevitably play with the innocent. It is because the innocent stir in the sophisticated distant memories of other ways of being and feeling that the children of the Age — however much they may deny it — look upon them with longing disguised as amusement.

And it is while Michael is contemplating all of this that Madeleine looks up from the cinder path in response to Bunny Rabbit's playful question, her face dramatically half lit in the fading autumn sun. Every gesture — the slightly raised eyebrow, the flick of the fringe across her forehead, the pursed lips, the defiant stare (eyes proud, like a servant turning upon a master and discovering for the first time how well she wears the look) — is perfect. She is her own melodrama. And those proud, defiant eyes are turned directly towards Bunny Rabbit, and whatever it was he was saying he is not saying any more because nobody is listening. Everybody is watching Madeleine. It is a look that commands total attention. A look that will not settle for anything less. A look that is breathtaking in the way it refuses to even countenance the possibility of anybody looking elsewhere. In the political parlance of the day, it is a coup. Bunny Rabbit has been silenced, routed, and in a way that Michael has never seen Bunny Rabbit silenced before. And without a word being spoken. For Madeleine has drawn from within her a look that somehow makes everybody — Michael included — feel like children of a lesser age. Tatty. Plastic. No longer serious. She does this, Madeleine. Just when he thinks he knows her, she looks up with a defiance in her eyes that says 'Enough!' like she has just now, and he realises he doesn't know her at all.

Madeleine possesses a beauty that is *not* of the Age. Not that it doesn't call her beautiful, but it is not a beauty that the Age calls its own. Her beauty is distant, like old films. It is a beauty that the world might imagine touching, but only in the way that you can touch the celluloid — not the fact.

Then the look is gone, but its work is done. An eerie calm settles on the park. She has changed everything with a look. Bunny Rabbit and Pussy Cat no longer gaze upon her with playful amusement in their eyes but with a kind of marvel that wasn't there before. Even trepidation, for they are almost wary of her as they quit the park and wave goodnight, leaving Michael and Madeleine alone. There was even, for a moment, the briefest of exchanges between Madeleine and Pussy Cat, a look that not only said 'Well done', but acknowledged some sort of understanding. Michael is left wondering just what it was that Pussy Cat was acknowledging in Madeleine that she had not seen until now. And he quickly concludes that what Pussy Cat saw in Madeleine was the kind of strength that comes from having sung songs of Experience, not Innocence. And his impulse, on evenings such as these, to see them as that rare thing, an old-fashioned couple in a radical age, looks silly.

13.

Lurch

Midway through the next morning, as Madeleine goes about her duties at the hospital, and Bunny Rabbit and Pussy Cat either rise from or take to their bed, Michael is walking down the corridor of his old school. Even after a month of being back (and he never applied for his old school, but simply accepted his appointment as evidence of the invisible hand of Fate at work), there is still a distinct feeling of discomfort at walking through the door in front of him. The schoolboy Michael always waited outside that door marked 'Staff Room' all his schoolboy life. Michael the teacher enters. The years in between aren't all that many, but they're enough. Enough for the lifeblood of the corridors to have experienced a complete transfusion and now be populated with what seem like intruders. Every now and then, on a bench here and there or a study that once served as a Senior Master's office, he'll see himself being detained for some minor misdemeanour, the nature of which has long since been forgotten by everyone concerned but which seemed so grave at the time.

It is one of those schools that the frontier suburbs got. Grey, flat, porous brick slapped onto match-stick frames. All of them flung up overnight. Built to fall down a generation later. In fact, in the years to come, when the generation that made the school a necessity has moved on and a new generation of young families follows the frontier further and yet further inland, the school will be bull-dozed and match-stick townhouses will spring up on the site in the place of a match-stick school.

Michael pauses before passing through the door, gazing down the corridor. The years in between aren't all that much, but enough. Enough to have him musing on the difference between then and now. For there is a difference. A quality lacking in what he sees around him. He calls that quality Order, and everywhere, in the classrooms, corridors, playing fields and even in the streets surrounding the school, he sees the demise of the Order that characterised his years at the school. Something, long destined to cave in, was, in fact, in the process of caving in. And it wasn't just the slapped-on grey bricks and match-stick frames of the building itself that were falling apart; something else was.

And it is while Michael is contemplating what the decline of his old school might herald that he sees his old geography teacher turn the corner at the general office and into the A Block corridor; the tall, stooped, slow-moving figure of 'Lurch'. With his hair still resolutely parted down the middle, a hint of greying sideburn being his only concession to the passage of time and the arrival of fashions other than those that fashioned him, he is a figure from another world. And he always was. Even then. He hasn't changed, not much. But the corridor through which he moves has changed utterly. Whereas he once moved — and 'moved' is the word, it occurs to Michael, for Lurch never really walked, but progressed (like a warm or cold front, depending on the day) from one point to another — through these corridors in complete possession of them, he now wanders about them like a stranger. And with that vague, lost look in his eyes that strangers in a strange place have. The look that people have when the world around them moves on and they are left gazing about for signs of the Old Life to hang on to.

No student ever called him Lurch to his face back then (although word would undoubtedly have reached him, even though a character from an American television comedy would have meant nothing to him), and the name has now fallen into disuse.

As he nears, Michael nods good morning, and Lurch looks at him at first wondering who on earth he is. Then there is recognition. The faintest hint of a smile, and Lurch is once again in possession of at least one small part of the corridor. And as he nods back it strikes Michael that he is one of those signs of the Old World that the Lurches of life, caught up in changing times, look for to hang on to, so that the world they find themselves inhabiting will not seem so strange after all.

There is even a touch of the old irony in the raised eyebrows and wrinkled forehead, as he tacitly shares his observations of the corridor with Michael. But it is communicated in such a way as to suggest that his trademark irony isn't much called for these days. That, indeed, irony is wasted on days like these.

Michael leans his hand on the staff-room door, pushes it open, and watches as the tall, stooped figure enters the room, the stoop more pronounced than he remembered. Lurch, it seems to Michael, is a bit like an old vine that will, in the not-too-distant future, require the stake of a walking stick.

At his desk, Michael is thumbing through an English textbook that he used as a student when the headmaster taps him on the shoulder and drops a letter in front of him. It is, he says, slightly amused, from something calling itself the Centenary Suburb Committee and they're looking for someone who is young and who grew up in the suburb. With that the headmaster turns to leave, suggesting as he goes that there might be a bit of time off in this for the young Michael. Then he adds, correcting himself, a bit more time off, aware of the concessions the teacher in charge of the school's timetable has made so that Michael might complete his studies.

Low clouds of cigarette smoke hang in the air, groups cluster about each other's desks as if having been arranged that way by some resident Dutch master, and in the reflexive way of the herd that suggests this happens every day. And while he notes that he just might get to like these routines (for he has always been one for routines), he also senses that a bit of time off out there mightn't be so bad. Even for this odd thing that calls itself the Centenary Suburb Committee.

14.

A Letter is Written

Less than a mile from the school, as Michael sits at his staff-room desk and Lurch (cryptic crossword in front of him) lights the kind of old-fashioned cork-tipped cigarette that Vic smoked at formal social occasions, Rita takes Florentine writing paper from her bedroom drawer and begins with a simple 'Dear Vic'.

She is then distracted by the day. A bright, autumn thing. Her roses, glowing in their second blooming like the whole street's. The leaves of the birch, silver and green, in the centre of the lawn. The street is mid-week quiet, except for the stocky figure of Mrs K across the road pounding the summer dust out of a rug with hands and meaty forearms that look, equally, like those of a strangler and a pastry cook, for she is well known along the street for her heavy Ukrainian doughnuts that come with at least three eggs. Having given the rug a thorough belting, she pauses and wipes her brow, for all the world like a peasant in a field of swaying wheat. She seems, this woman from a far part of the earth, to be no particular age. Or, one of those women who grow old while still young. She was old when she came here, not long after Rita, Vic and Michael did, and she's just stayed that way. She hasn't aged, because she was aged in the first place. But, Rita reflects, the poor woman might only be in her forties or less. She's never really asked herself before how old Mrs K might be, and she now concludes that it's impossible to say.

None of this goes into the letter. Dear Vic. At first it was odd to be writing to him, then she got to like it, and now (after seven quick years) she's quite attached to what has become a weekly ritual. Did you know, she opens, that we're a hundred years old? Not us, the suburb. Somebody's got it into their head that this is the year — God only knows how — but it's official. Centenary Suburb. That's us. It's going to be stamped on all official letters, she says. There's going to be posters. Street signs will be altered. Names will be changed. There will be events. And she can see Vic laughing at all this because she is too. Then she adds that someone will do well out of all this — that mayor for a start. That the whole thing has a bit of a smell about it.

From there she moves on to the topic of the Webster house and Mrs Webster, then to Michael, who now talks to her like one of his students (and she wishes he wouldn't). And the house. Michael is always telling her to sell it and go. And it's always good when Vic says stay there, girl, if that's what you want, in that way of his — and she can always hear his voice coming off the letter. The voice of her Vic, conjured up by his words, so that she doesn't so much read his letters as hear them. And it doesn't matter what he says; they're usually about nothing much in particular. They never really told each other much anyway. It's just good to hear his voice, and every time she opens his letters (and he's a good letter writer), that voice is there. Vic's voice. Vic's words. No one puts words together in quite the same combinations and order as Vic does. So when she reads his words, his words are inseparable from his voice. And it's not always like that, she pauses, reflecting on letters and styles. Most people don't have a voice at all when they put words down. You can't hear anything. But not with Vic. When he puts words on the page, he seems to throw the whole of himself into it — his whole body — like he does when he laughs. His whole body laughs when he's *really* laughing, and his whole body writes when he's writing.

And, as she finishes her letter and slips it into the envelope and addresses it to that little box of his at the post office, she wonders if he hears her voice as clearly as she hears his. And there is also that part of her that wonders just how Vic is. How he really is. Because he never says. And she's not sure if it's her imagination, but his handwriting lately looks a little shaky. And it never did before. He always had such beautiful handwriting. Firm, flowing and confident, just like Vic. But it's looking, well, it's looking a bit old lately. And she can't help but ask herself if the Vic she remembers, *her* Vic, is the same Vic who writes the letters and reads hers. Or has he changed like his handwriting? There's nothing sadder than watching a big booming man grow old and shaky, until the boom goes out of him altogether. She's seen it happen in others, big booming men, with booming laughs, and she couldn't bear to see it in Vic. And there's the silences between letters. They can go for weeks. And during them she's always half waiting for the inevitable phone call in the night. For he lives alone, with a bunch of strangers for friends who'll only talk to him as long as he's propped up at the bar (and who probably couldn't care who's propped up at the bar beside them as long as someone is), and sometimes it can take days for anybody to find you. If something happens, that is. And that's why she jumps when the phone rings at night. There's a fatalistic part of her (which she sees in Michael too) that immediately tells her it's bound to be bad news. Only it rarely rings at night, and she'll be happy if it stays that way.

So when she writes these letters, she never says just anything, as though you've got all the time in the world to write a proper one later. Each letter counts. And every time she drops them in the post, she's got to be content that she's written the right letter.

She seals it and looks up. Mrs K has gone, the dust from the rug having been expelled into the still autumn air, and now, presumably, has settled onto the lawn and the flowers of her garden.

Such is the life of the street, and all the streets around it. And such is all she has to report. A rug is aired, a letter is written, and the voice of a loved-one returns for a moment while a silver birch glistens in the autumn sun and somewhere out there a committee prepares to sit. All around, the infinitely complex organism of the suburb is going about its business, unnoticed, and as unconscious of itself as the birch is of the pleasure its shining leaves give to anyone who cares to pause long enough to observe it.

15.

The Search for a
Crowning Event

She knows who he is, all right, the way you know
things around the suburb. This is Rita's boy, although
he's hardly a boy any more. She's seen him round and
about the suburb over the years. This is the first time
they've met. And it's an unsettling meeting. If that's the
word. Although his hand is shaking hers and his lips are
turned up into a smile, his eyes are doing something else.
They're watching. No, more than watching. They're
judging. And although the smile is there, it comes with
the shadow of a sneer. He is a teacher at the local school
and he is on the committee because he is young. He is
what they call the younger generation. Mrs Webster's
round from home to factory and home again rarely takes
in Michael and his kind, and this is the first time she has
ever officially met him, or them, and both he and they
have got her back up already. 'Smug' is the word that first

comes to her, and 'smug' is the word that stays with her throughout the meeting. His lips curl into a smile as his hand shakes hers, but his eyes are judging her, and, she is convinced, he doesn't approve of what he sees. And, what's more, it is a judgment delivered with an air of invulnerability.

You can't touch me, that look says. You ride through our streets like cardboard royalty, and, as you nod and greet the passers-by released from your factory floor or on their way to it, you register their weekly worth: Charlie Monger, foreman, forty-two of these new-fangled dollars and thirty cents; Les Lott, machinist, twenty-eight dollars and no cents; Teresa Krylov, secretary, not much. You ride through our streets like cardboard royalty and calculate the total cost of the labour you pass along the way. But you can't touch me. I'm beyond your touch and your calculations.

This, sure as eggs, is what the look says as he smiles and shakes her hand, and this is what the look says to all of them throughout most of the meeting. He has this thing — they all do, this generation. This thing that is written into their features, this thing that enables them to smile and judge simultaneously, this air of knowing more than they let on — this *learning*. For, in the end, it wasn't speed that took Michael out of his street and his suburb — and, yes, she remembers how cricket-mad he was, as did the whole suburb. No, it wasn't speed that got him out in the end; it was a university degree. And she inwardly pronounces the two words with deliberate, bouncing irony. It was this *learning*. The learning that they take with them wherever they go, and, yes, they will go places, this lot, for their learning is written across their faces. And there is a word for faces like Michael's, the one that first comes to her and the one that stays with her throughout the meeting. And, for the one and only time in her life (if what his smile says is at all true — that he is beyond her touch), she deeply regrets that another human being is beyond her grasp. For, although she has affection for Rita, she has to confess that she would dearly love to wipe the smugness off her son's face. Off all their faces, for that matter. Yet, as soon as she registers this thought, she corrects it. And not out of fairness or some inexplicable rush of generosity. No, it is simply that she knows such thoughts are the thoughts of the old, of those who, like her machines, have been superseded, and Mrs Webster is not yet prepared to call herself old.

It is not only Mrs Webster who is looking at the room differently now. So too are the others. Whether it's the hair, the sideburns or the amused look in his eyes as he takes in all their names, they can't tell. But 'smug' is the word that occurs to all of them, although no one says as much. And Mrs Webster is seriously wondering if the damage to her dining room will be permanent. For it seems as though this revolution of which they all speak, this lot (and he does wear a red badge mysteriously inscribed with the word 'moratorium' on his coat lapel), in the same way, it seems to her, that the mayor talks of Progress, has already occurred and its representative is now seated among them, not so much as an equal member but as an inspector, here to report back later to all the others who, like himself, wear the red badges and amused grins of their kind. Their kind, and this Whitlam of theirs, who speaks to the whole country in the same way that Michael and his kind speak to the rest of us. This Whitlam of theirs of whom they speak as if he were not so much a person as a historical Movement. And, although she would never let on to Michael, she has, in fact, met this Whitlam of theirs at the opening of a new wing at a nearby hospital. He seemed, to her, to move about the room like a mountainous statue on wheels. And this mountain on wheels, she knew even then, was History. This much she felt compelled to concede. This Whitlam of theirs, this mountain with the gift of speech, who moved about the room like a public monument that knows its moment has come, was History. The streets have not yet prevailed, but this young man is an intimation of what it will be like when they do. His presence is a disruptive one and there is a part of her that is not quite sure if she will ever be able to look at her dining room again without picturing the slightly raised eyebrow that she is observing now as the mayor (no doubt an amusing old geezer in Michael's eyes, although only forty-three) explains the task of the meeting.

Michael is there at the invitation of the committee, but now they are all quietly wondering about the wisdom of their impulse. As a first-year teacher at the school — his old school — and someone still engaged in university studies, he is Youth. The quality they all mutually recognised they didn't have and which they sought. Now all feel the disruption of his presence. All tacitly acknowledge, without even so much as the occasional communication of a raised eyebrow, that they have never really sat down with Youth before (not quite like this, not to make *decisions*) and there is a general, unuttered agreement that they don't much like the feeling, especially with someone who has the air about him of sitting down to Sunday afternoon tea with the old fogies, someone who gives every impression of wanting to get away as soon as possible and who doesn't say much because, presumably, he can't be bothered. But, there you are, it's done. And so they plunge onward.

It is an idea they seek. If they are to be Centenary Suburb then the activities must surely all revolve around something that could possibly be termed a Crowning Event. But what?

Silence settles on the room like a sudden dull patch in an otherwise bright day. This long silence — a thinking silence — is punctuated with sputtered suggestions (a concert, a ball, a gala cricket match) all of which are briefly considered then quickly dismissed.

It is then that Peter van Rijn, who has again said nothing to date, quietly suggests a mural.

'A what?' says the mayor.

'A large painting on a large public wall,' the vicar of St Matthew's says, in the manner of a translation.

The mayor is about to do two things: tell the vicar that he knows perfectly well what a bloody mural is, and then laugh at the suggestion itself. But he sees the two priests turn to Peter van Rijn and nod, encouragingly. As does the rest of the table. He realises that the suggestion is actually being taken seriously, and he is a little tired of

Peter van Rijn doing this, at the same time quietly congratulating himself now for having thrown that brick through his window all those years before.

'He means,' adds the priest of St Patrick's, 'something, well, for the purposes of illustration, along the lines of the Sistine Chapel.'

'Yes, yes, I know what he means.'

'Only not so grand, of course,' he adds, with a nasally laugh.

There is a brief silence, then the mayor, reluctantly warming to the idea asks: 'Do we have such a wall?'

Each member of the Centenary Committee then bows their head, each contemplating the idea of a high, wide public wall in a public place. And whether the sheer force of the thinking conjures up the wall, or the wall announces itself to the deeply preoccupied mind of the vicar of St Matthew's, he finds himself saying, 'Of course.'

All heads turn to him as he announces — as if it were perfectly obvious and how did they ever miss it — that the newly completed town hall has just such a wall in its grand foyer.

The mayor is about to quash the idea, as if the vicar is proposing to paint the entrance hall of his house, when the rush of enthusiasm silences him. There are general nods, each to each, young and old, and the mayor finds himself once again nodding.

The phrase 'That's it' is uttered all around the room and everybody congratulates themselves on a job well done. But not completely, they all concede. For, what shall this mural be of? What will it depict? And then, as if all have hatched the idea at once — a mark of its inspired nature, too grand for a single mind — they all announce, simultaneously, over one another, overlapping one another, weaving in and out of each other's words, that this grand wall will depict nothing less than the history of the suburb itself, from its sheep-farming origins, when that first fragile shop went up, to now. Of course, 'all' doesn't include Michael, who is smiling along with the rest of them, but it is a smile, Mrs Webster notes, of a different kind. Nonetheless, it is as though a wave of common thought has passed through Mrs Webster's dining room and uplifted them all. As if the idea itself — the Crowning Event — came from out there somewhere. From the streets, the footpaths, driveways, sporting fields, the public and private houses of the suburb itself, and rolled towards them, gathering in momentum as it went, with the inevitability of an idea that had not been dreamt up but that had always been there waiting for its day to be summoned — as if the suburb itself had spoken *through* them. How else could they all think and utter exactly the same idea at exactly the same time? The vicar of St Matthew's announces that there is, in fact, a German word for this sort of thing, then adds that it is so long he's quite forgotten it.

And it is then, as everybody leans back in their seats and stretches, that Michael announces that he knows just such an artist. One who paints walls. One who has trained in Europe where great walls are painted. He doesn't say that this artist lives downstairs in Michael's student house and that he is known only as Mulligan. Instead, he paints a picture of a latter-day Michelangelo with whom he happens to be on good terms, and the committee turns to him (pleased that he is actually talking to them, and noting with the collective pride of the suburb that raised him that he can actually string a sentence together), each of them now tacitly congratulating themselves on having invited Youth into their circle (and inwardly conceding that Youth might not be so bad, after all). And all the time they are secretly imagining a grand wall of truly majestic appeal, to which, one day, people would come from all over the suburb and beyond. A place of pilgrimage even, and all sprung from the inner circle of the Centenary Suburb Committee, now seated at Mrs Webster's dining-room table.

But as Mrs Webster farewells them all from her doorstep, she is secretly eyeing a distant corner of the garden — Webster's corner, where the garage is — and she is no longer thinking of public walls and crowning events, but quietly contemplating Webster's one trifling infidelity.

16.

The Guitar and the Decade

That evening, after having knocked on Mulligan's door and entered the welcoming mess of his room to tell Mulligan he had a job for him, Michael is sitting with Madeleine in the lounge room of her flat. There is a guitar on the floor. Everywhere, Michael imagines, in all the houses, on all the floors, there are guitars. The guitar and the decade go together. Once, it was the Age of the Piano. Pianos, he imagines, marked the leisurely passing of time in a more leisurely age than this. Pianos spoke of ease and calm in that recently vanished world of their grandparents, the time signature of which was forever *adagio*. In that once-upon-a-time world where the piano ruled, the hours passed unhurried, and days were long. And the music that came from pianos was as ordered as the lives of the people who played them, and as long as the days through which they lived and played. At least, this is the way Michael, currently lounging on the floor in front of Madeleine, thinks of the piano.

This, by contrast, is the Age of the Guitar. Wherever you may be, a guitar is never far away. But this is not an instrument that is content to mark the slow passage of time as music did in that once-upon-a-time world that resisted the ruffian of change. The guitar is an instrument that shakes things up. The piano is made for living rooms and quiet houses. As much a resident of the house as the family in it. The guitar is like something blown in off the street. It has the look of trouble about it. Like a stranger on the doorstep, who slips into the house, unwanted and uninvited, by dint of sheer front. Unpredictable, with an attitude suggestive of it being permanently up to no good.

He could share these thoughts with Madeleine, and he would, if he knew her just a little more. If he was at ease with her as his lounging attitude would suggest, if he knew her just a little more he could relax, deliver his thoughts on the contrasting characteristics of the Age of the Piano and that of the guitar in such a way as to amuse her. He may even make her laugh (and he is convinced he doesn't make her laugh enough). But in the end he keeps these thoughts to himself, convinced that thoughts sound best inside the head and silly in the open air, like quotes remembered, stored up and trotted out to impress some girl if the occasion should arise.

There is a guitar on the floor in front of them, and it also possesses, it occurs to Michael, when looked at from a different angle (he's tilting his head to one side), a certain air of wantonness. This guitar is no longer a ruffian, but a vamp. Lounging there on the floor, all curves and trouble, lying on the floor like a challenge, not so much waiting to be picked up but daring anybody to do so.

Madeleine sits on the sofa, the communal garden outside lit up by a line of full moons suspended on dark staffs, the foliage silver and white, not quite vegetable. Her knees together, she wears a short skirt — as is the fashion — and knee-high leather boots. She's talking of travel, of the journey home, the one she's been planning ever since the day she arrived here with her family on a ten-pound ticket (did she only ever agree to come for the boat trip, she's not sure).

'You know,' she says, laughing, in that northern English, sing-song voice, 'I've been talking about this for so long there are some people who think I've already gone and come back.'

He too laughs, but his is a different kind of laughter, a laughter that, in part, wishes it were true — that she had gone, and that she was back. His is, in short, glum laughter. And, implied in what she says is the fact that he knew from the start that she was going. That he would only have her for a short time. She's never withheld this from him. In the brief time they've been together, it's been out there, in the open. You knew this, you always knew, Michael, so don't go glum on me. This is what she may as well be saying.

It is while he is contemplating this (thoughts of the committee meeting that afternoon banished to the back of his mind) that she reaches out for the guitar and places it on her knees, ready to play. Madeleine is learning the thing, but not seriously. As an amusement, for company almost, in much the same way that his father's generation took up the harmonica. She holds the guitar like a non-smoker holding a cigarette for someone else, then assembles her fingers into the familiar triangle of the D Major chord. She then strums the strings and grimaces as a muffled sound emerges. She has strangled the chord. Possibly killed it forever. He returns the grimace, then suggests she try again, but to hold the strings down properly this time and at just the right distance from the metal fret. She complies, only to replicate the crime. And he is not quite sure how many lives the D Major chord has, so he is quite relieved when she gives up.

'I'll never get it,' she says, handing the thing over to him.

He rises from the floor and, while resting on his knees in front of her, takes the guitar. His fingers assemble unbidden (he has played the instrument for years, ever since fast bowling left his world and the guitar walked in), and without really being conscious of the relative complexity of the process, he strums the same chord. And from the moment he strikes the chord, one single chord, he realises he has never struck a chord in anything like the same way before. It is as though he has unwittingly brought this thing, this instrument of the Age, to life (and the devil that lurks in its woodwork), for the sound seems to expand and grow in the room like vegetable matter. The whole room, all four corners, is filled with sound, and he looks down at the instrument as if he were holding an entire orchestra in his hands, not a familiar, cheap classical copy from a city store. And, with the sound still swelling, he looks up to Madeleine as if for an explanation, and sees only bewilderment in her eyes. For this sound has transformed the room, and has now transformed them. They not only hear the sound, they feel it. The sound enters them, enters the vast network of their nervous systems and is registered throughout their bodies in the same way that touch might be registered. And as much as she might now look upon Michael as the magician who produced this effect, Michael looks back at Madeleine in such a way as to suggest that the whole thing is a complete mystery to him. And, after sharing this moment of mystification, their eyes drift down to the guitar and now gaze at it in mutual wonder.

And it is then that she leans forward, her eyes now firmly on his, takes the guitar from him and slides it onto the carpeted floor. He has never seen her like this, her eyes open and direct. Foreign, a Madeleine he has never known. Although she says nothing, she is willing him, asking him, inviting him to kiss her. She will not move, the look says. He will now come to her and she will receive him. And, with the sound of that single chord still in their ears, he pauses so that he might return the extraordinary directness of her stare, delve into the depths of her eyes (which still might be blue or green), because he knows they have never shared an experience such as this before. This, he is saying to himself, this is Madeleine. This is *her*. The Madeleine that neither he nor quite possibly anybody else has ever witnessed before. And then he is kissing her.

He knows little of kissing (he assumes that neither of them really do), but he knows instantly that they have never kissed in this manner before. For not only is he kissing her, she is kissing him, the faint residue of wine still on her lips from the evening mass. She is both receiving him and seeking him out, at once playing him and being played, and all through the lips. No other parts of their bodies are touching; not hands, arms, thighs, bodies — only the lips. And everything about this moment that has overtaken them is being poured from one to the other through the margins of their mouths, these organs of speech that seem to have acquired a life of their own and no longer feel the need of speech; that have, in fact, shed the need, and, in this delirious exchange, have discovered a higher order of communication altogether. And so deep is the craving there seems to be no end to it. And just when he imagines that this might very well go on forever — and he is content to let it — he feels her arms encircle his neck and draw him back onto the sofa with her. And not once do her lips leave his, or his hers. It is almost as though they have melded, become one, a pose set in marble that will leave them kissing forever, a spectacle frozen in time and destined for museum gardens, one that will outlive both time itself and the elements.

At first this other sound enters their ears like a door opening and closing in a distant universe. A door of no consequence in a faraway world — where two people (recognisable as Madeleine and Michael) lie on an identical sofa in a flat indistinguishable from the one they are in. But it is not a door of no consequence. It is theirs, and they spring from the sofa, their lips finally parting, and are almost sitting upright as Madeleine's sister enters the lounge room, which, throughout the whole exchange, has been left in full light — the curtains not drawn, the room open to the casual or inquiring eyes of the flats opposite them.

Her sister excuses herself, is about to retreat from the room, but they implore her to stay. But, as if having trespassed, as if in the company of two people who ought to be familiar but who seem disconcertingly foreign, she begins her retreat. They stop her. She sits. She sits, she knows, because if normality is to be returned she must sit and chat as if nothing has happened. And at some stage during the talk that follows, while uncertain conversation floats back and forth between them, Madeleine rises slowly from the sofa, picks the guitar up from the floor where it has been left to languish, and places it upright in the corner of the room. And, for a second, she fancies that it is staring back at her, satisfied with itself, its work done. She can still feel his lips, and he still feels hers as he watches her deposit the thing in the corner, both of them wondering what came over them, while staring at the guitar in the corner of the room as if the answer might be found in the infinity of chords contained within it, each just waiting for the right moment to be struck.

17.

The Letter is Received

I t could be any of the mornings of his life in the town. Vic has just come from the greengrocer's and has left carrying a small bag of potatoes and beans. After the greengrocer's, his walk takes him to the post office, where he checks his mail.

And, on this morning, before he even opens his post box, he senses there is a letter from Rita. He turns the key, draws the tiny door back, and there is one of those fancy Florentine envelopes that she sends her letters in, this one written a few days before at the small desk in her bedroom. It's either that or a fancy French envelope. He doesn't know where she finds these things. What takes him by surprise, though, is the anticipation he feels. Of looking forward to the letter, and knowing that he will be disappointed if his intuitions are false and the letter is not there.

He sits on a bench in the sun. The light is always good, and it's the perfect place to read these communications from a previous life. He unfolds the crisp, decorated paper and the old street, its houses and gardens, the entire suburb, open out with the letter. He holds the Old World in his hands, and it is both near and distant, something for which he feels both a curious affection and cold curiosity. You don't walk away from twenty years just like that. You always leave something behind, and you always bring part of that Old World with you, no matter how much you might imagine you haven't.

Not that Vic is someone who spends too much time dwelling on the past, because, as he tells himself, there's not too much time left in which to dwell. There's a lot more of the past now than there is of the future, and, besides, the past is gone, isn't it? All the same, something Rita says (a reference to the Tivoli Road hill and that big old house where Rita grew up), drags him back, as much as he doesn't want to be dragged but there is an emotional tide drawing him back into the former life, and soon he's not even reading the letter. He's back there. He's young, she's young. Impossibly so. Her eyes bright and brown, the adventure, that glorious shot at Life about to begin. The look, the eyes bright and blind to everyone around, they both had it. The look the young always have, for it's so easy to forget you had it too. And it is then, with a shock that moves him physically as if having been rocked by invisible hands (or the convulsion that his doctor tells him could come any day), it is then he remembers that they were once in love. He was once in love, she was once in love, they loved each other and together they spoke words of love. That this thing picked them both up and swept them along, and that they were happy to be swept along by a force so deliriously incomprehensible that it didn't bear thinking about. They only knew that this was a time of 'befores' and 'afters', that the power of the thing had to be trusted, and all that was left for them to do was go with it. Let it take them wherever it would. And so they gave themselves up to it. And such was the power of the thing that it gave them days and days delirious with happiness (all too easily forgotten), that it gave them their son, and that, to give their son room for his long legs (which he got from Vic) to run, it took them out to the fringes of the city where a frontier community was hovering between town and suburb, a suburb in the process of being born, and where, in time, between one weekday walk to the station and another trek home, they eventually forgot that they were ever in love in the first place and could remember little of the force that had swept them all the way out there.

Vic finishes reading Rita's letter and there are tears in his eyes. Where did they come from? He has no memory of the first tear or those that followed. A man, just doing the shopping, sits down in a public place to read a letter from his wife (from whom he is separated, but not divorced) and cries. Such a man is an event. And Vic is that man. People passing stare openly at the event of a man crying in a public place. And, as much as he is not a man given to crying in public places, he is not concerned. Vic is no stranger to crying, or ignorant of the wisdom of tears. He told Michael, often enough in those last few years in the old house and would tell him again any time, that crying is as natural as sweating. And Vic is a big sweater. And as the tears flow, Vic happy to let them, he contemplates how it is that we can forget such things. Such things should be unforgettable, and yet all too often they aren't. How was it that, until just then, he was able to forget the hour before meeting Rita? And how was it that he was able to forget the Vic that pedalled her back from the late-night dances, all the way up that Tivoli Road hill (an eighteen-year-old Rita balancing on the handle bars)? And how was it that he was able to forget cycling back home from Rita's in the early hours of morning, looking up to the stars and kissing the old life goodbye? How is it we so easily forget that something momentous once happened to us? Something so momentous we know intuitively that whatever we were up to until then was the 'before' of our lives, and whatever was about to follow, the 'after'.

Vic rises from his bench, wipes his eyes and looks about the town, which is suddenly alien to him. He places Rita's letter in his pocket. Somebody nods and wishes him a good morning, with a funny look in his eye. Vic nods back. Calls the man 'brother' in that familiar way of his, and returns the greeting, but is not really sure who he has just greeted.

18.

The Arrival of Speed

It arrives one afternoon, a week after the Centenary Suburb Committee found its Crowning Event, under a mellow autumn sun. There are no rough winds in May. The air is autumn still. Leaves flutter slowly onto the footpaths and streets, unhurried, landing softly on the ground above which they've hung all through the spring and summer. It glides through the suburb in black majesty, barely noticed for the suburb is either at work or school, not on the streets. It is the perfect time for speed to arrive. The few who do notice the thing, eye it in the same way the street does Rita's European dresses.

It speaks of somewhere else, of that far-away world out there where wonders such as this are made. But as much as those few who stand and stare on the footpaths of the suburb are wary of this imperial beast as it glides indifferently through their streets, they are drawn to it. It is an object complete in itself. Perfect, beyond either the reproach or approval of the place to which it has been brought. But, co-existing with that part of them that still retains a capacity for wonder is a ready sneer. To be roused to wonder is to be reminded that such things are not of the suburb and come from out there beyond its boundaries.

Just a week before (the very day public tears had turned Vic into a public event), Mrs Webster had ventured deep into Webster's corner of the garden where, in those last years of their marriage, he had kept his one harmless infidelity. That corner of the garden to which he came whenever the dark mood took him, the one he never spoke of. Where he took that one trifling infidelity that in the end made the marriage a lie. He brought it there — the mood; never to her. She had misread Webster, Webster the factory, to the extent that since his death she had been constantly preoccupied with the question of just who this man — with whom she had lived for over twenty years — just who this man was. She only knew, in the end, what everybody else did. And, after more than twenty years together, that wasn't enough.

The green wooden doors of the garage had been locked. As she'd yanked the doors free of all the weather and dirt that had glued them together and light entered the garage for the first time in a decade, she saw the neatly folded tarpaulin that had concealed the black majesty of the beast the garage once housed.

Shelves, tins, tools and cables had revealed themselves to a changed world. The scent of old oils, petrol and cleansers had risen to her nostrils, summoning another age when Webster walked from his garage with these very smells upon him and brought them into the house before changing for lunch or dinner — and making small talk that never suggested that he was engaged in anything more than a trifling indulgence. And, perhaps that is how it began, innocent enough. A trifling indulgence, until it became all-consuming and would not be denied, this need for speed.

She'd moved about the garage (which she had secretly eyed from her doorstep as she farewelled the committee), touching the tins that were closed one day and never re-opened, the tools that were put down and never picked up again. She wiped the dust from a cylinder and the letters and colours of a brand of motor oil no longer around revealed themselves. How little time it takes. The doors of the garage closed one day, Death folded up its belongings, life moved on, and the contents of the garage became those of a lost age. Yet, in those smells and the sudden familiarity of brand names long passed into social history, she'd felt Webster's presence with an aching intensity that she hadn't felt for years — and those feelings that she once gave to him she gave to the objects he once touched. And, it was then that she asked herself, reluctantly, if she would ever be over it.

Perhaps this is why she'd never opened the doors until then, because she knew what was waiting for her inside. That and a lifetime's practice of leaving Webster's corner to Webster. She'd moved about the shed, imagining that the musty air inside might have been the same air that Webster once breathed. Why not? The twin doors of the garage shut snugly on a concrete floor, and the windows were all locked and air-tight. There was even a brief sensation of having violated his tomb, but this passed as fresh air from the gardens circulated with the old and the last remains of Webster's breath had been carried out into the world by the breeze.

And it was then, while the old air was making way for the new, that she began to look upon the place as Webster might have. The overalls still hanging on the wall, the tools either on the workbench or in boxes, the grease and oil stains on the floor, all spoke of a function. This was the core of Webster's world, that all things had their function — humans, machines, tools. And the function of a garage was to house an automobile.

She'd closed the garage doors behind her that day and stepped out into the dappled greens, reds, yellows and purples of the gardens. This was the foundation belief of Webster's world, of someone with two feet planted firmly on the ground and a head full of thick hair that spoke of a man with years left in him. Before she'd even closed the garage door she knew she had resolved to bring back to the garage the very thing it lacked, and, in so doing, restore its function.

Now, a week later, Mrs Webster sits in the wide lounge room of the mansion, looking over the gardens, as the car completes its journey from the showroom to the suburb. It is mid-afternoon and the stillness of the day seems somehow wrong for such an arrival as this. This car — famous enough to adorn the exercise books of idle schoolboys — brings with it not only wonder and grace; it brings speed back to the suburb. The day should surely be unruly. The wind should stir the trees and leaves be scattered across the sky to mark the occasion. But the day remains still, and Mrs Webster rises from her chair as the black hood of the thing noses its way into the driveway, sniffing out its new home with the same indifference it sniffed out the suburb.

As she moves to the front door, she considers the possibility that the circumstances of the day might be right after all. That the very stillness of the day is perfect for the arrival of speed. A day, to all appearances, may remain still and yet be disturbed. As the car enters the gardens, it enters like one that has left waves behind it.

The transfer of the keys and papers of ownership takes place on the front step, and Mrs Webster (who has taken the afternoon off to receive her guest) is soon left standing alone with the thing. With its sweeping lines, which speak of an age of mechanical elegance, this vehicle appears to be moving when standing still. And when she sits behind the wheel and brings it to life, she is conscious of acquiring the feet, fingertips and central nervous system of Webster himself. Just as when she opens the garage doors and drives it inside, bringing it to rest on the concrete floor stained with the grease and oil of the previous occupant, she is aware, once again, of restoring to the garage the function for which it was created. And when she bolts the doors, bedding the indifferent guest down early, there is a faint thrill. The suburb has witnessed its arrival (those that were about or cared to notice) and it is no secret. Yet when she bolts the doors of the garage and cages the thing in, she feels that it could be her secret, feels the thrill of such a caged prize, as though it just might be her one harmless infidelity, her one harmless indulgence.

19.

Madeleine on the Old Street

The following Saturday, Michael and Madeleine are walking down his old street, under a ripe morning sun that pours its warmth onto the gardens, lawns and hedges of the suburb that Michael has brought her to see. George Bedser's roses are coming to the end of their second blooming, yellow, red and pink petals falling upon the lawn; Peter van Rijn is about to step into his car but pauses in mid-motion, waving to Michael with a look both happy and sad, for the boy is grown now and he is asking himself where all the years went. Then he is in his car driving to his television-and-radio shop in the Old Wheat Road, and his question is answered. The metal gate of Mr Malek (Michael never knew his Christian name), the fevered rattling of which did old man Malek's talking for him throughout his years in the suburb, is now silent. Bruchner, the street brute (every street had one), a crippled ruin after a car smash, will no doubt be sitting alone in one of the wide, empty rooms of his house, his dog long gone and the ashtrays, once piled high with the ashes of Joy Bruchner's dreams, long since cleared from the house. When his dog, old and slow, simply expired on the footpath in front of him one hot summer's day, Bruchner wept (the street observed) like a blubbering child, and he carried the broken beast in his once-strong plasterer's arms back into the yard where he'd regularly beaten it to the brink of death and (the street later heard) he buried the thing in the soft, summer twilight and lamented its passing like he never did for his wife, who died of cigarettes and anxiety.

It drew you back into it, the street. You didn't mean or want to be drawn, but you were. Michael eyed its length and was ten, twelve and sixteen all over again. Somewhere in Madeleine's tired eyes (she has come from an all-night shift at the hospital) she knows that the street is drawing him back and she lets him drift for the moment into that deeply private world.

They are pausing by the paddock next to the Bedsers'. To Michael, it is a source of wonder that this vacant paddock is still a vacant paddock, and that he and Madeleine should now be pausing at the very spot they all did — Vic, Rita and Michael — when, one Saturday night, in the distant world of his childhood, they all stood beneath a timeless peach-coloured sky on the way to Patsy Bedser's engagement party.

It had vanished, the world that saw Patsy Bedser dance out of the street and out of their lives, and which also saw the twelve-year-old Michael consume hour upon hour of his early years bowling a worn cork cricket ball against his back fence, chasing speed and never catching it. He hears once again the rifle shot of the ball ricocheting off his old fence, and imagines once more the muttered comments of the neighbourhood warning anybody in earshot that the boy will destroy the fence before the summer's gone. The suburb is no longer at the edge of the known world — as it was then — and that frontier bleakness is gone, for the frontier has moved relentlessly inland. The gardens have grown, the streets are paved, and the houses themselves have achieved a solidity that they never had when they were being thrown up, one after the other, when, all around them, a suburb was being born. All that really remained of that world, when Patsy Bedser had danced out of the street and out of their lives, was this vacant paddock. The tall khaki grass that had swayed that night in the summer breeze was now motionless in the autumn warmth, under a peach sun hanging up there in the sky like the last of the season's fruit, mute witness to all that had gone on in the years that had followed.

They move on, Michael and Madeleine, walking slowly back to the golf-course end of the street. And, as they stroll towards his old house, he is aware of the eyes of the street, in their lounge rooms, behind the shades and the drawn venetians, following the progress of the two young people out there. Those eyes will know him, a rare visitor to the street these days (which will be read as him feeling too good for the street), and their gaze will then shift to the unfamiliar figure of Madeleine. They will know that she is not of the street, and not of the suburb, for she has the look of having come from some other, quite possibly distant, place. And, for a moment, Michael observes her the way the street does, with suspicion, for she brings something with her — and they can't put their collective finger on it — something that speaks of the great world out there. And they view her with the same suspicion that they view the great world. The sons and daughters of the new families (of whom Michael knows little) have nothing better to do on this Saturday morning but stand on the paved footpath, lean against their front fences, and eye her as she passes. Michael, this son of the street, has dragged an outsider into their midst, and however fleeting her presence may be, it is an intrusion. An affront. And since she will be judged as just a bit too fancy for the street, with the stamp of somewhere else all over her, she will also be judged as one who will never blend with the street or learn its customs in such a way that she would no longer stand out, and those same eyes will be happy to see this intrusion off their land and out of their midst. At least, this is what Michael sees.

But as they pass the children of the street, lined up against the front fence of the Millers' old house, Madeleine nods to two young girls and they burst into smiles as radiant as the second blooming of George Bedser's roses. They are tender smiles, tender because the street hasn't got them yet and strangled the tenderness out of them. Michael imagines that once they have passed and the two young girls are inside, they will be told not to go smiling so readily at strangers.

Michael and Madeleine move on up the street until they come to the old house. Rita is away for the weekend visiting her sister. The key will be under the mat. They pause out the front. Once again the street draws him in, draws him back, and he is four years old. Possibly less. He is standing on a muddy dirt street holding his father's hand, looking at the bare framework that will become their house. His father, young and fit, is speaking. This, he says, pointing to the bare structure, is where we shall live. That will be your room. When there are walls and windows and a light and a bed, that will be your room and you will sleep in it. And there, he adds, pointing to another section of the bare structure, that will be the kitchen. And when there are cupboards and a table and chairs, you will eat there. And when you have finished eating in the evenings, you will go to the lounge room, where you will lie on the floor and listen to the radio. And when television comes to the street, you will sit on the floor in front of the heater (or in between your father's legs, telling him you will always sit there) and watch television. Just as one day you will hear the ring of the telephone in that room, for good and for bad. And you will hear the raised voices of your mother and father, fighting because your father has returned late from work again, late and drunk. You will hear words spoken in these rooms that you were never meant to hear and that you will never forget. Just as you will see things you were never meant to see. This is the nature of the house.

Later in the morning, when Madeleine has gone to sleep in his old room, in his old bed (and she will stay there most of the day), Michael wanders from room to room, observing the ghosts of the house. The three of them (Vic, Rita and Michael), as they will always be and will never be again, ghosts crossing each other's paths.

In the yard at the rear of the house, the last of the

summer fruit (which, to Michael's surprise, his mother has not raked up) is rotting on the ground, the plums, apricots and passionfruit lying where they have fallen. The lawn is autumn brown. The house has a bright new coat of white paint, and sparkles in the sun. Fancy drapes have transformed the porch, a modern clothesline has replaced the old, and a garden light that was never there before overlooks the scene. But on the back fence three white stumps are just visible, the paint having just survived the years of rain and sun, as faint as old pain. Inside the shed, a red plastic cricket ball lies on the workbench where it was casually dropped one day and never picked up again. The remains of the old life mingle with the new.

During the day he listens to music, reads, and explores the living museum he grew up in. That evening, before rousing Madeleine, he smokes in the kitchen and lounges at the table, much, it occurs to him as he blows smoke into the air, in the manner that his father once did. Likewise, he sips the beer he brought with him from the prized Pilsner glass that his father once drank from. And, for a moment, he *is* his father. And, for the course of the cigarette and for the remains of the beer, he registers the sensations that come with this, as if he is being given a foretaste of what he will become. Eventually, he extinguishes the cigarette and places the ash and butt in the wastepaper bin, drops the beer can on top of it, and turns in the direction of his old room.

He slowly opens the door and pauses, watching the sleeping Madeleine. As deep as her sleep is, he will have to disturb her soon, not only because it is time to leave, but because the house itself, as the day has waned, has begun to unnerve him. Its ghosts are out and about. It is the very time of day, it has always seemed to Michael, when the hoo-ha's come to get you. The hoo-ha's, that's his father talking. Like many of his father's phrases, the phrases that come from his father's age, they have stood the test of time and he is content to use it. The heebie-jeebies is another. And perhaps it's appropriate that when he reaches for the words and phrases to describe the house at this hour he should find only those from another time, just as the life he lived here is now another life. Hoo-ha's. Heebie-jeebies. These, indeed, are the words that the house would use. And with the hour and the vocabulary that is written into its rooms reasserting itself with such ease, the whole house and the darkening street itself have now taken on a conspiratorial air, as though they would drag Madeleine, too, into its past and claim her. And with her, claim his new life. So he strokes her shoulder, and her eyes open to an unfamiliar room, adjusting to the light and staring at the figure of Michael standing by the bed.

'Did I call you?' Her eyes are wide.

'No.'

'I thought I called you.'

'I didn't hear.'

'I dreamt I called you, then.'

He shrugs as if to say only she can know that.

'But you're here,' she says, now sitting up in bed and grinning. 'I did call you. I called you from my dream and you heard. Explain that. No,' she adds, her arms now open, 'come here.'

The light in the room thickens, there is a chill in the air, and they stay close to each other. Then Michael hears the voice of Mrs Barlow next door, her voice with that high-pitched edge that has remained as consistent down through the decades as the things she says: the house is all wrong, the suburb ghastly and it's all Desmond's fault for dragging her out here in the first place. But Desmond is gone, and Michael imagines her addressing the empty room. A compulsion she barely understands herself any more, driving her to it, on and on. She has been here so long she can now no longer leave. But she can never admit this to herself, for to admit this would be to concede that she is, in fact, home. Over the years, this place and she have meshed, grown into each other, to such an extent that she would now be lost without it. Sometime, during all the years she fought so hard against the place, it became her centre. Desmond Barlow is gone (having coughed the last of his lungs into the last of his buckets) and Michael can only speculate about the scene being currently enacted in the Barlow lounge room and what (a photograph, a chair, a coat on a hook) she must be addressing.

He grins at Madeleine. She grins back.

'Who is she talking to?'

'Nobody.'

Her eyes pop, and she pauses.

'Does she talk to no one often?'

'Every night.'

'Every night?'

'Apparently.'

Then Mrs Barlow's voice rises on one last wave of hopeless rage and the grin falls from Michael's face.

Madeleine turns her ear to the house next door. They are in her thrall and it is almost with a sense of panic in his voice that he coaxes her from the bed, switches the light on and brings her shoes to her. He throws the quilt over the bed and when Madeleine suggests they make the bed properly, that his mother will notice, he tells her not to bother. They must leave, he says, as the voice next door finally collapses into silence, and Madeleine, glancing from the window looking onto the Barlow house and then back to Michael, nods, as much annoyed by Michael's high-handed manner as she is amused by the scene next door.

The autumn evening settles in. The children are out in the street, the way Michael once would have been, while Madeleine and he walk to the station, to the train that will take them back into the city and the Saturday night that awaits them. It's dark, the hoo-ha's have gone, and they are now safely beyond the reach of the street and the house and all its twilight phantoms. It can't claim them now. But she has seen it, the suburb, the world that he comes from and which he will take with him wherever he goes.

Outside the train window, the suburbs of his past rattle by; the lighted platforms of familiar stations come and go, and as they recede into the distance, they also recede into that comfortably sentimental part of the memory that sees the past under eternally honeyed street lights.

Inside the carriage, Madeleine talks about the town she left to come here. The place that she talks about often enough but doesn't miss. And, in the years ahead, when Michael will actually go there and see this town, he will know why. For it will have the look of a place, that, if you were Madeleine, you'd want to leave. He will pause by the park opposite the station one dank November night waiting for the Liverpool bus, not knowing what to make of the place until he recognises something of his old street in it, a touch of a closed-in world, and a town that always has one eye on the flat horizon because trouble is bound to be on the way and that's where it comes from.

The suburbs have given way to the city now. The eyes of the old street will have turned inward and will now be focused on their televisions. The protesting voice of Mrs Barlow will have been silenced for the day. The khaki grass of the vacant paddock will be silver under the moonlight. Inside the carriage, the city beckons and Saturday night awaits them. But as much as the prospect of the evening excites Michael, Madeleine is subdued, even sullen now, and still more than a little annoyed at having been bundled out of the house. She has said all she wants to say about this town she came from, and now she wants to just sit. He doesn't know it yet, but he is witnessing, for the first time, the unreachable Madeleine. The Madeleine who goes somewhere in her mind and doesn't take him, because she doesn't want him there. And, already, he is wishing he'd never taken her back to his old street. Everything goes rotten on the old street, and as much as he might just have viewed it through a sentimental lens, he is now cursing it, for it has given him this new, this unreachable, Madeleine, and he is convinced that he is cursed to carry the street wherever he goes.

20.

Perfume (1)

From the moment she enters the house on the Sunday evening, she knows someone else has been there. Michael had told her on the phone that he might drop in, and he has — but someone other than Michael has entered the house too. *Her* house. And the instant she asks herself why she knows this, she puts her nose to the air and smells it. Perfume. And not her own.

She's been visiting her sister on the other side of the city. And as much as she is happy to visit her sister, she is always happier to be home because Rita is not one of those people who settle easily — or at all — into other people's houses. Even if only for the weekend. And so she has been looking forward to this homecoming. When she would once more be surrounded by familiar walls, prints, chairs and all the carefully chosen decorative objects that give the place her touch — as well as the distinctive sounds and smells that make a house a home.

But the smell is all wrong. And she picked it as soon as

she opened the front door and stepped inside. Michael had said he might be coming out to the old place (might 'drop in' he'd said, with the same casual air, it seemed to Rita, that these friends of his 'drop out'), but he didn't mention that anybody else would. And she knows it must be this young woman he's been seeing. The one Rita hasn't met yet, because she hasn't been introduced. And her nose is out of joint about that. But even if Michael were to explain to his mother that their house was never that kind of house, it wouldn't matter. That their house was never the kind of house to which he could bring a girl back and introduce to everyone, that throughout the whole of his adolescence he knew it was not written into the laws of the house that a girl could be brought back to it, because it would always be the wrong girl. The wrong sort. For the girl — apart from surely bringing with her the wrong laugh, voice and clothes — would always bring with her the possibility of Michael's closed bedroom door and Rita would always be bursting that door open. Because some closed bedroom doors are unnatural. Not that Vic would care. Let him, Vic would say. Let him. If Rita were to just pause and think, she would recognise that it was always this way, and her nose shouldn't be out of joint because this girl of his hasn't been introduced. They never were. And she knows this even now, standing in the hallway of her house with all the wrong smells around her. At least, part of her does. The part that she doesn't talk to. And behind it all, there all the time (and once again Rita knew it then and knows it now without need of Michael telling her), there was always this business of the weight. The weight that she took from Vic and placed upon Michael, the weight that they could have called love but never did. The weight that eventually landed on Michael. Who else? For when love turns to weight, somebody has to carry it. So, the girl would always be wrong. And, throughout Michael's adolescence, no girls ever entered the house. If Rita were to just pause, she would see that it was always this way. But she doesn't. She's got the cheap reek of some tart's perfume up her nose.

And so Rita, dragging this ancient weight about with her and wishing she wasn't, now walks about the house smelling only the scent of intrusion. Of a stranger. Of deception. And, as she walks about the house, she is now aware of other smells, of cigarettes, yes cigarettes — and beer? She's sure she's got the whiff of old beer in her nostrils. She knows that smell, stale beer, from the night before — any night before. The smell of previous-night's-beer is unmistakable. And with the whiff of old beer she is simultaneously seeing Vic falling through the front door, stumbling through the house, and that old familiar feeling of wretchedness is upon her once again, and the memory of that wretched madness that swelled her heart to the point of exploding all those years ago is now more than a memory. It's a smell. And smells make things happen all over again. And she knows she doesn't want these memories again, but knows they won't go till the smell does. Then she sees further signs of disruption, even as she's dwelling on this business of smell and weight and love and why it had to be like that. For she has entered Michael's old bedroom, which has changed little since he left, and noticed immediately that the bed has been disturbed. Slept in. And with the observation comes an involuntary shiver. A half-hearted attempt has been made to make it, a quilt thrown over the bed almost contemptuously. Brazenly. And as this stranger's perfume — which she knows to be a common, cheap scent that young girls these days go for — as this stranger's perfume mingles with the sight of the shabbily remade bed, the word 'tart' comes to her again. And she is convinced that Michael has not only sneaked back into the house when she was not there like some creature with guilt written all over its face, he has dragged a tart back into *their* house, *her* house, with him. And she knows straight away that this is not the act of *her* Michael, upon whom she rested the weight of the love she was left with (when Vic wouldn't carry it any more), *her* Michael who had always told her that her dresses were just right when the street sneered. No, it wasn't him, but some other Michael with a tart in his ear.

She has been at her sister's all weekend, looking forward to being back in her own house. With its own sounds and smells, but now all that has been ruined. And, although it is chilly, she is opening the windows of Michael's old bedroom and pulling the quilt, blankets and sheets from the bed. And as she lifts the sheets she notices that the perfume — this common drop that, no doubt, common girls go for — rises, stronger than ever from the pillow slip. And soon, the whole intrusion, the whole violation, is bundled up and dropped into the washing machine in the laundry where the scent can be washed from it. The thought of some girl that she's never met sleeping in the house — if 'sleeping' is the word — without Rita even being consulted is not only an intrusion but a betrayal. And, if he can treat this place like some kind of doss-house, she is also asking herself just how well she knows this other Michael who mixes with all his university types and the sorts of girls — that she can well imagine — who hang around them.

For an hour — or is it more? — she's wretched. Ridiculous. As angry with herself as she is about the bed and everything else. She's spent all her life either waiting for the men in her life, or watching them move on, just wishing they'd stand still long enough for her to get a grip on them. And noting, more sad than angry, the happiness with which they move on, when they finally do. And maybe all the staying when everybody told her to go, all the care she poured into the house, was just another way of telling herself, and telling the street, that the world hadn't expired the day Vic moved on. A way of telling herself and everybody else that the house was still here, she was still here, things would go on, and the damage wasn't so bad really. But, perhaps, in the end, the only one she convinced was herself.

Later, when the bed has been changed and the evening breeze has done its work, when the kettle is boiling and kitchen smells fill the house and the television is creating its own distinctive sounds (for each television is different), she tells herself that the house is *hers* again.

For a moment it slipped from her, its ghosts rose up from where they were resting and she felt the weight of old love doing its work all over again. And with that moment, possibly acknowledged for the first time with any sense of inevitability, or even urgency, was the feeling that Michael might be right after all, that her sister might be right, they all might be right — that the ghosts of the house would be forever in residence. And so, after all the care she's showered on the house and the sense of home the house gave her when a sense of home was needed, after all that, the time for parting company might be upon them.

She looks around her, wondering what the feeling might be like — to finally say goodbye to the place — and if (for the memory of old love and old wretchedness has exhausted her) she would ever have the strength to do it.

21.

Vic's Detour

This is the part of Vic's wanderings through the town that he doesn't have to take. But for reasons he is not quite sure of, he does. And perhaps 'reasons' isn't the right word, for he is driven by the kind of impulse that an animal might be driven by, uncomprehending, but utterly accepting. Therefore, once a week (usually a Monday, as it is today), even on those midsummer mornings when nobody should be about, Vic goes out of his way and strolls past the funeral director's in a small street behind the post office.

He has, in fact, just come from the post office and on this day there is no letter from Rita (currently noting that the whiff of intrusion has been expunged from the house overnight). He enters the side street that takes him round the back of the funeral parlour. The roller doors are up, a long, gleaming hearse sits waiting for its hour, and near it a beautifully polished and lacquered coffin has been placed on a metal stand. Three men in white shirts and dark suit trousers, and a woman in gumboots, all stand about in a circle, chatting, laughing and smoking, the way anybody would before work. They could just as easily be a road gang taking a break, or drivers in between shifts.

As he passes he nods and they all return the greeting, but it is the tall, grey-haired, senior member of the group who makes eye contact with Vic. An amiable face, a grin that is happy enough. But at the still centre of his smiling face are the eyes that know a few things about Death. We greet Death in the mornings, this man's eyes say. We mix with Death's family and friends, we drive Death to a lonely plot and we bury it. Or we burn it, and put it in a jar. But before we do all that, we like to hang about out the back here and have a bit of a smoke and a laugh.

On this morning though, Vic recognises something more than all that in his eyes. The coolness on the dark side of the affable undertaker. A professional interest, and Vic the object of his interest. It is a passing moment of scrutiny, of calculation. Up and down the length of Vic's frame. Of measurement. In short, a fitting. Unspoken, but there. They all come to us in the end, the look says. Whether you like it or not, we will, you and I, do business one day. And Death does a steady trade in this town.

Has he got a smell about him? A smell that Vic himself can't pick up, or anybody else for that matter, except for those who deal with bodies every day. Vic could swear, as this affable undertaker narrowed his eyes, he also lifted his nose as if detecting the unmistakable scent of business.

He walks by, the men put their suit coats on and prepare to go to work, and the woman in gumboots gives the tyres of the sleek, dark limousine a final squirt with the hose. Vic remembers, years before, the doctor in the suburb telling him that the pills for his head and his heart were useless with the grog, that he'd die, and he remembered telling him he couldn't care less. And he still doesn't. But when the buggers start sniffing you out from the crowd, when you've got some sort of scent on you that you can't even smell yourself, you know that it really is getting near dying time. Dying time, that's what Vic calls it. And when the time comes, Vic, like any animal, will know what to do. Find a nice spot and just lie down and let it happen. If it doesn't ambush him.

He doesn't have to pass by the funeral director's, but once a week he takes that detour, goes out of his way to pass the back of this place, just so he can look upon it and the men in the dark suits of their trade who stand about in between jaunts, smoking and laughing and chatting about all the usual things. He doesn't have to pass this way, but he does. And they're all acquainted with one another by now. They're all, more or less, on familiar terms.

By the time he hits the bottom of the street, he's ready for a beer. And it's always the same after this little detour. The bar always glows in the morning light, and that bold, crass and wonderful sub-tropical sun always pours in through the stained-glass windows of the pub and lights it up like a vast cathedral. Light is brighter, warmth warmer, and when he raises that first beer of the morning, when his lips kiss the glass, part and receive the blessing of malt, hops and barley, he knows he will feel more alive at that moment than he will be for the rest of the day.

22.

Perfume (2)

Michael is standing alone on the footpath near the taxi rank outside the city hospital. It is a cold Friday evening, the first of the bad nights, and it seems to come without warning. The first of the nights when Madeleine pronounces everything wrong, and Michael can't understand because everything is right. More right than it's ever been. The first of the nights when the unreachable Madeleine he'd glimpsed that last weekend in the train carriage stares at him with that sorry look in her eyes that he will now see more and more of. Just as he will know more and more of the unreachable Madeleine.

Nine miles to the north, the weekday business of the suburb is concluded: the school is closed and dark until Monday; Lurch has returned to his home, his wife and daughters (something Michael is surprised to learn, for there is a touch of the eternal bachelor about him); with a flick of the switch Rita brings the full-moon lights in the garden to Friday-night life; and the sleek, black beast in Webster's corner waits to be sparked into motion.

And here, at the front of the hospital, Madeleine has just driven away in the taxi that was meant for them both. The taxi that would take them to the city station, and then on to that jumble of rooms by the sea where her parents and sister lived and where she and Michael were to spend the weekend. But the bag he packed earlier in the afternoon is at his feet and this Friday is now going to be different from the one he imagined when he packed it.

Then he is conscious of it for the first time. Perfume. It does not suddenly overpower him, this scent. It is infinitely more subtle than that. It does not regale him, but gently taps him on the shoulder, saying (as it will whenever he smells it in the years to come when Madeleine is long gone from his life) remember me? He is oblivious of it one minute, and the next he is drawn to it to the extent that he is now oblivious to everything around him. He knows this perfume. Knows it now, and forever. And from the moment that he inhales it he sees once again the deep blue cashmere sweater she wore tonight, sees once again her neck and the simple gold cross suspended round it. He closes his eyes and breathes her in, Madeleine.

She is physically close again. Close enough for him to feel her warmth, and close enough for him to smell the faint trace of wine left on her lips from the six o'clock evening mass from which she came this evening before meeting Michael (and as he tries to imagine her in church, he can't; he sees only a shadowy, kneeling figure, whispering in candlelight, another mystery again). Around him the world goes on, but, as he breathes deep on the scent, he feels it slipping from him, as if he were slipping irresistibly into a dream or a narcotic doze.

Suddenly Madeleine is there in front of him, looking down at the footpath, the taxi rank behind her, the Friday-night taxis lined up in the chilly evening air in front of the cream-brick hospital which is lit up in the night. She is shaking her head and telling him that everything is wrong as he hears his imitation leather bag fall at his feet and watches again as she walks to the taxi alone. Watches as she alone takes the taxi they'd both been waiting for, glances at him with that soon-to-be-familiar sorry look in her eyes that she will always be giving him, then slides into the back seat and is gone.

Now standing on the same spot, Madeleine gone, he's wondering how it is that he can smell her perfume as if she were in front of him, and he concludes that because the air is so calm this invisible cloud of perfume has remained, hovering round him, and he is reluctant to leave because as long as he has the scent of her he still possesses some part of her. He still has her. But this scent stays and stays, and taxis come and go, and it seems that he'll have to either give her up or be prepared to stand all night on the same spot, delirious, in the midst of a cloud that, to the rest of the passing street, isn't there. For, anybody strolling by would simply see a young man staring up at the cross-hatched branches of the bare trees that line the street for an inordinate amount of time and for no apparent reason. Longer than the street would deem normal.

And just when it seems that he will have to stay all night, he lowers his head and the scent becomes even stronger. It is then that he lifts his woollen pullover to his nose and realises that the scent is there, that there is no cloud, that the perfume is on him and he carries it with him. He remembers now her face resting on his chest, pressed into his pullover, just before she told him that something wasn't right tonight and that she'd rather spend it alone. Just before she'd told him how good he was to her and how rotten she was to him (when he knew he was never so good, and she was never so rotten), and just before she turned and took the taxi they had both waited for.

No longer captive to the invisible cloud of Madeleine, he is now free to move. He carries her with him. And so he picks his bag up and walks away, happy.

But in those years waiting for him, after Madeleine has gone, this perfume, whenever he smells it on the street or in shops or trams, will always be the scent of absence and will always work on his senses and his mind with all the power of a magic potion. If he knew what it was, even now, walking back from the taxi rank, he would buy it and have Madeleine in phial — to be drawn in and inhaled like some sweet narcotic at will. But, even as he plays with the thought, he knows he doesn't want it. Knows that if he were to have his Madeleine in a phial by his bed, to be inhaled at will, that the sweet narcotic of instant remembrance would surely lose its potency, and like all such potions would eventually lose its power altogether. And Madeleine, the Madeleine that he now draws from his pullover into his lungs and arteries, would be forever lost to him.

23.

The Artist Meets With His Wall

For many years he has been one of those people who are only ever known by their surnames. Mulligan. He has other names but nobody ever uses them. Not Michael, nor Bunny Rabbit nor Pussy Cat. Mulligan — like Rembrandt — says it all. And so, on this overcast Friday morning, Mulligan gazes upon the wall with bright, hungry eyes. He has sought such a wall all his life. He has seen such walls during his travels and his studies in foreign countries, but they were never *his*. A wall such as this, he knows only too well, comes along once in a lifetime. It is high and wide and dominates the entire foyer of the town hall. Once done, he knows, his name will live as long as the wall itself and this wall looks like it's not going anywhere in a hurry. It's only just come into the world.

Mulligan is in his early thirties, not old, but old enough to feel immortality slipping away from him. Besides, he has a pact with himself that if he doesn't make his mark by the time he's thirty-three he will give up and accept the slow suicide of the public service or teaching. Or, he just might hasten the whole process and do himself in altogether on the spot. Thirty-third birthday. He's not sure. He has been at it — painting, that is — for most of his life and as he stares up at the vast expanse of wall before him he suspects that this is what the labour was all for. This is where the study and the sheer slog of learning his craft were leading all along. The wall was waiting for him. And there is an unmistakable sense of the twain converging, wall and man, meeting for the first time as they were always destined to. For this is *his* wall, and if it hasn't got his name written all over it, it soon will.

He paces back and forth across the foyer, black beard shining, black hair flopping over his forehead, intense, glinting eyes that, at times such as these, bear a striking resemblance to a Rasputin who never quite found his patron — a resemblance that has been commented on before. He did, in fact, train to be a Catholic priest when he was too young to know any better, and the significance of choosing his thirty-third birthday as his year of reckoning has not escaped him. He continues pacing about, ignoring the committee members gathered about him, as he contemplates just what he will do with this gift of a wall, this wall that has come to him and was always meant to.

The committee, in turn, eyes him with a mixture of wariness and intrigue, not quite sure of what it is that they are letting into their midst, but the two priests recognise in this man the religious zeal that fired their youthful ambitions, and Mrs Webster recognises the look. She had seen it in Webster from the first, this *will* that seeks to impress itself on the world, and she sees it in this young painter, now gazing up in wonder at the wall.

When he is gone and they all confer, after viewing his folio, complete with photographs of his previous works, they all agree that there is indeed something curious about him but it wouldn't be the first time a curious character got a council contract. Besides, that is artists. That is their way. They can be a funny bunch. But no funnier than others. Just as long as he can do the job, and the evidence is that he can.

24.

Paths That Cross and Uncross

That night Mulligan and the whole house (as they often do on Friday nights) drink in the pub opposite. It is a simple pub owned by an Italian family, and on most nights, towards closing time, the older Italian men at the bar, who drink little and talk a lot, sing like a heavenly choir and warm the pub and everybody inside. They have not yet begun to sing. Mulligan is loud, talkative and expansive. He has found his wall. Michael is silent. He has just lost his Madeleine (driven away alone in a taxi that was meant for two), the first of the many times that he will lose her before losing her altogether. Pussy Cat and Bunny Rabbit are restless at the end of the table at which they all sit.

Rita, vaguely aware of that Friday-night feeling out there in the streets and houses of the suburb, puts her feet up on the coffee table in the lounge room and sips wine while eyeing the empty rooms of the house and listening to the television. Mrs Webster, her chosen whisky in hand, stands at the drawing-room window dwelling on the corner of the gardens where Webster kept his one trifling infidelity, the keys to the newly installed resident in her dress pocket. Peter van Rijn, having stayed back late, shuts the door of his shop, while the lights of the Chinese take-away burn brightly and the evening bells of St Matthew's roll softly over the dark streets of Centenary Suburb. Travelling south, on the last part of the long train journey down to where her parents and sister live by the sea, Madeleine sits in an empty carriage staring at her reflection in the window beside her, sad to acknowledge that she is happy being alone tonight, while, a thousand miles to the north of her, Vic sits in his usual chair in the Twin Towns Services Club and looks out through the wide windows of the club, onto the sprinkled stardust of the town's lights, his hand wrapped round one of the evening's many beers.

Lives cross and uncross, meet, merge or go singly through this Friday night. And those, like Pussy Cat and Bunny Rabbit, who sit restlessly beside each other, are, in some part of their wandering minds, preparing themselves for those Friday nights that will be spent separately. While those, like Michael and Madeleine, who crossed and parted on the one night, gaze from separate windows into the blackness and wonder just how many times there are left for their lives to cross and part before parting forever.

Everybody, looking forward or looking back, on this late-autumn Friday night, the last of the sodden leaves trampled into the footpaths outside, the low clouds of winter already settling in for the season. Everybody, either looking back to a not-so-distant time when the adventures of life were new and fresh enough to sustain storybook identities, or, like Madeleine, looking forward to when 'real' life can begin, or those like Mrs Webster and Rita, hovering over that blurred line that separates what was from what might be. Needing only the slightest of nudges to cross over. But not tonight. Tonight everybody takes a deep breath. It's Friday evening. The harking back, the straining forward, can stop for a few hours and everybody can give themselves over to the bright face of television, lose themselves in the noise of crowded places or in chosen solitariness.

Mulligan floats over it all, buoyed by the day. Mulligan doesn't need people. He doesn't need the past or the future. Mulligan has his wall, and this wall of his isn't going anywhere in a hurry. He calls to the table for more beers. And it is then that they start up, the older Italian men at the bar who drink little and talk a lot. One moment they are ordinary drinkers at a bar, changed out of their tradesmen's overalls and dressed in their Friday best, and the next they are a heavenly choir and the whole pub lifts with their voices.

And all the time, the living suburb is constantly evolving, through night and day, weekend and working week, sunshine and rain, ever forward, ever onward, until that perfect day arrives, surely not too far away, when the straight line of History can lie down in its perfect summer gardens and pronounce its job done.

Part Three

Winter

25

Pussy Cat and Bunny Rabbit Copulate, then Talk Afterwards

It begins slowly and quietly. A low moan, followed by ripples of laughter. But it is clearly the beginning of something. Of some secret ritual, inadvertently made public. Without knowing any more, without being told anything and without speaking, Michael and Madeleine (both sitting on Michael's bed) know that this is the beginning of the thing. And soon they will hear the sound of two people at it.

It is late in the afternoon and clearly Pussy Cat and Bunny Rabbit think they have the house to themselves. Michael and Madeleine heard them tramping up the stairs, push open the door, then neglect to close it. And, even though Michael's door is closed, the sound travels easily from one room to another when doors are left open. First there is the sound of heavy objects (shoes, possibly) hitting the floor, then the first of the low, quiet moans and both Michael and Madeleine know it is just starting.

And, although they have done nothing but be in Michael's room at this particular hour (and not be noticed), they are now compromised. Two people have begun to copulate in the room opposite, while two people sit on a bed with no choice — seemingly — but to sit, listen and wait for an opportunity to leave discreetly. And Michael knows the noise will grow louder because he has heard them copulate before. That and because of the structure of the house itself. It is a Victorian terrace and upstairs there are three rooms: a large balcony room facing the street, which is Michael's, another on the side of the stairs (in which Mulligan stores his paints and materials) and another facing the back yard. This last room is the room of Pussy Cat and Bunny Rabbit. Its door faces the stairwell, and when the house is quiet, as it is this afternoon (Mulligan is with his wall), the stairwell amplifies all the sounds that come from their room. With the door open, every movement, every utterance, every moan, echoes and swells in the open air of the stairwell. And, along with these sounds, the distinctive scent of tobacco and hash flows into the house.

And although the moans and laughter begin quietly, they soon grow in intensity and volume. Michael and Madeleine are caught. They could, it is true, rise quickly and leave the house, whistling on the stairs and in the hallway to announce the nonchalance of their departure. Or Michael could simply close Pussy Cat and Bunny Rabbit's door, confident they would scarcely notice or care. Or, they can simply wait for it all to be over. Without speaking, they choose the last of the options and prepare to sit it out. It is a decision that automatically compromises them, as though they have chosen to remain near, chosen to listen to these sounds that are growing louder and more insistent by the minute.

And soon it seems to be all around them, as though the two lovers are right there in front of Michael and Madeleine and not in the room opposite them. The grunts of effort and labour and the squeals of pleasure mingle and pour through the open doorway into the ears of Michael and Madeleine. And as much as they never wanted to be eavesdroppers, they are now. Each drawn irresistibly, if guiltily, to the sounds that tell them that a process older than words, older than laughter, is now taking place. And they can't help but listen. Its elemental simplicity demands their attention, and so they sit in silence, an almost childlike fascination written on their faces while the mystery dance unfolds.

Michael is staring out the window, Madeleine at the floor. And although they try to avoid each other's eyes, they can't. And the look in Madeleine's eyes (that mixture of the troubled and fascinated, in spite of everything) is surely mirrored in his. Had they been watching Pussy Cat and Bunny Rabbit going at it in their room, had they been sitting beside them observing the spectacle, it could not have been a more awkward matter. For that mixture of the troubled and fascinated has been made all the more intense for not having been witnessed but imagined. They both avert their eyes from each other, then find other things to look at in the room. And, as they do, there is a sudden collapse of sound, a sense of bodies flopping in the dying afternoon light, and of the thing being done.

In the silence that follows, it seems to Michael and Madeleine that Pussy Cat and Bunny Rabbit have fallen into instant sleep, expired or even died. So complete is the silence. And, at last, after having been trapped in the room for what feels like the better part of the afternoon, they prepare to leave.

'Oh fuck, the door!' Pussy Cat's voice is so loud there is, once again, the feeling that she may as well be in the room with them.

'Nobody's in.'

'Oh, what the fuck. Who cares, anyway?' Pussy Cat, who must have jumped up in alarm, now falls backwards, sending tremors through the old bed. 'Be good for them.'

'Who?'

'Them.' And Michael and Madeleine can imagine Pussy Cat's soft, white paw pointing in their direction. 'What do you suppose they do?'

'I suppose they don't do anything.'

'I don't believe that. I can't believe they don't find ways of, well . . . letting nature take its course.'

'Never. She's a good Catholic girl.'

'So was Heloise.'

'She was a sinning Catholic. They're different.'

Pussy Cat bubbles with laughter as Madeleine breathes in deeply and exhales sharply.

'Pity,' Bunny Rabbit goes on. 'Bit of a waste. I rather fancy her, actually.'

There is a sudden short silence.

'You what?' Pussy Cat pounces, nothing playful in her tone.

Michael and Madeleine know that menace is in the air. Its presence is confirmed with the strange hiss of language that follows.

'Don't you *ever* fancy anybody else.'

'Calm down.'

But Pussy Cat won't be calmed.

'You ever, *ever* go near anybody else and I swear I'll kill myself. I might even kill you.'

It is all delivered in a loud, hoarse whisper.

'Well,' and there is a fragile flippancy to Bunny Rabbit's voice. He is not someone to be frightened easily but he is now. 'Well,' he goes on, 'if you're going to kill both of us, don't forget to kill me first.'

There is a sudden explosion of shrill laughter, their door slams, and the whole house trembles and shakes with the impact. And then comes the muffled sound of their bed swaying and squeaking as Pussy Cat and Bunny Rabbit return to what they do best.

Michael and Madeleine rise, flee the room, and carefully negotiate the carpet-covered stairs, breathing easily once out on the footpath. They walk quickly back towards the hospital.

'Sorry.'

'What for?' Madeleine says, not looking round at him.

'That's just it. I'm not sure.'

It is then that she turns upon him.

'Then don't say sorry till you know why.'

But she has no sooner said it than she reaches out for his hand. Behind them, up in their room, Pussy Cat and Bunny Rabbit have collapsed into sleep, a long, late-afternoon doze that will go into the evening and leave Pussy Cat irritable and touchy upon waking. And the more her Bunny Rabbit tries to smooth her fur, the more she will arch. And, later that night, when they are drinking and laughing with friends in the pub across the street where the Italian men sing each night like a heavenly choir, she will look for her Bunny Rabbit and find him staring out the window.

26.

Rita Begins Webster's Museum

The first job is to clear out the old room to make space. Mrs Webster calls it the Games Room. It is at the back of the house and has its own entrance. It is, she says, perfect.

At some stage, it seems, during the last meeting of this Centenary Suburb Committee, it was decided there should be a museum, a dedication to Webster's Engineering. Not just the man, but the establishment itself. There would be photographs, documents, old desks and chairs, bits of machinery, scraps of metal, and displays of the bits and pieces that the factory produced. Workers, old and new, could come and view the history of their life's labours. As he had so often said himself, the Websters of this world would be impossible without labour. They had, between them, he had told his staff, created this thing that had been the centre of their working lives for most of their collective memory. Webster may well have brought this noise of his, this beast of production to the suburb, but he could never have done it alone. Ultimately, his gift, the beast of production, was a two-headed one. And so this museum would be a dedication to anyone who ever stepped inside the place, and everyone who still does.

This committee (and Michael tells Rita about it from time to time, how it is like stepping back into an old British comedy, and how he can only ever see them all as players from that old black-and-white world that gave them so many laughs when the laughs were needed), this committee seems to have money. Enough to put on a show like this. And so Rita stands at the doorway surveying the cluttered jumble of gaming tables and chairs and rolled-up rugs, all covered with successive layers of dust that would have taken decades to gather.

As much, Mrs Webster had told her earlier in the week, as much as she would love to look after the whole business herself, there just wasn't time. Did she, Rita, understand? Besides, she went on, she might be too close to it all, and perhaps they would be better off with a clean pair of eyes, someone from outside the place, who had never stepped in, someone — she eventually suggested — like Rita. And as much as Rita declared that she couldn't do it, she eventually nodded and the job was hers. And it was a job; she would be paid. This committee had money indeed.

Immediately, they moved on to the practicalities of the task at hand, Mrs Webster's tone and words, brisk and brief, the kind of tone people use when they've just hired someone. The kind of tone Rita herself has slipped into when she, too, has hired any of the many tradesmen, who, over the years, have transformed her house into what it is today. But there's something else about Mrs Webster's tone. And it tells Rita that for all her talk about being too close to everything, there was a distinct touch of just not caring any more. Not so much too close as just plain removed. Someone who was quite relieved to have the matter taken out of their hands. She's a curious case. And she's *always* Mrs Webster, too. Rita is always Rita, but there is no hint that Mrs Webster will ever melt into Val. And Rita doesn't take it personally, because she knows from Michael that even the members of this committee call her Mrs Webster. Even the mayor. It's as though it's not a name any more, but a title. Conferred upon her by the suburb. A title she's happy to receive. One that suits her purposes. One that allows her to walk the same streets of the suburb as everybody else, but (like some sort of homegrown nobility) to be removed from it at the same time.

So here is Rita, standing at the door of the Games Room that smells like it hasn't been aired in years, mulling over the curious case of Mrs Webster and contemplating the job at hand. Behind her, parked on the gravel drive at the back of the estate, the removalist's van sits under a low, suffocating sky that gives every impression of settling in for the season. And, as the two men join her in the doorway, she finds herself employing the same tone of voice that Mrs Webster used when she employed Rita. The billiard table is a monster of a thing and will have to be dismantled before it is removed. The whole room, she informs them, will have to be cleared before she can begin. Tables, chairs in varying states of disrepair, sideboards, mantelpieces, and boxes, boxes, stuffed with all the things that are eventually stuffed into boxes, which are then sealed and forgotten.

Throughout the morning and early afternoon (as Pussy Cat and Bunny Rabbit merge into one amid moans and howls of laughter, and while Michael and Madeleine sit in his room waiting for it all to be over), the room is slowly, laboriously, cleared. And, late in the day, Rita has a view of the room: its dimensions, shape, and the light — not much of it — that the windows let in. And, as she sits there, amid the stirred dust and relics of Webster's life, she compiles a list of what must be done.

And it is while she is compiling this list that there is a sudden explosion in the room. She looks up, not fearful but puzzled to see that a number of boxes have fallen from the top of an old bookshelf and crashed onto the bare floorboards. A cloud of dust rises, particles swirling skywards in a shaft of light, spearing into the room through the trees outside. The balance that for so long has held this room together and kept it stable has been disturbed. And, as fanciful as it seems, it is as though the room, after all these years of silence, has something to say.

She puts her pen and paper down on the floor. The cardboard boxes are heavy, sealed with thick tape (as if whoever sealed them never intended them to be re-opened), but one of them has burst open upon impact. The others, which she can barely lift, she pushes against the wall. The contents of the broken box have spilled out onto the floor and she kneels, placing the collection of scattered items — the tools of office work, stamps, inkpads and official paper — one by one back into the box.

The small black business notebook amongst it all, for appointments and meetings, is for the year 1959. Her first impulse is to put the thing back in the box. Her second, upon reading the year, is to open it. This is not Rita's way. She would be horrified at the thought of anybody reading her private papers. Everyone has a right to a private life, even when they're dead, and she respects the rights of others as she would expect hers to be respected. But she can feel, even as she pauses with the slim black volume in her hands, that she is giving herself licence to pry. She has, after all, been entrusted with the task of preparing the room for the exhibits. And although Rita is only meant to prepare the room, not to select the items (the local historians and someone from the city library will do that), she is, nonetheless, involved. And, as the gold numbering of the year draws her in and bids her read, she tells herself that the box fell for a reason.

She is wondering why the year 1959 should feel significant, when she remembers that Webster died (if it can be called dying), that Webster 'left' this world in the summer of 1960 and she realises that this notebook is the business record of his last year as Webster the factory.

They are everyday entries. Regulation matters. Contacts, delivery dates, meetings (with people whose names mean nothing to Rita and who may or may not be around any more), addresses, phone numbers and so on. At first the entries are detailed, the names and places written in full.

But, as the year progresses, the entries become more and more basic, until towards the final pages they are punched in in a kind of shorthand. Names have simply become first letters, places abbreviations. They are the entries, Rita suspects at first, of someone who is too busy to write things in full, someone who feels the pace of the year gathering and for whom the luxury of full sentences and complete names is no longer affordable. But as she flicks through the pages, these last official days of Webster the factory, a second suspicion occurs to her: that these just might be the entries of a man who simply doesn't care any more.

And it is then that she flicks a page over and comes to the oddest thing. Not just full sentences but a whole paragraph of them. And not scribbled but carefully written down. But, however carefully they may be written, the words themselves make no sense. None at all.

A lonely impulse of delight drove to this tumult in the clouds

What? It's as though he had lost his wits, taken leave of his senses, and poured gibberish onto the page. The scribblings of someone who, after a lifetime of strict order and routine, had discovered, caved in to, the delights of gibberish and gobbledegook. It is only as she reads on that she realises she is reading poetry, that Webster may have written the words down carefully, but, for some reason, hadn't bothered to arrange the words on the page the way the poet would have. For there is rhyme in there, and the more she reads this little entry, the more she sees there is also reason. But he wrote it out like you would anything else. Perhaps he was just crammed for space on the page, for on this day, November 27, 1959, he had three meetings, the details of which took up most of the page. And jammed in between was this odd business.

I balanced all, brought all to mind the years to come
seemed a waste of breath, a waste of breath the years
behind, in balance with this life, this death

Poetry? Webster? The man who, Mrs Webster had assured her often enough, had never read any of the books on his shelf. That they were there for decoration and that it was she, Mrs Webster, who was the reader of the house. An odd thing to find in a business notebook, this outbreak of ... what do you call it? She pauses, drumming the page with her fingers before the word bursts from her ... humanity. An odd thing, this outbreak of humanity. The handwriting, she notes, looks like Vic's. It was the way they were taught, the Vics and Websters of the world — and all the other children they played with in all those distant playgrounds before they became what they did. And while she is thinking this she remembers that it was Vic's habit to write bits of verse and poetry on the backs of envelopes and in notepads, and then file them away in his wallet. But Webster the factory? It's odd, even disturbing. And she can't say why. And while she doesn't know what it all means, because she never knew Webster, she has the distinct, unnerving feeling that something is wrong here. She's been given a glimpse into something she was never intended to read. This, she tells herself in her mother's voice, is what you get for prying. And if this is what the room has to say, then she doesn't want to hear — and the room has no business blabbing.

What has disturbed her is the fact that she is now the recipient of knowledge. And she'd rather not be. For she now has to decide what to do with it. And, after quick and decisive thought, she decides to put the thing straight back in the box and seal it with the same thick tape — this time properly.

The only person who could possibly be interested in the contents of the notebook is Mrs Webster, but Rita, putting herself in Mrs Webster's position, concludes that she would rather not know. Rita concludes, with utter certainty, that Mrs Webster would rather not know that the years of her marriage to Webster had been a waste of breath. If, indeed, that is the way to read it. And Rita, mentally arranging the jumble of words on the page as they ought to be, can see no other way. And the thought that her husband might very well have driven into oblivion and been delighted to do so is not something a wife wants to hear. Nor does the suburb, which knows — and chooses to believe or not believe — that a most unfortunate accident took place. Nothing more mysterious than that. And it's best kept that way.

With this all in mind, she places the notebook back into the box, along with the stamps and inkpads and the official paper. When the workmen are back, she points to the boxes and suggests they tape up the broken one, properly this time.

A few moments later, the boxes are all in the back of the removalist's van. With everything else, they will be taken away, stored and forgotten.

It will take what's left of the day and the next morning to clear the old Games Room, but already it is less cluttered, and Rita is beginning to see it as an exhibition space. And so she now turns her mind to the happy task of sweeping the dust and debris away and transforming the room.

27.

At the Pub Window

How was it they ever knew what to do? Vic may be staring out through the pub window at the comings and goings of the town (while Rita clears Webster's Games Room), but he doesn't see any of it. He is looking at a field from long ago, a sodden paddock, one that may or may not be still there if he was to go back and try to find it. This field is cold and damp with evening dew, but it doesn't concern the young couple walking across it. The young woman is called Jessie. And he says it again, for the name has not been on his lips for many years now. She is sixteen. An old sixteen, as all sixteens were then. Perhaps this is why they knew what to do. They didn't, but she did.

There is no reason for this, none that Vic can find, to explain why he should be back there. No spark, no face in the crowd. No scent, no taste. But there it is again, this field he once shot rabbits in and which he dreamt of earlier in the summer, popping up again, clear enough to step into, a sudden rush of memory strong enough to turn day into night. So strong a memory that he is not looking out the pub window as he was just a few seconds before, but staring into a night of country darkness in which the moon is good. The field, the trees and the jagged fence posts are coated in a silvery film. The yellow squares of house lights that define the hamlet and the country intersection provide the only colour. The two young people on the damp field don't notice the hamlet, but the old Vic, the one watching, looks over their shoulders to that distant clump of colour, distant but warm, and memory opens the door of the small wooden shack of a farm house where a family is gathered round the fire: the father smoking, the mother watching the flames from her chair, two boys reading on a rough mat. They seem not to notice that their daughter is missing, as is the young Vic, who lives throughout the week in the town nearby with his mother and with this family on weekends, Vic who is now like one of the family and whose rabbit (the rabbit he shot earlier that same morning) has just fed everybody. It is acknowledged that Vic is a good shot, the best shot of the whole bunch, and it is not uncommon for them to feed on rabbit during these weekends that he comes to stay. But, for the moment, nobody seems to notice that he and their daughter are not there.

And just as memory opened the door of the house, memory now closes it again and once more he is gazing upon the two figures in the field, wondering how on earth they knew what it was that had to be done. And with this puzzle vaguely occupying his mind, he watches the condensation rise from their mouths as they settle into the thick grass beside the crumbled remains of a stone wall. There they were, there they are, and there they will always be. Breath rising from their bodies.

A cow munches on silver daisies at the far end of the paddock, the lights of the farm house burn, sleepy and warm, but the minutes are precious as they always are when there is urgency in the air. And there is urgency in the way this sixteen-year-old Jessie pulls her skirt up above her waist, and urgency in the way the fourteen-year-old Vic tugs at his belt and pulls his first pair of long trousers down to his knees. The lights of the hamlet burn orange and gold, but not for long. Life shuts down early in the hills around the town. And so there is urgency in the way she pulls him to her without kissing, for although they know what kisses are, it is agreed without speaking that there is no time for them. There is urgency too in the way he is dragged down upon her, with all the force of a strong young woman used to handling young animals far larger and stronger than this stringy fourteen-year-old with a shooting eye good enough to fill the house with rabbits and game every weekend. She's not looking at the bright squares of orange and gold that define the farm house, but she knows they're there and that the time is short, so she throws her arms out as they fall back together onto the field, a human star of arms and legs gazing up at the silvery sky. And in that cold night, with the dew already turning to frost around them, the heat of their bodies as they touch sucks his breath away, and it is all over, the end as urgent as the beginning.

That is it, one, possibly two seconds. And whatever the sound is that he releases, it is enough for her hand to rise instantly and almost slap his mouth shut, sealing the sound in. And Vic can feel that hand, he can feel it now in the early-afternoon quiet of the public bar, he feels Jessie's warm hand almost stuck to his mouth. She keeps it there, her eyes wide, as she lies back, a quick flick, a nod of the head, indicating the low mounds of sleeping cattle behind them and the importance of not stirring them. For, if troubled, the sounds of their disturbance will rouse the house and both of them will be in for it. And so she keeps her hand across his mouth, long, long after the sound has been stifled. And it's still there, even now, the wet warmth of Jessie's hand.

With the same urgency she had pulled her dress up, she now pushes it down, watching the young Vic buckling his belt as she does. And when they rise, quickly looking about them, they turn their eyes briefly back to the patch of field where they have just been and notice for the first time that something looking like a four-limbed star has been pressed into the sodden grass. Into the silver field that would be white by morning, except for a damp star that would be there for all to see.

There is a smile on Vic's face, a quiet, private smile in a public bar. Night turns to morning and he now observes his fourteen-year-old self, stomping across the same field with the farmer and his two sons the next day. They come to a sudden stop. The scene is still and silent. The old farmer is scratching his chin, his hat pushed back from his forehead, his eyes fixed, the eyes of the old Vic, the young Vic and the two sons following his deeply puzzled gaze. These are his paddocks; he is as attuned to them as is a rabbit or any of the wildlife that live in them. He can read in them the day's and evening's events, as easily as his sons read their serials or his wife her novels. But here is something he can't explain. And this doesn't happen, not on his land. And he continues staring at the cause of his concern as if it had dropped overnight from the sky, fallen into one of his paddocks. The field is white with a heavy, snow-like frost. And it is all around them, except for one place. A deep, star-shaped impression has been left in the ground. And as his forefinger and thumb rub the clean-shaven point of his chin, he turns to the other three, seeking an explanation or an opinion. For, and it is written in the eyes of the farmer and his sons, it is as though some extraordinary visitation has taken place in the night while they were sleeping and the cattle looked on. For a second, everyone is exchanging glances. The old man and his sons (who shrug their shoulders) and turn in unison to Vic as though the eyes of the sharpshooter might see something they can't. And there is a moment as he gazes without responding upon the spot where the two of them had been the previous evening, upon that pattern in the grass, when he is certain that they have read his face and are now aware that he knows more than he says. But when he shrugs his shoulders just like the others, there is universal agreement that it is indeed a puzzling business. One that brings with it a vague, uncomfortable sense of intrusion. That some alien matter had stolen into their fields in the night and left its mark on their land, an act that had brought with it not only a sense of intrusion, but violation as well. Whatever has left this mark, there is the disturbing possibility that it is not one of them. It is not, the look on their faces suggests, the mark of a local. Not even a local animal.

Yet, even as Vic shrugs his shoulders, he is quietly, secretly amazed that it should all come so easily, so naturally, this business of saying one thing and knowing another; of going along with everyone, and not; of being at one with the group, while remaining apart.

It is then, while Vic is registering this sensation that is as new and grown-up as his long pants, that the old man looks back at the troubling impression and pronounces his verdict. One of the farm dogs, a fox come to rub its back on a choice piece of damp ground. Who knows what brings an animal out in the dark. That's the best he can do, has anybody got anything better? And they all shrug again, then move on.

Vic and the youngest son go to the school in the town, where Vic lives in the boarding house at which his mother cleans. The old man and the eldest son to the duties of the farm. There they are, forever trudging out across that field. And just as memory opened and closed the doors of the farm house, it now opens the gate of the school, the door to his old classroom, and after school the door of the boarding house just down the street where Vic's mother (if you follow the verandah around to the laundry) is washing white sheets in a steaming copper. And, if you're lucky, she'll give you a big smile as she looks up, for you're her boy, the only thing she's got in this world. And she'll die for you. And she did. She died in small doses, slowly, working herself to death for her boy who now sits at the pub window staring back across the years at that big smile of hers, all eyes for her boy.

And out beyond the town, the pale winter sun has melted the frost. Jessie is carrying fresh milk to the van in the dirt drive. The star is gone and Jessie sees you, takes you in at a glance, but she's giving nothing away. And neither will you.

Vic's head is bowed, and he's oblivious of the broken, muffled talk around him in the public bar, as he shakes his head ever so slightly to the unspoken question in Jessie's sixteen-year-old eyes. He never gave anything away. He was as good as his word. Not even when he arrived at the farm one weekend, months later, and found Jessie gone from the house. Jessie gone, and everybody carrying on as though she'd never been there. Not a word about her, or where she might be. It was only later that he learnt she'd gone to the nuns. And the fourteen-year-old Vic thought nothing more of that. Except for those times, every now and then, when, for no apparent reason, he remembers the look in Jessie's eyes. And with the look, he always hears again the soft, knowing talk of the town, saying that Jessie had gone to the nuns. Then a nod, as if to say we all know what that means.

The public bar is now noisy, lunchtime laughter explodes from the four corners of the room, and Jessie recedes from view. Melts like the silvery frost on that far-away paddock and evaporates like the starry impression they left behind in the ground one dewy night when the minutes were precious and urgency was in the air.

As it all evaporates, there is a sudden emptiness in Vic's eyes. And it is then that he rises from his stool, his glass half full, and takes his empty eyes out into the full glare of the afternoon sun where no one will notice them.

28.

How Terribly Strange to be Seventy

A few days later, Michael is with Madeleine. There is a song playing. There is always a song playing. Madeleine is sitting by a window overlooking a rain-sodden communal garden, with that look on her face. Michael is sitting with his back against the wall, beside the stereo.

Neither of them is speaking. Nor have they for some time. In their poses and the attitudes they have struck, they might easily pass for one of those paintings depicting a nineteenth-century couple whiling away a wet Sunday afternoon. But then they would each be holding a book of verse, or she might be writing a letter while he carefully brushed the dust from a local fossil, and the silence in the room would be there because they were so immersed in their respective activities that they hadn't thought to talk. But they have neither books nor letters nor fossils. They have nothing. They do not speak. The stereo speaks for them.

She does not move and he has no desire to disturb her. He knows that look and knows that behind it lies impatience with this little world she's been dropped into. This little world is in her way. And everybody and everything in it are barriers between her and home — which is out there beyond the window and the sad communal garden of sodden shrubs. He knows the look and he chooses to say nothing. Besides, while she sits absorbed in speculations of home, he is free to observe her: the auburn hair folded across her shoulder, the elbow resting on the window, the nose in profile, the eyebrows that rise playfully when playfulness is in her. The girl with the kaleidoscopic eyes is a cameo, or a detail from a domestic scene in which he feels himself to be a peripheral part. Her face is turned away, the look is outward.

It is after days such as these (and they will become more and more numerous in the lead-up to her departure) that she will enter the books and poems that he reads. Or is it that he will impose her upon them? Turn characters into her and therefore catch her in the pages of his books like pressed flowers. In this way, Dorothea, trapped in the provincial confines of *Middlemarch* becomes Madeleine. Eliot's crying girl, who weaves the sunlight in her hair, becomes Madeleine. And so on. It will not be a conscious process — just a way of holding on, or letting go. If she becomes books, becomes poems, she ceases to be the she who is leaving, and the books will become a repository for the emotions that he won't know what to do with any more when she is gone. And imaginary characters will become the recipients of these feelings. Madeleine will have gone, but not the emotions she stirred. He will have nowhere to take them, except to these characters in books and poems. And they will, of course, accept the burden of this love of his that has nowhere else to go. It will become a way of reading that will bring characters alive in a way that they never were before, and in time, in the hollow years that will follow her departure, this facility will become so precious a lifeline that he will, in the end, not be sure which he prefers — the fact of Madeleine or the idea of Madeleine. And he will reach a point where he has become so attached to his lifeline that he will not know how to choose should she return some day, out of the blue (announcing her return on the telephone or in a letter).

But, for the moment, it is the fact of Madeleine that reclines, motionless against the window, watching the Sunday drizzle. They are silent. The music plays, the stereo speaks for them. And, as it does, this song begins to preoccupy Michael. It is a speculation on the strangeness of being seventy, and it assumes that the very idea of being seventy is somehow incomprehensible. But Michael is not so sure that it is so strange after all, and that is when he turns towards Madeleine.

'Perhaps we'll meet again when we're seventy.'

Madeleine does not look round from the garden. She barely seems to hear, and, just when he has all but given up on receiving a reply, she speaks in a flat monotone consistent with the mood of the day.

'How sad.'

'All those wasted years,' he says, idly.

But she turns from the window, all the cooped-up frustration of the afternoon in her eyes and the sudden dismissive tone of her voice.

'No, that's not it. That's not what I meant.'

She stops talking as quickly as she started. Why don't you understand, she is almost saying. Do I have to explain? And she shoots him a glance, as if to say (or so Michael thinks) I can imagine someone else there, right where you're sitting. Someone who might understand, without being told. I can, the look says, see someone else where you are. Not their face, not their hair. Nothing like that. Just the possibility of someone else being there. A substitution that, in Madeleine's mind, would have the power to transform the afternoon. Someone who would understand exactly what she means without need of speech. But not Michael.

He is surprised by the intensity of her response and her impatience with him, until he realises that she is denying him the assumption of all those years, denying him the right to all those years (even as wasted years, for to call them wasted is in some way tantamount to appropriating them). Somewhere in her impatience she has taken this idle remark of his to mean that he is saying she is making the wrong decision in leaving. Perhaps he is without knowing it. Perhaps Madeleine has discovered his intention before him. And, clearly, she is having none of it.

He is surprised, but he also has to admit — if only to himself, for Madeleine has resumed her pose and is once again watching the heavens drain themselves onto the garden — he has to admit she is right. It is not the point. The sadness inherent in the idea of two people parting in youth and not meeting again until they are seventy is not to be found in any sense of lost or wasted years. It is something else altogether, which neither of them can name at this particular point. And so he leaves it. They return to their respective silences. The song finishes, another begins.

29.

The Discovery of Speed (1)

She feels the cold tonight. Winter's in the air. The keys rattle in her hand, jangling in the night as she steps out along the gravel path of the gardens to the garage. She looks up, and — the oddest thing — a child's balloon floats high up above before drifting into one of the estate's many trees and landing on a forked branch, where it sits, as if watching her.

A shiver runs through her as she pulls the door open, and moonlight falls across the curved snout of the car. Not for the first time this evening, she considers turning back and going to bed. But she is dressed for a drive and she wouldn't be able to sleep now, anyway. And besides, this new addition to the household is, she imagines, happy to be let out. It's been promised a run, and can't be disappointed now.

Behind the wheel, she slips on the black leather gloves and notices a slight tremor in her hand as she reaches for the ignition, pausing for a moment before bringing the thing to life. It groans with the turning of the key, then settles immediately to a low, happy hum.

She points the car north, out towards the new frontier that lies just the other side of the recent housing developments. There are two main roads in the suburb, the one running east–west, the other (which becomes a country highway of sorts) running north–south. If she follows the road running north for long enough, she will eventually come to a point where, either side of her, the paved roads give way to dirt, and the houses give way to scotch thistle. When this happens, she will have reached the new frontier, where the suburbs stop and the open country begins, where that last line of backyard fences marks the outermost borders of settlement. She will be in the thistle country, where the fences run along the rim of the old river valley like medieval town walls against the darkness without. Where it is now fashionable to build large, double-storey houses on cheap land. Large houses that look more deserted than roomy. There she will find the straight stretch of paved road that calls itself a highway. A straight stretch of road along which one can accelerate into life, or into death.

Soon, and with little memory of the ride, she is idling by the side of the road, the paddocks of grass and thistle beside her, a long thin line of paved road stretching out into the night in front of her. There are no other headlights in sight. This excuse for a highway is hers.

Outside, and she winds down the window in order to feel the elements against her cheek, this place to which she has come (which, no doubt, in a few years' time will be as thick with houses as it is now with thistle) has the kind of stillness and chilly quiet that is only found in the country. The only sound is the low murmur of the engine.

Did Webster pause before releasing the power of the thing? Did he take a moment to consider the darkness of the road — the black void out there that is neither suburb nor country nor earth, nor anything to which one can put a name? For she feels that she could fly completely off the road and out into the night. And it is tempting.

Oh, it is so tempting. To penetrate the night, to go where Webster went — whether by accident or design, to catch some intimation of Webster himself, who drove out of this world and into another.

Mrs Webster feels a dreaded, longed-for, rolling wave lift her heart, and she knows she has reached that point where she no longer controls events. And, when the car takes off, the sound, the sudden explosion of acceleration, is already part of the world she has just left behind. Distant thunder. Somebody else's thunder, in somebody else's world. Not only is she not controlling events any more, they are also being experienced by someone other than Mrs Webster. There is a woman sitting at the wheel who, for all intents and purposes, resembles (in every detail) Mrs Webster, but from whom she feels sufficiently detached to observe — as if she were witnessing the event, not the driver in it. And throughout the next few minutes, when she will have accelerated into that part of the night where the minutes don't exist because they've been obliterated by speed, she will remain a spectator to events and of herself.

It is only when she eventually slips back into the suburb, slips back into the network of streets that leads back to her house and registers the trembling in her hands and feet that the experience becomes *felt*, and she knows *she* was that woman out there on that excuse for a highway where you could just as easily accelerate into life as into death, depending on the driver and depending on the night.

As she parks the car in the garage, the silvery gardens shimmering all around her, she is wondering if Webster chose, or if he had simply reached that point where he no longer controlled events and choice was obliterated by speed.

30.

An Unfashionable Jealousy

'I knew I shouldn't have told you.'

Madeleine is not angry, but annoyed. And it is possibly this which disturbs him more than what she says. For this annoyance is as much as she can muster for now. Her anger, he concludes, she keeps for another time and someone else. He receives her annoyance. It is, like her gratitude, the best she can offer. There is, she implies with a shrug of the shoulders, insufficient reason for anger.

Madeleine has just made casual mention of what she did the night before. She went, she says, to a nice little Chinese restaurant in the city with some work friends and, she adds with a glint in her eyes, a doctor whom all the nurses regard as handsome though, as they say, 'taken'. But a bit of a 'hunk' all the same. He has never heard her use such words as 'hunk' before and it comes as quite a shock to Michael to hear the word so casually drop from her lips — a word whose company she has kept before, and not without a certain ease of manner. But the sound is all wrong, and the shock of it is not so much the shock that an obscene word or phrase from an unlikely source can produce, as the shock of inferior words or phrases from an unlikely source. Hunks, presumably, like the word itself, are beneath her. It is not a Madeleine word, at least not *his* Madeleine. But he is no sooner contemplating *his* Madeleine, than he is thinking of this *other* Madeleine who keeps the company of lesser words. And there is a light in her eyes when she speaks of him, a glint that is intended to be playfully teasing but which he now takes as excitement. And for a moment Michael cannot help but wonder just what sort of a roving eye his Madeleine has and how many men have caught it. He tries to ignore her playful teasing but glumness falls across his features. He has seen this look on his father's face, a silly, childish brooding that his father was powerless to stop, and that Michael now feels likewise powerless to arrest. With the glumness, silence descends upon him. Glum silence. He is a child, like he always seems to be in her presence. And that is when she says it.

'I knew I shouldn't have told you.'

And it is said in the way that an older sister might speak to a younger brother. Implying that he annoys her at times such as these, the way a nagging little brother would, a nagging little brother you just want to be rid of. He is not yet, this comment implies, mature enough to be told such things. Not, at least, without behaving like a child and ruining a perfectly good evening and turning all glum on her.

And it's true. He is one of those who bring their own dark clouds wherever they go. He keeps them on a string. They are always there, even on the brightest of days. It takes only a chance remark and he tugs their strings, drags them down, and blots out the sun.

Jealousy is not so much out of fashion as out of favour. And she sees this out-of-favour jealousy in his eyes immediately. It is written all over his features, for this dark cloud he has dragged down on a string from the heavens is the dark cloud of jealousy. But the source of her annoyance is not so much the fact that he feels jealousy; it is her obvious belief that he has no right to feel it. Jealousy is for the privileged few upon whom anger — and love — are bestowed. To assume jealousy is to assume possession of her. And underlying the assumption of possession is the assumption that she is his property — and this assumption of property is what makes jealousy unfashionable.

She sees in his glum jealousy the assumption of possession, and she rejects both his jealousy and his presumption with her mere annoyance. She gives no hint — as they continue walking (and he desperately tries to wipe the schoolboy glumness from his features, but the more he tries the more it resists and settles in, threatening to remain there all evening) — she gives no hint of disliking the idea of a jealous response. But not from him. His is the jealousy of the eternal sixteen-year-old. The result is a disdain that is consistent with the Age — but not because of it.

As the minutes drag by, he realises that if he doesn't soon wipe the glumness from his features she will also become bored with him — not simply annoyed — and so, to avoid compounding the error of his ways, he determines to wipe his hand across his face and smile.

'Why did the chicken cross the road?'

'I don't know,' she says, eyeing the wintry trees along the street, quite possibly too bored already to say much more.

'To get to the other side,' he grins. 'Any turkey knows that.'

The trace of a smile lights her face and she takes his hand and warms it.

'I wish you wouldn't get like that.'

'So do I.'

'There's no need to. Nothing to fear.'

'It's genetic. It's come down to me through the years. I had no choice.'

'You poor thing.'

'I know. But, you see, it's gone. All finished. A sun shower.'

They cross the road. The annoyance leaves her features, the fourth-form glumness departs his. They are now a happy young couple. Holding hands, chatting freely, because the young don't have a care in the world.

But his voice is a fraction too loud, his laughter a fraction too ready. It is an effort, this carefree chat. For, although the schoolboy sullenness has left his features, the memory of an older man with the air about him of someone used to the company of women, the possible hunk in question, relaxed in their company and possessing the gift of setting them at ease, stays with him. Michael has only ever seen him twice, but it is a persistent memory. And while they laugh and chat in the carefree manner of the young, an image hovers in the back of his mind. This man's eyes resting upon Madeleine just that bit too long at the ball, before departing. Is this what he saw, or what he now sees in his mind's eye? It is all part of this unfashionable jealousy, but Michael can't help asking himself if this man knows her in ways that he knows her. Does he know the smell of her — her perfume, the hint of red wine always on her lips after coming from evening mass? Are these things the possession of this other, older married man the same way they are the possession of Michael? Does he know her smell and does he carry it with him on his clothes and his surgeon's fingers that are so at ease with women and presumably do the talking for him when his lips have tired of speech?

And then a thought, more troubling than the possibility that they both might possess knowledge of Madeleine in equal shares, occurs to him: that he might also know her in ways that Michael doesn't. That they might not possess knowledge of Madeleine in equal shares after all.

These thoughts — and he is as much troubled by the fact that he can even think them as by the thoughts themselves — lodge at the back of his mind as he strolls, hand in hand, with his Madeleine, making the light and carefree chat of the young.

They come, they go — these silly thoughts. As Michael and Madeleine cross the road and a small, inner-city picture theatre comes into view, as they cross the serpentine tram tracks of the university terminus where a green rattler is preparing for its return run back down into the city and over the territorial border of the river, it is not only his moodiness and her annoyance that have gone. Having exhausted itself for now, this unfashionable jealousy of his also retires from his conscious mind and slips out of sight into those realms where it can get on with its business, unseen and untroubled.

They enter the cinema and surrender to its welcome darkness, while, back in the suburb, Mrs Webster nervously jiggles the keys of a black sports car in her hand, her shoes crunching the gravel pathway that leads to the garage, every step taking her closer and closer to that point where she will no longer control events but events will control her on that excuse for a highway out there in the country darkness of the new suburban frontier.

Inside the cinema, Michael takes Madeleine's hand and is uplifted by a reassuring squeeze, small but unmistakable, enough to send the balloon of glumness out into the night and far, far away.

31.

Sitting for Immortality

It was something of a surprise when Mulligan (the name that he signs on his works) approached the mayor, suggesting that if the mural were to be a history of the suburb then the story of the suburb ought to finish in the present day — and would His Worship, as a community leader, like to be in the painting? Mulligan, in the paint-spattered trousers of his trade, sat opposite the mayor, bulging eyes peeping through the fringe of black hair that was forever flopping over his face.

Until then, if the mayor had bothered to think much about this artist the committee commissioned for the mural, he would probably have pronounced him a prick (barely looked at the committee, or the mayor, only had eyes, and pretty weird ones at that, for the wall). And, of course, nobody wants to hire a prick. But, after viewing his folio, they'd all had to concede that — though a prick he might be — he could paint. So, he got the job, despite the vague, uneasy feeling that they'd let someone into their ranks with — how did they all put it? — a touch of the ticking bomb about him.

After Mulligan had approached him, he found himself re-appraising the man. Perhaps they got it right, the committee. Perhaps, even, it was an inspired choice. Here was a man, after all, who had studied in the great schools of Europe and who was now informing the mayor that there is a long tradition of such public portraiture. Rembrandt did it. The rest of the Dutch masters did it. They all did it. Only back then, of course, public figures paid to have their faces in the paintings of a master. It was, Mulligan had explained, their stab at immortality. For if the master's work lasted into the centuries to come, so would they, through their faces up there on the walls of their cities and the framed canvases in their galleries. That, he further explained with a smile, is why they always wore their best clothes.

And that explains why the mayor is now wearing his best suit. In an empty room at the back of the town hall, with the curtains drawn back and the afternoon light streaming in through the high windows, the mayor is standing, looking intently into that future where his painted face will live on long after the suit has fallen apart and the body inside it has turned to compost. He has been standing like this long enough for his back and neck to begin aching. Not that Mulligan notices. He works frantically with charcoal and paper, large sheets of butcher's paper strewn about him on the floor. None of which the mayor is permitted to see. Even when he asks.

'Only ever show children and fools unfinished work,' Mulligan explains, not even looking up from the easel, 'and, I assume, you are neither.'

And so it goes throughout most of the afternoon: the mayor, dressed for immortality in his best suit (and with a new-found interest in the group portraits of the Dutch masters), and Mulligan, layering sketch after sketch upon the floor, as he commits the eyes, ears, nose, forehead, mouth, chin, trunk and limbs of His Worship the mayor of Centenary Suburb to paper, so that, when the time comes, he can, without thinking, commit it to the wall in the foyer of the town hall, where it will stay for as long as the town hall does.

When they are finished, Mulligan rolls the sheets up and secures them with string. At no stage is the mayor permitted to see any of it. And, the artist explains, it will be the same with the wall. He explains that when he finally begins work on the real thing he will work behind a large drape. And it will stay that way until he has completed the job for which he was commissioned. No sticky-beaks, no prying eyes, no unwanted, intrusive observations floating up to the decking upon which he will stand or recline, intent, his body motionless, fingers only, brush in hand, silently scuttling across the wall behind the drape. No one else, just the artist and this wall for which, he is convinced, he has been destined all his working life. He, Mulligan, and not a committee, will paint this wall.

The mayor returns to his office as the day shuts down outside (winter is only a month old, yet seems to have been around forever), contemplating this Mulligan, Michael and the whole bunch of them. They seem to be more of a giant club than a generation. A very big but exclusive club. They all seem to recognise each other — Mulligan, Michael and their kind. And this Whitlam of theirs, around whom they gather. And it is then that he sits at his desk and seals the official letter he has written to this Whitlam of theirs, requesting that he open a new sports ground. Harold Ford trades in politics, but he doesn't believe any of it. He has seen them come and go over the years, and he has a nose for History in the making. He has looked at Michael, Mulligan and this Whitlam of theirs, and he sees History heading straight for him like the *Spirit of Progress* on bright new shiny rails. You mightn't like this particular train, Harold Ford (he tells himself), but you've got two choices: you can stand there and get run down by it, or you can book a first-class seat right now and be there when it pulls into that platform marked Destiny. And for this reason he has invited this Whitlam of theirs to Centenary Suburb.

The mayor will not be the only one to sit for immortality. Over the next few weeks, the local member will sit for Mulligan, along with a councillor or two and the aptly named Charles Draper, whose clothing store has fitted the school, the sporting clubs and the families of the suburb for two decades. Their faces, trunks and limbs will be committed to sketching paper after a series of sittings, and, when the time comes, their distinctive features will join a group portrait on the town-hall wall, their images part of the grand narrative of the suburb, and upon which the children of the future will gaze. But they will all, at a later date, concur that there was always something vaguely unsettling about sitting for Mulligan. Something unsettling about the way Mulligan looked at them, as though they ceased to be community leaders, and, under his scrutiny, became curiosities. As though there was something inherently amusing about them standing up there in his makeshift studio in the town hall for hours on end in their best clothes. And they all confessed to a certain feeling of, well, silliness afterwards.

It was, however, a small price to pay for immortality. And each of the sitters, in turn, shrugged this vaguely unsettling feeling off at the conclusion of each sitting, convinced that they were imagining things.

32.

Bunny Rabbit Eyes
the Horizon

While Michael is being driven back from the school by the kindly maths master who has designed the teaching timetable to allow for Michael's studies (and who likes a chat and likes the company), Pussy Cat is set to pounce upon her Bunny Rabbit in the shambles of their room.

'I was watching you. When you didn't think I was. Your eyes were crawling all over her.'

Bunny Rabbit, who is studying law, is learning, day by day, the need for words to be exact. People get into all sorts of muddles — his case studies tell him — simply because they think they've said what they mean, and they haven't. And, more than just acquiring a growing respect for precision in language, he is also rapidly acquiring an intolerance of sloppiness.

'Eyes don't crawl,' he taunts. 'Have eyes got legs? Or arms? Or any other implements of crawling?'

'You know what I mean.'

'No, I don't,' he continues, still taunting her. 'And neither do you. Eyes don't crawl.'

Pussy Cat is studying literature. She respects words for the possibilities inherent in them every bit as much as Bunny Rabbit respects them for their precision. She is happy to be ambushed by the unexpected and arrested by the inexplicable. She gives words licence to break the rules.

'Yours do.'

He laughs, then continues to taunt her. But he is composed. Part of him has had enough of Pussy Cat's funny little ways — which are becoming funnier and funnier by the day — and is genuinely angry. The other part is detached enough to feel a certain satisfaction at the words coming so effortlessly from him. He is even finding time for a quiet, private chuckle before uttering them. He is, in short, performing. He is taunting his Pussy Cat, but he is also honing his skills. The skills that will stand him in such good stead in those days in the future when he is a well-known barrister, an important back-room boy on the conservative side of politics, famous for his courtroom jibes and the cut of his French suits. But, for the moment, he is still wearing flared jeans and shirts purloined from his father's wardrobe. His long, dark hair — which he will lose very quickly (along with the droopy moustache), making him virtually unrecognisable in later years, even to those who knew him well — hangs down to his shoulders. There is a square of hash the size of a piece of chocolate in his shirt pocket. A song is playing on the portable hi-fi about the marines landing on the shores of Santo Domingo. A well-thumbed, popular poetic study lies open on the desk, while the voluminous eighteenth-century novels, anthologies and law journals fraternise on the floor. He is a child of the Age. But, even as he taunts his Pussy Cat, he is aware of the fact that he is honing the skills that will make him master of another, less poetic age. And he will know his skills are honed when the poetic age of youth is sufficiently enough behind him to be amusing. Far enough behind him to become the stuff of light, confessional anecdote.

Pussy Cat, or that part of Pussy Cat that is not trembling with anger about the way he lectures her on what her words do and don't mean, can see all this. The flourishes, the hand gestures, the sheer acting of it all is leading to one place only — that future of his, already rolling out like a carpet before him, and across which he will stroll with accepting ease into the horizon of good fortune. And when he has crossed that imaginary line that separates today from tomorrow, he will have assumed what he will, by then, come to think of as his true condition, his true self. But Pussy Cat knows better. She knows they are trembling between two conditions: what they can be, and what everything and everybody tells them they will inevitably be when they finally grow up. She won't accept that Bunny Rabbit has already chosen. And so, standing there in what she sees as the endearing shambles of their room (and which he proclaims a mess), the part of Pussy Cat that isn't shouting at Bunny Rabbit at the top of her voice is moved by something so shattering she can barely contain it. Or barely name it. Then she can. For she has heard and been drawn by the most haunting of calls: not the desire for love, or to kill the thing you love, but the desire to save him. One part of Pussy Cat won't accept that her Bunny Rabbit has already chosen. The other part, the part that is shouting and on the verge of spluttering tears, would dearly love to tear his crawling eyes out.

It is late in the afternoon, a dead, dreary time. The mayor has completed his sitting and consigned his best suit to the office wardrobe, and Michael has just finished school. He stamps his feet as he mounts the stairs, but Pussy Cat and Bunny Rabbit don't hear. They fight often now. There are raised voices coming from their room every day and every day they fail to notice what is outside the confines of their room. So he walks past and slams his door and they continue, it seems to Michael, like the loud, unhappy couples from his old street, when, it seemed, there were days when everybody was fighting and nobody's lives were private.

Even in his room, with the door closed, he hears them. They go on and on. It's in his eyes, she says. In his eyes he is leaving her. And the more he taunts, the more she shouts. Until she is swearing, she is swearing once again — as she has before — that she will kill herself, or both of them, if his body ever dares follow his eyes. And he taunts her once more, Bunny Rabbit taunts his Pussy Cat. Do it, he cries. Do it. There is a short, tense silence and Michael is listening more to the silence than he was to the fighting. Then Bunny Rabbit's voice returns, cool and restrained. But you know you won't. I know you won't. Those who talk about it never do it. And as Michael listens to his sad taunts, a chill passes through him. There is a story — and he has long forgotten its name or who wrote it — in which a man says he will kill himself, and his friend, bored with the all-too-familiar threats, says the same thing: that those who talk about it never do it. And, from that moment on, the man who threatened to kill himself knew he had to, otherwise his life would just amount to so much talk. A handful of words. And this is why Michael experiences this sudden chill, because he is convinced that exactly the same thought, at exactly the same time, is passing through Pussy Cat's mind.

The silence that follows this final taunt is succeeded by quiet sobbing, and the sound of what Michael assumes to be drawers being opened and closed. Nothing is said. The drawers are opened and closed. Bunny Rabbit stomps about the room. He ceases to stomp. And Michael knows, without being witness to the events inside the room, that they have reached that point they can no longer avoid.

A door opens. He hears Bunny Rabbit scurrying down the stairs.

'I will! You just wait. I will!'

A door slams. The house is silent. For a moment. The sobbing starts again. Soft, then loud. So loud, Michael concludes that Pussy Cat has opened the door in order to sob to the house. It is, he knows, an invitation. A call for company. An inquiry if there is anybody out there after all. And, of course, there is. There is Michael. And he knows he can't ignore the call, and so he rises from his desk, opens the door, and finds her sitting on the landing. She looks up, this Juliet who should be leaning from her balcony with carefree, provocative innocence, then pulls her long, dark hair back from her temples and forehead. Her face is smudged, her eyes red, her look is — and this is the only word Michael can find to fit her face — lost. No longer Pussy Cat, Louise, Lou, looks about as if having just been thrown into the world for the first time and not sure where she is or what is expected of her. And, for all this, that face is more entrancing, more beautiful than ever. And more distant.

'I've lost my pills,' she says, her eyes more blank than lost now.

'What pills?'

'*My* pills. Don't you know?'

'No.'

'I've looked everywhere.'

Michael looks about in the stairwell for other signs of life in the house.

'Where's Peter?'

She doesn't answer. She simply rises, looks at Michael and nods, almost dismissing him. 'I'll find them. They can't be far,' she adds, more or less to herself, before closing the door.

Michael pauses for a moment, lingers by the door, then decides to leave her alone. Decides that this is what she wants, and that she is beyond any words he might have at hand and that he could offer, anyway. He is, he tells himself, close at hand.

A song rises from her room — already it is hers, not theirs — as he steps into his own. Over the next hour — the day is golden, one of those eternal winter afternoons and he has lost track of time — she plays it again and again and he drifts into a doze listening to its slow, almost dirge-like rhythms.

On the floor beside the bed (he has no bedside table) is a book he has just begun to read. Lurch approached him that afternoon in the staff room, and in the quiet, understated manner that is his hallmark informed Michael that he reads too much of the black-spined classics by authors with unpronounceable names. He had, it seemed, been observing Michael's reading habits and concluded that he didn't read enough of the books about his own place and time. And this surprised Michael, because he always thought of Lurch as Victorian and withdrawn, with the reading habits and tastes of the withdrawn Victorian. But he had thrust a book into Michael's hand and said, 'Here, try this.'

As he lies on the bed, the sobbing of Pussy Cat and the dirge-like music rising and falling, he reaches down to the floor for the book. He stares at the cover, the title *My Brother Jack* (not a good title), the author's name, George Johnston (he has never heard of him), then opens the book where he left off. He has only just begun to read it, but he already knows he is doing more than just reading another book. There is something about the reading of this book that feels like what he can only call an event. He is not simply reading another book; it is, he knows, much, much more than that. For when he reads this book, he sees, for the first time in his reading life, the world from which he comes. His world — his past and present (and quite probably his future) — has been made different by a book. And that is the event. It is a special book in the same way Mr Maugham had written a special book (just, it seemed, for him), and he knows that one day he will share this book with the right person, but, oddly, he is not so sure he can share it with Madeleine in the same way that they had shared the Maugham. And this is a puzzling thought because it implies that the person with whom he will share this book he has not yet met. And that is puzzling because he does not *want* to meet anyone else. He has met Madeleine.

He does not know that the writer, this George Johnston he has only just heard of, is a dying man living his last days in Sydney and who saw his death foretold in X-rays the previous month while Michael bared his unfashionable jealousy for Madeleine to see. Two people cross a tram line and enter a picture theatre; a dying man, skin on a stick, refuses to enter a hospital because he wants to die among friends; the book he wrote a few years before is thrust into Michael's hand from an unlikely source; and already the dying man lives on.

The dirge-like music in the room opposite stops. Michael's eyes move from line to line across the page, his mind moves upon silence. The music starts up again, but he doesn't notice. He is lost in the event of this book. He is somewhere else, someplace else, at once familiar and strange. He is somewhere else, both home and not home. Like it or not, want it or not, he will carry home wherever he goes, will be forever going back to it, or being dragged back to it, while forever just wanting to be rid of the whole damn place. And it is, he knows, the same for the character in this book, and its author, this Johnston, this skin on a stick who will die before winter finishes.

33.

Vic Eyes the Horizon

It's the socks in the variety-store window that catch his eye. White, knee-high and good quality. Golf socks. And going for a song. Vic rarely stops here, but he needs new socks. And so, while Michael begins his last class of the day before going home and witnessing the final, sad scene in the adventures of Pussy Cat and Bunny Rabbit, Vic is entering the front door of the variety shop. At first he takes only one pair, but, on his way to the counter, he goes back and picks up a second, because that is his way. If something's worth getting once, it's worth getting twice.

An hour later he's out on the fairway, his feet snug inside the new socks. And it's odd how a little thing like a new pair of socks can make you feel good and lift your whole day (it's not often, after all, you think about your feet). So, when Vic tees off he's got socks on his mind, and congratulating himself that he had the foresight to buy the second pair. And when the ball is sent skyward (a sweet meeting of club and ball, not one against the other but a pleasing result achieved by their collaboration), Vic puts it down to the firmness of his stance, the good feeling in his feet, and the socks that made it all possible. As he watches the ball arc across the fairway, he feels part of a sweet, continuous act that will end only when the ball finally plops down onto the grass. And, for those few seconds, he is aware of that small touch of what he can only call the sublime.

It's while this sudden intake of wonder is flowing through his veins, alerting him to the sparkle of the moment, that he feels a familiar shortness of breath coming on as his chest tightens up and a cold, dramatic sweat breaks out across his forehead. He drops his club, taking in short, sharp mouthfuls of air, while he reaches for the pills he always carries in his pocket. And as he drops one into his mouth and chews on it, he feels, almost straight away, the magic pill performing its little miracle once again and in a few minutes his breathing is better and he wipes the sweat from his forehead before bending down carefully to retrieve his club from the ground. His playing companions, having already set off as soon as Vic's ball was launched, have their backs to Vic and have not noticed anything, being so caught up in the tasks at hand, walking to their balls, finding them, and deciding what to do with them. Though they play together often, the four of them (different types united by the game), they rarely have anything to do with each other outside the golf course.

As he drops the club back into the bag, he leans against the buggy, exhausted, dwelling upon this all-too-familiar intrusion. Vic has mixed with various types all his life. He likes to mix, likes to move among people —

not only to feel their variety, but because he likes to find the best in them. And that can take some finding, for, when you mix, you come up against rough company from time to time. As much as you don't want to. But they're out there, rough company, and they will intrude. Even when you're happy. Especially then. They don't like to see you happy. And just when you are, just when you're watching a harmless white ball doing all the things you've ever wanted it to do, this rough type intrudes and tells you he doesn't like the happy look on your face. And you could tell him why he doesn't but you'd be wasting your breath. There's only one response, and that's to ignore him. To turn your back and walk away. But, even as Vic takes the handle of his buggy and walks quietly away from the tee (the rest of the foursome by now turning to see where he is), he knows there comes a time, and will always come a time, when the rough company that life throws up won't let you go that easily, won't cop the insult of your turned back. There are times when it wants action, for no good reason. Vic waves the rest of the foursome on, indicating that he'll catch up. The thug of Death there on the tee lets him be for now, but he'll be back.

As he strolls onto the fairway, the world opens up again, as it always does out here, and the horizon looks good: the long, sweeping fairways, the distant view of the coast, and, running alongside it, the black stitching of the railway line.

He knows the sun will shine and that the surf will be good on the day that he dies. Or, if it is at night, or in the early morning, he knows that the air will be balmy. Sweet even. And he knows that the pain will be more than he can bear. And he will know the moment is upon him when he can see no way through the pain, and that the only way to ease it is to submit to it. And so, in sunshine or in balmy night, he can picture this world of his on the day he leaves it. And the very predictability of the occasion, during this quiet, reflective break on the golf course, has the effect of making Death just something else he will do that day.

What he doesn't know about are the black plastic rubbish bags. How they will be sitting outside his flat by mid-afternoon waiting to be collected so that the next tenant can move in (Progress having not yet done its job, and small, cheap flats such as Vic's being at a premium). How they will contain the few things he needed to kick on from day to day — the hairbrush with his grey curls still caught in its teeth, the shaver with his whiskers still wedged in between the twin razors, and the new, unwrapped pair of knee-length golf socks that he never got around to opening because he still hadn't worn out the first pair.

The white caps in the distance tumble and crash into one another, and somewhere out there on the wide, rolling fairways of the golf course, voices are calling. As his eyes leave the horizon and he turns in their direction, he realises they are calling his name. And, as he turns to them, the rest of the foursome now gathered on the green and waving him on up the fairway, he observes the group, this once-or-twice-a-week order of friendship, with distant eyes.

34.

Speed and After

There is an odd calm surrounding Mrs Webster. She sits at the kitchen table looking out over the front path and the gardens (ignited by the mid-winter spring) of her domain. She sees it all, and she does not see it. The sway of the eucalypts, the shimmer of the shrubs, the quiet industry of the gardener are all perfectly visible to her. But the world they inhabit does not impinge upon hers. Mrs Webster has the quiet calm of someone who has been away, and never quite come back. The abstracted air of someone who has been somewhere mysterious and never wholly returned, the air of someone over whom a question mark hovers. She knows full well that if she were to walk out into the garden she would feel upon her face the breeze that ruffles the shrubbery, smell the air and hear the distant rattle of a suburban train if one were to pass. But, for all this, the world does not touch her. She's been somewhere, and not wholly come back.

Earlier in the morning, and it is a work day, the gardener had spoken to her about a clump of winter flowers he had recently introduced to the gardens and had invited her to inspect his handiwork. And she had accepted his invitation and followed him, all the time knowing that the gardener and his handiwork belonged to another earlier dispensation. She has begun to understand the temptation of speed, the lure of utter obliteration, and with that has acquired a glimpse of Webster that Webster himself had never offered her. And she has begun to know why. He had been somewhere and never wholly come back. And each time he went, less and less of him returned. Until, finally, he never came back at all.

In those last days, before Webster left forever, she remembered waking in the early morning as he slept, remembered staring at the strangely alien figure of Webster beside her, and for the first time in her life asking consciously, 'Who are you?' It was, she knew, not an uncommon question for couples to ask. But it was one that, until now, others had asked. Not her. Or — and of this she felt sure — him. She had then rolled over and returned to sleep. Although hardly apparent at the time, she now thinks of it as an intimation. As though some part of her sensed that she didn't really know him at all, not where it mattered, and something was out of whack. But what?

In the months that followed his death, she went through all his possessions — papers, photographs, letters, notes, cards (no diary, he never kept one) — repeating again and again the same question she had posed herself in the early morning while he'd slept beside her, only now it was couched in the past tense: 'Who was he?' And the more she looked, the more she realised that there was nothing to be found in all of it that might even provide a glimpse of an answer. Most disturbing, most striking of all, was the realisation that in the personal papers of Webster, there was no hint, not even the slightest trace, of something revealing. Nothing that was utterly personal. No sign that might foretell what was to happen. Nothing that could conceivably be the source of some deep unhappiness, loss or shame, were it to be discovered. No irrelevant, sentimental observations. Nothing. And all of these papers and notes and cards and letters (the carbon copies of which he had retained) that should have been personal were utterly impersonal. Could have been written by anyone. Did not need the hand of Webster to be written. And the source of that emptiness — which she knows must surely have existed — which only speed could fill was nowhere in evidence. No sign of its source to be revealed in any of his papers, all of which read like the public records of a public figure whom she knew to be Webster.

The fashionably dressed figure of Rita (too fashionable for this suburb) glides by the wide windows of the lounge room, to which Mrs Webster has moved. This woman with a flair for rearranging things, as she is currently doing with the old Games Room, seems to drift across the gravel pathway like someone, it occurs to Mrs Webster, used to living in the retreat of the imagination; like someone who is also hovering between two lives — what *is* and what can be dreamt, what she has known and what she doesn't yet know. And what Rita doesn't yet know, and which Mrs Webster suspects, is that she is leaving the past behind faster than she realises. It is, Mrs Webster notes, the kind of intimation that friends have of each other. Rita drifts across the pathway unaware that she is being observed. Soon she will arrive at the front door, ring the bell, and Mrs Webster will be required to talk. But, as much as she has the sneaking feeling that this woman could become her friend, she is also in no mood to talk. She continues to wear the look of someone who has been somewhere, and not quite returned.

Rita rings the doorbell, and from the moment the front door opens and sunshine fans the doorway, she notices. Mrs Webster is different. Not obviously or dramatically so. But it's there, this difference. And Rita sees it, although she is not sure in what manner or in what gesture this difference reveals itself. But it is immediately apparent, and, as they talk about the Games Room and the appropriate colours for the exhibition, Rita is distracted by this air of difference and the need to locate its source, place a finger upon it. But it is difficult. She only knows that there is a question mark above Mrs Webster's head.

Mrs Webster is always respectful in her manner, and enthusiastic in the way she engages Rita in conversation. But although they are talking the way they normally would, Rita splashing a palette of possibilities before her, something isn't there. And Rita's not sure just what it is for some time, until she finally realises it's the enthusiasm that's missing. Mrs Webster is talking like a woman who would really rather not be talking at all. And it's not just the nature of the words that she does muster; it's that strange calm that surrounds her in the silences between sentences — the calm of someone who's not really there. She may be in the room, right in front of you, yet somewhere else altogether.

It is a question that will preoccupy Rita throughout the remainder of the conversation, but which she will forget about upon returning to the old Games Room and experiencing a surge of excitement lift her like a wave, the way, she imagines, some of the old painters must have been lifted when shown a blank wall and told to fill it.

Rita is left alone to contemplate her task. But the question returns to her when she takes a break later and strolls around the gardens. She has never done so before, but her employment at the place tells her that she now has the licence to amble through those parts of the estate she previously felt she couldn't. And as she wanders about (convinced that she has the place to herself, that Mrs Webster is at work), thinking about the job at hand and vaguely contemplating the strange but absurdly real possibility of getting lost in these gardens, she comes to a halt in a far corner of the grounds. The estate, as the suburb calls it, is still. Except for a sudden, disruptive movement at the edge of her vision. Perhaps if the scene had not been so still she would not have noticed. As she turns she gives an involuntary gasp, surprised by the figure of Mrs Webster, no more than a cricket pitch away, about to close the double doors of the shed — or garage. And, as Rita takes in the figure of Mrs Webster, she also takes in the shining, black snout of the thing parked inside.

When Mrs Webster realises she has been spotted, she behaves, for a split second, like someone who would prefer not to be noticed, indeed, like someone intent on pretending she hasn't been noticed. This is followed by the slightest shrug of annoyance, a glance that might well have been accompanied by an inaudible 'Damn'. Then a smile and the slamming of the garage door.

'Out for a stroll?'

Rita nods.

'It's a good day for it.'

And with that she walks off to the famous old Bentley parked in the driveway.

Over the next few weeks a report will be passed on from the chemist (who lives in a new, spacious suburb to the north where it is now fashionable to build large, double-storey houses on cheap land) to Rita of a car in the night, travelling at great speed along that narrow strip of bitumen that calls itself a highway. The frontier might have shifted, but the suburb is still the suburb, and nothing stays secret for long.

The portrait Mrs Webster stands beneath that evening in the study — part of her still cursing Rita's prying suburban eyes, convinced now that she could never be a friend — this portrait, she concludes, could have been painted any time in the last hundred years and could really be a portrait of just about anybody. It is, in fact, a portrait of Webster, commissioned at the peak of his productivity. Four factories, over a thousand workers, and the brand of his name, Webster's Engineering, written in cast-iron over the doorways of his plants, a constant reminder to all who entered or passed by that Webster the factory was in residence and that their lives, no matter how tangentially, were touched by his.

Yet, for all this, it could be a portrait of just about anybody. Oh yes, she confesses to the empty room, it looks like Webster all right; the fired eyes are there, the self-made brow and the head of hair of a man with years of productive life left in him (the wisps of grey notwithstanding). But it was a portrait of anybody, all the same. The kind of portrait that hangs in council chambers, boardrooms, town halls and the dining rooms of houses such as this all over the country. The artist could be the same, the subject the same. The individual subject is, more or less, unimportant. Irrelevant. For these portraits are never portraits of individuals (no matter how much the times might prize the idea of the individual); they are portraits of Progress. And the people who make Progress. But they are not portraits of people. They are portraits of the same, the one thing — portraits of the belief that drives the pistons, that drive the machines, that drive the Age. The incidentals, those individual agents of Progress, change from sitting to sitting, as do the commissioned artists, but the portrait remains the same. Short, squat, tall, thin, bald, thick with hair, young, old, at the peak of their industrial powers or with a sunset glaze across their eyes — it doesn't matter. The individual sitters are only there because somebody has to be, and the signature at the bottom of the canvas may as well be one artist as another. The subject is always Progress, in its many and changing suits, its many attitudes, in its many faces — be they bald, round or lean.

And it is this, above all, that Mrs Webster notices as she studies the image. And the more she stares at the thing, the less she feels herself to be in the presence of Webster. The Webster she first saw on a tennis court not far from the suburb when she was a young woman. Webster in his mid-twenties. The Webster who won his matches not so much out of talent, but through sheer will. It was the serve she noticed: direct, uncompromising, and fuelled by a cast-iron belief in the inevitability of a triumphal outcome. He ground opponents down with his will, and got what he wanted the same way. And she now has to concede the definite possibility that she may well have chosen Webster while watching him play tennis. *This man will have whatever he sets his mind on.* It is a sentiment that was never, to the best of her recollections, uttered, but it is a sentiment that she unquestionably felt and which may well have determined the course of her life.

And it also occurs to her at the same time that she may well not have chosen the man himself, but what he embodied. Did she merely choose, Mrs Webster is seriously asking herself as she stands beneath the portrait, did she choose the Spirit of the Age and was Webster simply the name it went by when she met it? Another day, another place, and she may well have met the Spirit of the Age in one of its many other guises — short, squat, tall or lean.

There is, she knows, no point standing beneath the portrait demanding *Why? Why? Why* of it. Webster the man isn't there, and he never was.

The attributes that had been conferred upon him by the Age — the vision to see factories on plains of thistle, a steady hand that could just as easily operate a machine as calculate profit and loss, and a cast-iron faith in the Spirit of the Age as unbreakable as his cast-iron name above the factory door — became the attributes by which the suburb and everybody eventually knew him. And through which he knew himself: Webster the factory.

But somewhere along the way, she imagines in the emptiness of the wide dining room, something odd happened. That cast-iron faith either snapped one morning or afternoon, or just gradually rusted away, and that agglomeration of attributes that was Webster fell apart. And, somewhere along the way he became a man without attributes. And when that happened, she once more imagines (the whisky in her glass gone, and the thought of another passing through her mind simultaneous to her contemplations of Webster's portrait), when the attributes had all fallen away and he stood without them, he must also have discovered for the first time that there was nothing left that he could happily call himself — nothing, at least, that he could put his finger on. Nothing ready to hand that he could point to and say, 'That is Webster.' Webster, it must have seemed to him, independent of the Age that fell upon him with all its attributes, didn't exist. And she realises also that this must have puzzled him deeply. At first. And later, this deeply puzzling fact of life would have become something more than puzzling, and the quietly astonished remains of Webster might well have turned to something to occupy his mind or obliterate it.

But she never noticed any of this. Nor did he ever inform her or let on. He gave her, in the end, nothing more than he gave everybody else. And this, until now, was her most disturbing discovery. But another was now dawning upon her. Is it possible, she asks herself (at first not even sure if she wants to give the thought the air of being uttered, if only to herself), is it just possible that Webster had never informed her of all that had quietly astonished him because he had also made the deeply disturbing discovery that she too was another of his attributes? That the marriage was the mirror image of his world of production and exchange, and they were no more a portrait of a modern marriage than the painting on the wall above was a portrait of Webster? And a man who, for whatever reasons (if reasons even need be sought), has shed all those qualities that he acquired through being born into an age that saw History as a soon-to-be-concluded journey to Perfection does not tell a discarded attribute that she is no longer required; that the accumulation of qualities and attributes that had combined to be Him, Her and Them had fallen apart, like machinery that had finally given up the ghost. And as for the question 'Who was he?' — well, she concludes, gazing about the wide room that will keep her confidences, that question was answered, after all, years before by the suburb. He was Webster the factory.

35.

Let It Be

Two weeks later, Michael is standing at the front of the local picture theatre with two tickets in his hand. There is a newspaper in his pocket and he has just read (hastily, for he has other things on his mind) a small notice in the paper telling him that George Johnston is dead. That he died early that morning in his sleep while he, Michael, slept soundly in another city. It is sad and it is annoying because he has only just met this Johnston. This Johnston who gave him the event of the right book at the right time, and turned familiar streets and houses and crappy milk bars into the unfamiliar stuff that is good enough for books.

At the moment, though, Michael is stuck with two tickets and behind him the queue is disappearing into the cinema. He has been standing on the footpath with two tickets in his hand for a long time. Long enough for the queue to dwindle. Long enough to know that Madeleine won't be coming. And as much as he scans the street and footpaths around him — still expecting her to materialise beside him, breathless with apology — he knows she won't be coming. The usher draws his attention to the lateness of the hour and Michael turns reluctantly from the street, leaves the unclaimed ticket on the counter of the ticket booth (with Madeleine's name), and enters the cinema.

The sixties ended and the seventies began, he would later reflect, the night he sat alone watching George Harrison tell Paul McCartney during the recording of *Let It Be* that he wouldn't play at all, if he — McCartney — didn't want him to. McCartney, fingers playing with his beard under the spotlights shining on what appears to be a vast warehouse, is trying to put into words the sound he wants to hear for a certain song. Harrison is shaking his head, both of them are scratching nervously at the strings of their guitars. Around them, the others are either shifting in their seats or gazing about them, quite possibly asking themselves if this cold, ugly warehouse is where their story ends. Playtime, Michael saw, was concluding, and the players of the day were tired of playing.

The decade they had all shared (the songs, the dance halls — each the possession of all) was over. The decade in which they'd all grown up, or died too soon, was ending up there on the screen. A new one had begun. And now it seemed inevitable that everybody would rise from where they were sitting, or turn if standing, and walk away to whatever was out there in those years that would constitute the rest of everybody's lives. It is an intimation of what is to come, of Madeleine leaving, as he knows she soon will.

Everybody knew that sooner or later they would all be called upon to stand and wave goodbye to this time in which they had all grown up together. Everybody except McCartney, who is pouring words into Harrison's deaf ears, as if, by virtue of his words and his will alone, he might yet hold on to this time they have all shared.

Michael watches from the dark stalls, thinking of Madeleine. His impulse, too, is to hold on and not let slip from them this thing they have, knowing full well that once it has been let slip and falls apart it will not come back together again. This, for Michael, is an immutable law, as heavy and incontrovertible as gravity: things once scattered never come back. When you rose and walked away, you rose and walked away for good. He wants to say this to Madeleine one day. And, although he feels like a child so often in her company, he is convinced that the years have given him at least this much wisdom. And Michael suspects that, up there on the screen, only McCartney sees what he, Michael, does, that when things are let slip, when people rise and walk away, they do so forever.

Paul McCartney has stopped pouring words into the deaf ears of George Harrison, who, in mind and spirit, has long since risen and left, his body only remaining, hunched over the guitar that he will play or not play at all, if he — McCartney — doesn't want him to. The others too have all but risen and left. They talk, in this wide, cold warehouse, but it is the kind of talk that is uttered when everything is over. And there are the cameras, everywhere, watching them. And when the cameras have done their work, when they have created the film that will make public these private moments, everybody will share the end of it all, just as they shared the beginning and the middle of it all, in a thousand dark cinemas where audiences will sit and see what the cameras saw.

The brittle smiles, the awkward sentences that end nowhere, the vacant seat beside him all become the one sorrow with a public and private face, one that is happening up there on the screen and right beside him. And the world grows that bit sadder during the ninety minutes that the film runs and the seat beside him remains vacant.

He does not know what happened to Madeleine this evening. Perhaps she was held back at work at the last minute, and, of course, could get no word to him for there is no phone in his house. Perhaps there'd been a mix-up and they'd got their nights wrong. Perhaps. When he finally emerges from the theatre, the first thing he sees is the unclaimed ticket, lying exactly where he left it.

On the street, he manoeuvres his way through the crowd. The footpaths are clean and shining, and the sky is clear. This is the way it happens. Before something can begin, something else must end. A band breaks up, a newly discovered favourite author dies. Ages come and go, orders of feeling rise and fall. Tonight she wasn't there. Tonight he realised that he must prepare himself. That somehow, somewhere within him he must find a way of letting go as a preparation for that time when he will have no choice *but* to let go.

At the same time he wonders how long it will stay there, Madeleine's unclaimed ticket, before someone sweeps it off the counter and into the wastepaper basket. And will this act be occasioned by a brief pause for thought? For an unclaimed ticket is a story, there to be read by those who choose, and in any way they choose. Or, not at all.

This is how it will end. Suddenly she won't be there, and he will no longer see her, touch her, smell the perfume that is hers and hers alone, or register the faint taste of wine upon her lips after coming from the evening service. This is how it will end, and that which had previously only beckoned — the idea of Madeleine — will be all that remains.

36.

Rita Observes Webster's People

Where have they all come from? All evening (the same evening Michael stands at the front of the cinema with Madeleine's ticket in his hand), they've been coming, in their best suits. Faces shining under the lights from the close shave these people always give themselves before stepping out. All evening they've been coming, whole families of them, Webster's people. For they are not simply stepping out. This is not simply a social event, party, wedding or funeral, and there is none of the false laughter and stiff talk that people unused to society always fall into. No, there is something taking place here for which Rita was not prepared.

The speeches have finished, everybody has been thanked for the work they've put in (the Historical Society, the adviser from the State Library who knew all about pedestals and glass boxes, and special mention to Rita), the exhibition is open, and Webster's people are gazing upon the fragments of their lives, past and present.

Bits of machinery, bits of lives, the spare parts they produced, here and there a wheelbarrow or a lawnmower illustrating the whole, the complete object, to which they contributed, are all on display in glass cabinets or perched on pedestals. Levers they once pulled, buttons they once pushed, are now either marked 'Don't Touch' or are out of reach behind panes of clear, polished glass. The objects around which their working days had revolved were now History. Or something else. Something untouchable. Not theirs any more, but the property of those who know about these things. Those who know how to order and arrange the tools of other people's days in such a way as to tell them what they were doing back then because no one really has the time to stand back and have a good look at things when they're in the thick of production.

As Rita watches from a quiet spot at the back of the room she remade, she observes Webster's people as they recognise machines they actually worked on, objects that they made and which they now look upon with a kind of wonder because, in the end, it all made sense. And it occurs to Rita that perhaps they have never felt closer to their work than they do now, looking at things from a distance. And isn't that always the pity of it, she's musing, that you can't have the days and the distance at the same time.

Of course, they all knew the bits and pieces they produced would eventually come together as something or other, but it's easy to forget that when you only get the bits to make. And, as she's watching them all, she's also remembering Vic, and that Ryan mate (who was really no mate at all), and all the rest of them talking about engines and rail and speed and the different touches they all brought to the art of engine driving, and she wonders if you find that in a factory.

Mrs Webster passed through early in the evening, thanked Rita, then got out, as if the whole thing was just a bit too much like work. Strangers, the ones with the familiar faces and the ones without, step quietly and respectfully around the equipment they once kicked and cursed, and gaze with quiet curiosity on the assembled parts of their working lives as if seeing them for the first time. Amongst them, the tall, stooped figure of the local geography teacher the students call Lurch, and she smiles briefly at the aptness of the name, then the smile drops from her face as he turns, looking vaguely about the room (his wife at his elbow, supporting him), and Rita can see in his face that he's not well. And she remembers what Michael told her, that Lurch had taken a little holiday, as they say, and wasn't coming to school for a while. One look (Lurch is now being steered towards the door) and Rita suspects that he won't be going to school again.

There is low laughter as a small group of workers discover the staff photographs taken over the years, and the newspaper clippings, the sick books, accident reports, and all the little and big things that filled their days and weren't much noticed at the time but which now feel like History.

And all the time, as Webster's people circle the room, as Michael takes his seat alone in the cinema, as the skeletal, consumptive frame of George Johnston who expired in his sleep earlier that morning is taken from the house in which he died, and as the life of the suburb goes on out there heedless of the significance of glass boxes and pedestals, Rita retains the memory of that small business notebook of Webster's, the bit that's not on display here tonight, the bit that's not behind glass, and about which only she knows. For in that distant place of storage to which the removalists drove, there is an ordinary-looking cardboard box that would take some opening, even if anybody ever cared to.

When it is all over and the old Games Room is shut up for the night (although the exhibition will continue to draw the suburb in for weeks after, some families returning two and three times), Mrs Webster invites Rita into the study for a drink to toast her success. They stand — Rita is not asked to sit (and from this she concludes that their drink will be a short one) — beneath a large portrait of Webster, and in a lull in conversation both gaze up at it.

'What was he like?'

The question is asked almost absentmindedly and is no sooner asked than withdrawn.

'I'm sorry.'

Mrs Webster can see that the question is spontaneous, unpremeditated, like a reflex. She does not take offence. She is touched even. For the question is fuelled by a certain wonder. 'What was he like?' being the polite, the discreet, version of what was he *really* like? Behind the public figure, the question asks, behind the cast-iron façade of Webster's Engineering, what was Webster the factory really like? It is all implied in the sheer spontaneity of the question. Even more, for this innocent

225

question is also asking 'What was it like to live with History?' What does History do when the gates are closed on everybody else out there (to whom History merely happens), when the doors are shut on the outside world, what does History do when it puts its feet up?

'I'd never met anyone quite like him. I knew that from the first and I haven't doubted it since. It was always going to be the journey of a lifetime. A once-in-a-lifetime adventure. Together. We shared everything.'

And here Mrs Webster fixes Rita with a silent stare that says, 'Nobody knew Webster like I did. We were two halves of the one life. The one adventure. You ask me what History does when it puts its feet up. I could tell you, because no one knew Webster better than I did, but forgive me if I don't tell you. These are private matters. And these private things are all I have left now. You'll excuse me if I keep them private.'

Then, with a faint, sad smile, she turns to the portrait.

'He was very loyal to the people he employed. Tremendously loyal. They were all ... all a kind of family. If something happened to them, it happened to him. You understand?'

Rita nods.

'He was true. A true spirit.' Here Mrs Webster dwells on the portrait in silence for a moment. 'He had a spirit as true, as clear as those mid-winter mornings when the sun is out and everything is bright with promise. Untouched. And every day was the same. He was as true as that. It was a privilege just to be there.'

Rita is silent. She has never heard anybody talk quite

like this before. Never before heard a woman talk quite like this about her husband. It is not the answer she expected, if she expected anything. And she ought to be moved, as moved as Mrs Webster appears to be. But she is not. Rita doesn't know anybody who talks like this, who talks the way books read. And although she is prepared to be moved by a book, she is not prepared to be moved by someone talking like a book. Then again, she has never met anybody quite like Mrs Webster before. Mrs Webster is what Rita calls rich. And perhaps, perhaps it might be as they say: that the rich are different. Different from the likes of Rita and Vic, and the whole street which she reluctantly acknowledges houses her kind of people. Mrs Webster is not the type of person Rita normally brushes with. Perhaps they are different. Not so much a different species but a different form, a different branch of the same species. And although they all bear the same family resemblances, they are different — with subtly different feelings, and ways of seeing the world that demand the kinds of words that ordinarily belong in books. She inwardly makes these allowances, but although she knows she ought to be moved by Mrs Webster's words, she isn't.

For a moment she is even anxious that this may be apparent to Mrs Webster, that this may appear tactless. But she is relieved to see that Mrs Webster is still engrossed in the portrait, the same faint, sad smile that was on her lips now in her eyes as well. And at the same time Rita notes that Mrs Webster is, in fact, on the verge of tears; that she, Rita, was not moved by Mrs Webster's words, but Mrs Webster was.

When Mrs Webster finally shifts that sad gaze from the portrait to Rita, she looks at her as if not quite recognising her, as though she could be just anybody.

It is, Rita is beginning to realise, the public face Mrs Webster keeps for public occasions. No doubt she has worn that face before when she has given speeches at community events, when she has spoken of her husband as if speaking of a statue or like someone who has completely forgotten whatever it was that existed before the statue came along. And she can understand why the public face is required for public occasions. But why now? Unless all those words that Rita ought to have been moved by, that have the sound of public words, words that belong in the books that record History's lives, are all that's left now.

Then the public smile fades and a look of curiosity crosses Mrs Webster's features. 'Your husband …' Here she pauses, waiting for Rita to supply his name because she has never asked of him before.

'Vic.'

'Vic,' and she stops, almost smiling, as if (it seems to Rita) on the verge of pronouncing it wonderfully uncluttered. Or, perhaps that's Vic himself talking. For, although he's gone, Vic still lurks within her and talks through Rita when the occasion arises, and his distrust of types like Mrs Webster is always there more or less, depending on the day.

'What was he like, your Vic?'

'I don't know. I realise that must sound pathetic after twenty years. But I'm not sure who he was. Not really. He just seemed to come and now he's gone. And I can't help but feel that either I never really tried hard enough to pick his brains in all that time, or he never let me.'

Rita knows she is overstating things, and already suspects that there was an honesty between her and Vic that the Websters of this world never have, but Mrs Webster has driven her to overstatement. And to resolutely using words that don't go in books. Suddenly the public smile is completely gone from Mrs Webster's face and she returns the most minute of nods to Rita. A nod of reflexive agreement. Or was it? There is also something else in Mrs Webster's eyes. You speak, she seems to say, as if the whole thing is behind you. As though it doesn't touch you any more. And you almost get away with it.

Rita finishes the last of her sherry as Mrs Webster downs her scotch in such a way, it seems to Rita, that suggests it will not be the last of the evening. They part at the front door, and with her coat buttoned to the chin and a scarf wrapped round her neck for good measure, Rita strolls, through moonlight and shadow, out along the wide driveway. The suburb, which inside these walls would be so easy to forget existed, lies still and silent, like houses gone under the sea.

The garage. The shiny black snout of the thing parked inside. The look that silently said 'Damn'. The closing of the double doors. The furtiveness of it. The Secrecy. The long, low beast that some say they saw slouching through the suburb in black majesty weeks before, the reports passed on from the chemist of a car speeding through the new frontier of cheap land and large houses in the middle of the night (reports which the street has now heard of), and that involuntary nod of agreement. Later that night, Rita brings all of this with her to the lounge room that was once too small to contain the silence of an unhappy family, but which is now large enough to contain hers. She imagines the doors of Mrs Webster's garage opening onto the night in another part of the suburb, and she turns her head towards the railway lines and the road that leads from them up to Webster's mansion as if half expecting to hear the faint, familiar call of the beast.

It's the feeling that Mrs Webster has discovered something, something special, that stays with Rita throughout a sleepless night. The house, the suburb all around her, is silent. No growl to break the silence, but she's up to something all right. A rare letter from Vic sits on the bedside table. She's read it twice, and, like all Vic's letters, she detects no sign of sadness, loss or regret. They describe what he does, each day more or less the same as the one before and the one to come. But he likes it that way. He shops, he walks, he's found a nice little pub (I'll bet he has, she nods to herself in the dark) where each day he has a fish lunch, then a round of golf and off home to shower and dress for the club. The rapacious jaws of Progress are eating up 'his' little town, he says at the end, and it's the only note of lament in all the letters he's sent her. He was always happiest walking away, and now that he has walked away he is at last content. Of course, she knows he should never have married. Not the marrying kind. Always happiest by himself, with those strangers he calls friends for company. She doesn't want him back, or any of the time they had, but some sense of regret that it hadn't all worked out, that a miracle never came their way and they never got it right, some intimation that they hadn't merely fulfilled a biological function (the subtleties and details of which they were oblivious), and that, in the end, twenty years hadn't just been the coming together of two life forms to produce another, would be a comfort at moments such as these when the sleep won't come and there's no end to the night.

When she wakes in the dark like this, and it is more often than not lately, her mind goes back and she wonders if she truly has the will to go forward, on her own. Or, if something in her broke back there when it all fell apart and she acquired the unmistakable look that men and women get when they have been left. A damaged look that others see or sense, but which very quickly becomes normal to those upon whom the look falls. Did this happen without her knowing, and did she stay in the house too long because she lacked the will to leave, until the house itself came to wear the same look?

Then the first glimmer of light is there, visible at the venetians. There's a bird out there somewhere. She could almost laugh. Nights do end, after all. There's a bird out there somewhere and a finger of light touches the blinds.

37.

A Passing Visit

When the cinema is shut and Michael returns to his room (while Rita is discovering the public and private faces of Mrs Webster), he sees the note that has been slipped under the door in his absence. He takes his coat off, drops the newspaper onto his desk and opens the envelope. She is desperately sorry. Work. Last-minute stuff. Had to fill in for someone. Impossibility of letting him know (no phone). Feels awful. Misses him dreadfully. Dropped by hoping to catch him. Call her in the morning. Madeleine.

He folds the note and places it in the drawer where he keeps her letters (the same letters that he will, when she is gone from his life, drop into a battered metal bin one inevitably rainy rubbish day). Something not right, he muses. It's crisp, plausible, says all the right things — but something's not right. And he can't put his finger on it. But it's there all the same. Nicely written, though. And perhaps that's it. It is 'written'. Crafted in shorthand. As apart from being thrown on the page, as you do when you're in a state. Perhaps it's the 'dreadfully'. Writers use words such as 'dreadfully'. Certain writers use words such as that in their diaries and their memoirs, and that's why diaries and memoirs always sound fake to Michael. Writers putting on airs use words such as that, not people who have had their nights thrown out. Something not right. Definitely. He shuts the drawer.

When he has finished mulling over the note, he slips back into his coat (brown corduroy, which he bought with Madeleine, who insisted he buy it when she discovered he didn't own one). Even though the evening is really getting on, he strolls downstairs and into the street, past the pub opposite, where the Italian drinkers sing like a heavenly choir in the evenings. But tonight there are no angelic notes to warm the cold winter air. The pub is shut. The night is still, and his footsteps (that will eventually lead to Madeleine's place, and which are as soft as a burglar's) blend with the mid-week quiet. Tomorrow is the last day of winter, and if he was to drag himself away from his thoughts he just might notice the scents in the air that herald the coming spring.

Not long after, he is pacing up and down the footpath at the front of Madeleine's. He's been there for five, ten, even fifteen minutes for all he knows. From below he can see that Madeleine's light is on. She's in. Doing something. It is, he has been telling himself over and over again, a perfectly reasonable thing to do. To drop in. He got her note, and here he is. He is, he tells himself, passing by, but he has walked well out of his way to be here and at such a late hour. If he admits it, it is a contrived situation. And it is this contrivance that is troubling him and making him march up and down the footpath when he should just march on in. If he had just come from visiting a friend, become lost to the world contemplating all the things they'd talked about, wandered off into the night afterwards not noticing where he was and looked up to find himself in Madeleine's street (she has recently moved into the upper floor of a house with her sister), he would simply have rung her bell without thinking. A surprise visit. But he has knowingly walked out of his way, not aimlessly strolled, and there is that undeniable element of calculation to his visit. Besides, she said call, not drop in. Without ever saying as much, Michael had concluded very early on, and has always assumed since, that Madeleine is not to be 'dropped in' on. Consequently, he never has. And, although it should feel perfectly natural, he is conscious of stepping outside the bounds — however tacitly agreed, or, indeed, imagined — of their 'going out'.

Two thoughts prevent him from ringing her bell: that this element of contrivance might show on his face and that he is not entirely sure of what he might find inside. The look of contrivance on his face will tell her that he is prying — that this is not a surprise visit, but simple snooping. And this simple snooping (to which he now feels himself reduced) will, he fears, from the moment he steps in the house, become a self-fulfilling exercise, conjuring up the very thing he dreads. It is, of course, ridiculous. But he is increasingly drawn to the ridiculous these days, and, even as he pronounces the thought ridiculous, he is aware of being in its thrall.

It is then that the voice of his all-too-patient, all-too-indulgent common sense, its tolerance finally run out, snaps him to attention and he strides through the gate, raps on the front door, his knocks seeming to reverberate around the neighbourhood houses and the park opposite. He is, he rehearses once more, just passing.

Inside he hears footfalls on the stairs. As her steps near, he feels the skin on his face tighten and his eyes widen and knows that his face will betray him when he casually lets her know that he was just passing.

The door suddenly opens on the night and she is standing there, at first not recognising him in the dull light, then smiling.

'Hi,' he says quickly. 'Do you mind?'

With a quick shake of her head, still smiling, she takes his hand and draws him into the house, closing the door behind them.

'I'm so sorry about tonight.'

'It's all right.'

'No, it's not. I felt awful, but I couldn't get away. And I wanted so dreadfully to be there.'

She says the word with such conviction, such unaffected poetry, that he believes her utterly. It is not the giveaway word of the fancy writer trading in fake feelings, but her word. And, being her word, it is his too. It is all right. All is well, he tells himself, and he was a fool to be standing out there in the dark all that time. She is, after all, his Madeleine, and he is just dropping in. She doesn't mind and he asks himself why he has never done this before. His face did not betray him, ridiculous words did not spring from his lips. He is inside and the only cause for wonder is that it took him so long. And, as she slips her hand from his, he resolves that that will never happen again.

She leads him up the stairs, and he can now unselfconsciously observe her. He notices for the first time that she is casually dressed. And then, and he wishes he hadn't but it is done before he knows it, he mentally substitutes the word 'hastily' for 'casually'. It is noteworthy, unusual even, because — unlike the female students he knows — Madeleine always dresses with care. Rarely in jeans and rarely in loose jumpers. But tonight she is wearing jeans and a sloppy pullover. The pullover — which he has never seen before, and which looks to be more a man's pullover than a woman's — has slid down one shoulder and he can see quite clearly the line of her collarbone, and her neck, and he notes also that she is not wearing a bra. Nor is she wearing a shirt. Beneath the pullover, she is naked. She is, in six months of them being together, as naked as she has ever been with him. And he concludes that he is right. She is hastily dressed.

On the landing she turns, kisses him briefly, then opens the door of the lounge room and pushes him in with a laugh, saying that she was just about to go to bed, that she needs to brush her hair at least, that she is not quite ready to be received. And when she murmurs the word 'received' it is with the italics of her raised eyebrows.

Then he is sitting on the sofa in the lounge room, the gas heater low, the moon casting a shifting, milky shaft of light through the curtains. He rises, walks to the window and stares down upon the footpath, calculating that no more than a minute has elapsed since ringing the bell. And this, this is the lighted room he gazed up at. The room is neat and ordered. It relaxes him. He is, once again, in her sphere. And as he is looking down on the footpath, he substitutes the word 'casually' for 'hastily' — which he now realises he was too quick in applying. She was, after all, about to go to bed. He never wears a watch but he can guess the hour. The lack of traffic, the deserted street and the high moon outside all tell him that the night is getting on. He relaxes, but resolves not to stay long for she must surely be working early in the morning. All is well again.

When Madeleine re-enters the room moments later, closing the door firmly behind her, her hair is up, pinned with a black velvet clip. She could almost be stepping out for the night instead of turning in. As they both lean back on the sofa, he sees that the pullover has been straightened and that she is now wearing a bra.

'You don't mind . . . me dropping in?' he asks again.

'No.'

'Sure?'

'Of course. But I haven't got my face on. You're seeing the real me.'

Once again, the word 'real' is delivered with the italics of her raised eyebrows. He hadn't even noticed or cared, but he now asks himself if he has ever seen her without make-up before and he concludes that he hasn't. And it is oddly thrilling, a kind of nakedness in itself. She thinks she looks plain, he hums inwardly. If only she knew. This, he tells himself, this is how she would look if ... This is how she would look if he were to wake with her in the mornings, the Madeleine he would see that nobody else would.

'I was just passing.'

'Good.'

'Are you pleased?'

'Can't you tell?'

And it is then that she rises, almost, it seems to Michael, on cue, and plays the record already there on the stereo. Music, the kind of music couples play late at night, romantic music — not the kind he associates with Madeleine. This music (which is beneath her in the same way that words such as 'hunk' are beneath her) swells and fills the room, like music at the end of a party rather than the end of an evening. And, when she sits back on the sofa, she places her arms round his neck without speaking and kisses him. It is a long, luxuriant kiss, and she is kissing him more than he is kissing her. And, when he inquires if he ought to leave because she must, after all, be working early the next morning (he feels guilty for detaining her), she pushes him firmly against the back of the sofa so that rising now would be difficult even if he wanted to, and resumes what feels like the same luxuriant kiss. But as he is about to lose himself in the oblivion of it all, he is suddenly disturbed by something out there. Footsteps. He swears he could hear, for all the world, somewhere out there beyond the music and their breathing and kissing, footfalls on the stairs. Then footfalls descending the stairs, out the front and fading into the street. And was that the distant thump of the front door or car door in the night?

He is tense, his ears alert for any sound. As he lifts his face, and for a moment extricates himself from the embrace, he looks intently at the window, the milky shaft of shifting moonlight still playing with the lace.

'What is it?' she asks, eyeing him with sudden alarm and concern.

His eyes are wide, asking, almost pleading, can I trust you?

'What is it?' she whispers.

She is troubled. Her face is now so close, her skin so warm, her eyes so alight with … with what he can only call care.

'Nothing,' he says, staring at the window, the moonlight, the room, then back to the nakedness of her face and this enthralling creature she calls the 'real' her.

When the music stops shortly afterwards, she reminds him that she is indeed working early the next morning, that it has been a lovely surprise, but that he perhaps ought to go now.

Downstairs, she stands framed in the doorway. The concern is still in his eyes, the phantom footfalls still in his ears. And it is then, her eyes gazing knowingly into his as if, indeed, reading his thoughts and drawing him back to her, that with a playful smile she pulls back the neck of the sweater (which he has never seen until tonight) to reveal the full length of her neck and the crest of her bared shoulder.

The effect is instantaneous. So much so that, at first, he does not see the invitation in the gesture.

There is no one out on the street. But there could be. At any moment. As his feet finally reach the doorway, his lips come to rest on her open neck (his eyes closed).

She does this. When he thinks he knows her, he realises he doesn't. And it is a puzzle, a constantly shifting puzzle. How she can be his Madeleine in private — the private, controlled Madeleine who goes so far and so far only when they are alone and nobody is looking — and then, as it were, fornicate with him in public. Fornicate with her shoulder and eyes and the line of her perfect neck.

Eyes still closed, his lips finally leave her neck and, as she draws the band of the sweater back into place, it is as though their accustomed places have been thrown into the air, and it is love that lights her eyes, and gratitude that opens his.

She smiles and takes one pace back into the hallway. She smiles playfully, both familiar and strange. The young woman he takes to be *his* Madeleine, always slipping from him. And, as he loses himself in her eyes, he is convinced he will never know her enough to keep her. She will always be leaving, even as she is drawing him back.

Then he is on the footpath and the honeyed wedge of light in her doorway disappears. The road curves up the hill to the university grounds, and, as he walks up the footpath, he occasionally glances back, half expecting to see something or someone, but not sure who or what.

In the years to come, he will know what it is to receive love and feel only gratitude in return. He will, in short, know what it is to be Madeleine. But on this night, on this street, Michael is experiencing the most important moments of his life until now and he knows it. Perhaps it is true, he is wondering. Perhaps it's true what the love-sick poems and books that he reads tell him — that we only ever fall in love once, and after that we may as well die. That the mind and the body can only ever deal with the earthquake of love once. By the time he reaches the top of the street and looks back down along the incline leading to the hospital and to Madeleine's door, one part of him is convinced it is true. The other is already rearranging the scene — and all their scenes — more satisfactorily.

When he returns to his room, he finds a pamphlet pinned to his door. It is from Bunny Rabbit, who must have slipped in when Pussy Cat was sleeping. There is a rally, it seems, at the university the next day. Be there or be square! But there is no room for meetings or rallies or marches in Michael's mind. It is a private Michael with a private mind that goes to bed and that wakes in the morning, indifferent to the public march of History out there on the streets around him.

38

The Last Day of Winter

Spring is in the air. On this last day of winter, although it is late in the afternoon, the darkness that always descends early in the thick of winter does not. Mrs Webster's gardens are still light and so too is the mood of the committee as they gather at the front door.

There is an air of congratulation. What seemed to be an improbable proposal when first put forward by Peter van Rijn that steamy January morning had now bloomed and blossomed like the flowers in Mrs Webster's garden. It was — and they had all eventually 'confessed their pleasant surprise to each other throughout the year — actually working. The suburb was more alive with events and celebrations than anybody could remember, for, once the idea had taken off, everybody wanted to be part of it. Small groups and societies that nobody even knew existed were writing to the committee applying to be part of the celebrations. A Scottish group was suggesting that the suburb be made the twin or sister town of a village somewhere in the highlands where the original sheep farmers who settled the suburb came from. Not to mention a statue of a farmer in the main street to remind everybody of their agrarian beginnings. Tiny religious organisations that seemed to have mushroomed overnight, sporting groups, amateur science foundations, reading groups — it was a revelation to the committee just what was going on in the suburb — were all writing to the committee for one reason or another, asking for money. The whole place was humming.

Michael, pleased to have the afternoon off teaching, is gazing out over the gardens, towards the garage in the far corner (out of view) where, as a teenager, he'd collected money from Webster for his cricket club, surprising him as he was cleaning the sleek, black sports car that was his one trifling infidelity — his one little secret that had been casually discovered by Michael, who had left with silver coins in a money bag for the club, and a ten-pound note in his shirt pocket for his silence. Webster's estate had felt like another country back then, and it still had that air, even though Webster and that sleek, black little sporting job of his were long gone.

And while he is dwelling on those days that seemed so distant, almost innocent now (although he knows perfectly well that no time ever is), the vicar of St Matthew's remarks on what a fine job Rita did with the exhibition. How everybody said so, and what a fantastic success the whole thing had been. Beyond anyone's imaginings. In fact, so successful had it been that it looks set to go on and on. It had touched a spot in the suburb that the suburb didn't even know was there, because it's easy to overlook the ordinary, familiar things that are around you every day of the year, because, well, they are. Until someone or something alerts everybody to the possibility that they just might not be so ordinary after all.

So, with spring already in the air, the mayor, Mrs Webster, the two priests, Peter van Rijn and Michael (the local member is 'sitting') all breathe in that hint of the new season and quietly congratulate each other on a job well done.

As they are about to break up, the mayor remarks on the mural. Still under wraps. Nobody allowed to look. Even peek. Bit odd, isn't it? What's Mulligan up to? For there is still a general feeling of unease about this artist who spends his days up the wall, suspended on a pulley like some latter-day Michelangelo. But aren't all these artistic types oddballs in one way or another (and here they all turn to Michael)? It is then that the mayor casually mentions to Michael that this Whitlam of theirs will be coming to the suburb soon to open a sports ground. Michael eyes the mayor as if looking upon an entirely different person, and the mayor, quietly, inwardly, congratulates himself on having knocked the smug smile off Michael's face. Catching, as he does so, the hint of a smile in Mrs Webster's eyes that says, 'Well done, Harold.'

With the year rapidly closing in on them, they all agree that their next meeting (and possibly their last) should finalise a date for the unveiling and that the artist should be told of the deadline. It is, after all, the Crowning Event of the year and will take a bit more planning than anything else so far. Speeches will have to be written, guest lists compiled and invitations sent out. The committee, of course, will all need to be there. And again they turn to Michael who, when the time comes, will be at one of those moratoriums that Mrs Webster (standing in her doorway and farewelling the committee) finds both amusing and annoying and that sum up Michael and his kind. For Michael, his kind and this Whitlam of theirs are a wave, she imagines, a wave that has been steadily building over the years and will not be stopped. They *are* History, their every word and gesture tells you. Michael and his kind, and she quickly looks him up and down, they're a bit like those kings who crown themselves without having the decency to wait for the hands of History to do it for them.

The group disbands and drifts back into a suburb contentedly humming with a new-found sense of itself, as the commerce of the Old Wheat Road prepares to shut down for the day and the street lights and house lights flicker and pop into existence on this last evening of winter.

Part Four

Spring

39.

The Invention of Death

Pussy Cat is at it again. The sobbing goes on night after night. It has been going on for weeks. Bunny Rabbit does not return. Pussy Cat, who will only ever fall in love once, sleeps through the days and will not answer her door. Nor does anybody see her come or go. During the days she is silent, and in the evenings it all begins again. Pussy Cat howls for her Bunny Rabbit in the night. But Bunny Rabbit has moved on and now nibbles ears other than hers.

She howls in the night, perhaps really believing that somewhere out there his ears will prick up and hear her call, her call that comes to him not only across the rooftops and chimneys of the city, but across those endless nights that have intervened since she last saw him. And perhaps she is also remembering, as she howls from her room, those times — and there were all too many of them towards the end — those times, those days and nights when they could do nothing right and it was clear that the adventures of Pussy Cat and Bunny Rabbit were over. Those nights when she bristled at everything he said or did, and the more he tried to smooth her fur the more she arched. Those nights when she offered him the choicest roots and clovers of her love, and his nose twitched and his eyes turned to the horizon. When taunts led to tears and tears to taunts, and they could each do nothing but wrong.

Michael falls asleep to the faint sounds of her sobbing. Downstairs, Mulligan walks loudly from his room to the kitchen, slamming doors, for Mulligan has only one thing on his mind. He has no time for anybody's sobbing. But the sobs continue. And it is like this the following evening, and the evening after. Then one night all the sobbing stops. Silence. The sorrow has run its course, she has run out of tears. The capital 'L' of life, Michael assumes (eyeing the closed door of her room before leaving in the morning) can begin again. The September sun has done its work. Pussy Cat will shed the burdensome fur of winter and spring into Life once more.

But when Michael returns later in the day from school, Bunny Rabbit is sitting on the landing, head in his hands. Pussy Cat's door is open, the room is empty.

When Michael stops halfway up the stairs upon seeing him, Bunny Rabbit lifts his head to speak, though he barely seems to notice Michael. It is the look of someone profoundly unprepared for the eventuality of life turning serious. And as soon as Michael sees that look in his eyes, he knows what has happened.

'She didn't mean it.'

It is as though having told her so often that she wouldn't do it, Bunny Rabbit couldn't conceive of the fact that she actually had. It was not written into her. It was not written into them. Therefore, it had to be a mistake, and his taunts, his careless words, had not killed her. Not, that is, if the whole thing had been an accident. Not if she didn't mean it.

Michael sits on the stairs below him and watches as the disbelieving face of Peter plops back into his hands. He had been Bunny Rabbit, she had been his Pussy Cat. Together they'd had the most wonderful adventures. And it occurs to Michael that they had had their innocence, after all. That, for all their talk and their ways, their joints, their drugs and their loud and frequent copulation, they were at heart — these children of the Age — more innocent than he'd ever imagined. Now his Pussy Cat was gone, and he would never play her Bunny Rabbit again. Not for her, or for anybody else. From now on, he would simply have to walk through the world as Peter. And those wonderful adventures he'd known in another incarnation — when love had metamorphosed them into storybook animals — would become the touchstones for measuring the value of all subsequent adventures.

Michael leaves him sitting on the landing at the top of the stairs. He retraces his steps and leaves the house. To simply go to his room and read, as he usually would at the end of the day, would be to act as though nothing had happened.

So we'll go no more a-roving. He can't remember who wrote it or even if he's got it right. Who cares? Pussy Cat is dead. And Bunny Rabbit and Pussy Cat will no longer go a-roving. Whatever that means. But it doesn't matter what it means. The right words have come at the right time. These, at the moment, as he crosses the street, past the hotel opposite, and through the drab playgrounds of the housing commission high-rise, are the only words that matter, even if their sense isn't readily apparent. For what the words are telling him — and which he will only realise much later — is that the poetic age of youth died in Pussy Cat's room, either late last night or early this morning. And, like old friends, these words come to us and stay with us until the thing that needs to be taken in is taken in.

As he leaves the high-rise grounds, he notes that the playground is deserted in the way that playgrounds that are rarely used are deserted.

And Bunny Rabbit? Bunny Rabbit will get over all this and eventually become what he was always destined to be. A lawyer. And a very good one. He is from a family of lawyers and his life will unroll before him like a carpet, and he will walk away from these aberrant days, from this landing upon which he is currently sitting with his head held in his hands, and meet that glittering horizon where he will find the prized life he was always destined for.

It will be a relatively easy stroll from here to there, from the poetic age of youth to the *real-politik* of the grown-up world. From time to time Michael will see his name in the papers, for he will achieve a kind of fame in the courts and in conservative politics. He will become especially well known for his courtroom taunts. And

Michael will inevitably wonder — whenever he reads these reports in the papers — if he ever reflects on the days when he lived for other adventures. Indeed, whether he ever looks into himself and finds in the public figure some long-denied vestige of the days when he played Bunny Rabbit to his Pussy Cat. And then he will also wonder if those skills — that gift for a telling courtroom jibe that now brings him newspaper fame — were the same skills that he honed in the room opposite Michael's and which killed his innocence.

His Pussy Cat was carried from the room earlier in the day. There was already a sheet over her when he'd arrived, after having been called to the house. He never looked into her dead eyes, for he couldn't bring himself to. But if he had, he might possibly have seen, written into them, the final realisation that, as much as she might have longed to, she couldn't save him and preserve him as Bunny Rabbit forever, because he was already out of reach and that was why, in the end, she stopped sobbing.

40.

Confessional

The afternoon sun, higher in the sky this time of year, slants through the double door of the garage, catching the cobwebs, the peeling paint on the walls and freshly cut flowers in a basket on the workbench. The day is sharp and tangy, and mingles with the smell of grease and oils, ancient and new. Mrs Webster pulls the old tarpaulin back and drops it on the smoothed brick floor. Rita has never cared for cars. Neither did Vic, or Michael. None of them did. Cars were no more a topic of conversation than a washing machine or a lawnmower. They all had functions, to clean or to cut. And the motor car's function was to carry you from one place to another, and, beyond that, there was nothing more to say. But this thing before her now, which seems to be crouching half asleep, ready to spring at any moment, is more than simply a vehicle that transports its cargo from one place to another. It is almost as though the fact of the car is not important; it is what it brings. It brings the possibility of speed. It brings the possibility of accelerating into life or into death, of going somewhere, and never quite coming back. Neither woman speaks. The sun continues to catch the cobwebs and peeling walls of the garage, the car remains crouching, half asleep, ready to spring into life.

What moved Mrs Webster to invite this woman into the garage? She had been standing in the gardens picking the first of the spring flowers when Rita appeared. Had she forgotten Rita was coming, or assumed she had more time? Whatever, she had been caught off-guard. They exchanged greetings and as they did Rita eyed the garage in the distance, just over Mrs Webster's shoulder. She had neither asked about the building nor spoken of it. But curiosity was in her eyes and Mrs Webster — dreamily, the basket of flowers in her arms — read the question there and turned to face the garage with her. What the hell, she's already seen the thing!

'Let's walk,' she said, and, without knowing why, directed Rita along the path that led to the green, wooden shed in the corner of the estate. Why? She would contemplate this later that night, but perhaps the time had come to share what she'd found with someone who would understand — and perhaps Rita was that someone. Perhaps, and the practically minded part of Mrs Webster scoffed at the idea, perhaps there was harmony in the person, the place and the time. And, without questioning the impulse (one that sprang from being caught off-guard), she had decided on sharing her experience with this woman who might yet be a friend of sorts. Decided that she could not or would not lie to this woman again as she did when Rita had, quite candidly, asked what he, Webster the factory, was *really* like.

So, when they reached the garage, Mrs Webster opened the doors on to the private world they hid and led Rita in, placing her flowers on the workbench and pulling the tarpaulin back in one swift, smooth movement.

'At first you ask yourself what on earth you're doing out there on the highway.' She laughs. 'Highway, they call it! Nobody else about. Just you. And the dark. Oh so dark. You really wonder if you haven't slowly gone round the twist, after all, only you haven't noticed. And then you think, I don't have to. If I just turn around and quietly slip back, none of this will have happened and I won't really be mad. No one saw me go, and no one sees me come back. I'm the only witness and I'm not telling. But then you think, I'm here. I'm not going back now only to lie in bed all night wondering what it might have been like.'

It is only a few minutes since they entered the garage and Mrs Webster can't even remember when she began talking. She pauses now, eyeing the freshly cut flowers in the basket as if wondering who on earth left them there. It's a long pause and Rita thinks she's finished. But when Mrs Webster starts talking again, it's as though there has been no break in the conversation at all.

'You can't imagine the kind of speed you can find out there. Everything beside you is a blur, but if you look straight ahead you could swear you're standing still. And so you press down on the pedal even more because, whatever you're doing, it's not enough. And the faster you go, the more you press the pedal down. And you keep at it and at it until you could swear your whole body is about to just blow away — and you're left with just your mind. No body. And as much as you're convinced you're barely moving at all, you're really about to take off to the moon. And the moon's just out there, over the next field. Not so far away. Not really.'

She stops and in the silence that follows Rita can almost hear the car humming in the afterglow of the tale. The garage is still, neither of the women speak. Mrs Webster is talking the way people talk in books again, only this time Rita doesn't mind. This must be her way, she concludes.

Outside, the doors closed and the basket of flowers once again through her arm, Mrs Webster gazes about the estate, the trees and flowering foliage ignited by the spring sun.

'I'm in no rush to die,' she says, 'but it's like driving to the point where you almost could, then coming back. I can see how you could get to like that feeling, how you might even come to need it or get to the point where you don't really care if you come back or not.'

Here she casts a knowing glance at Rita, and Rita knows she's not talking about herself any more. And it's at a moment like this that Rita could tell her about the box that fell from the bookshelf in the Games Room, the business diary and the funny poem inside. For, although she'd concluded then that Mrs Webster wouldn't want to know, Rita's not so sure now.

Then the moment is lost. Mrs Webster points Rita back along the same path in the direction of the house,

Rita wondering, if, apart from her afternoon greeting, she's since opened her mouth. At the house, Mrs Webster slips behind the wheel of the old Bentley and nods briefly before departing along the wide gravel drive out into the suburb. Rita turns and walks into the house to start the cleaning. Through the rest of the day (after Pussy Cat has been taken from her room, and Michael has encountered the disbelieving figure of Bunny Rabbit on the stairs), it is the look on Mrs Webster's face that stays with her: the almost ecstatic glow, the flush of someone looking about at the world from a great height, the look of someone who has been somewhere and never wholly come back.

The sun is dropping through the trees of the estate as Rita leaves. She has never been good at making friends, nor, she suspects, has Mrs Webster, which explains why she is still Mrs Webster, her employer, and not Val, her friend. For all her confidence, her position, her money, she doesn't seem to have friends nor does she talk of any. And, perhaps, this is what she sees in Rita, a woman — like herself — without friends. Precisely the kind of woman to whom she can talk. One who will not tell others because there is no one to tell. And Mrs Webster — who had to tell someone because the momentousness of what she had experienced demanded telling (there had now been a number of midnight drives) — had found her perfect listener. The perfect ears into which she could pour her confession. But, even this, Rita notes (as she turns into the wide street the estate fronts, and which will soon become Progress Avenue), is something to value. At the bottom of confidences such as the one Rita has just heard is the kind of trust that friends have for each other; the trust that she won't blab, and not just because she has no one to blab to, but because she is not the blabbing type. The thing Mrs Webster had experienced demanded to be told. For (like Webster himself, who told no one) she could see how you might become so entranced by the feeling of going away that one day — like Webster — you might not come back at all. Was this her fear? And did she look about for someone to share her fear with in order to release it?

This woman may or may not be a friend. She may, after a lifetime of not really having friends (of having lived the public life with public company for friends), be past the idea of friendship. But, all the same, they might still be a help to each other. Company. And this just might be a kind of friendship; the kind that cautious people allow themselves, without naming it so.

And if this is true, then she is more than happy to help Mrs Webster. To be a discreet ear. And not to blab. To be the kind of person upon whom the compliment of trust is bestowed. And, at the same time (as she rounds the corner into her street), it also occurs to her that Mrs Webster, having already found trust in Rita's taste for colour and material, found the next step no great matter.

That faintly rhapsodic glow on Mrs Webster's face as she spoke still preoccupies her, even haunts her, and Rita is left wondering just what it's like to feel as though you could almost take off, and to feel that the cool, distant sphere of the moon isn't so distant after all. And, as the weeks pass, this casual speculation will occupy her thoughts more and more and become a longing. An impatient one. And, as the ratty, spring winds pick up, this impatience will eventually demand to be spoken.

That same afternoon, Mrs Webster sits in her office overlooking the irrelevant industry taking place out there on the factory floor. Production is going on all around her, but, at the centre of it all, she sits unmoved. What on earth possessed her? She was, it now seems looking back on it, not so much talking as thinking out loud. And to a stranger. Well, more or less. She is not the sort of woman given to thinking out loud, only ever to Webster (and now she wonders if he was ever listening anyway), but this morning she did. Yet, somehow, she knew that the need to speak and the time to speak had come together. The moment was right, and she had no regrets.

Far from it, for as she had closed the doors of the garage that morning she had also realised that she felt no desire to open them again. She'd found what she wanted. She'd been to that place where Webster went — to which he had gone and never wholly come back, until eventually he had never come back at all. Now she knows. She's been there.

Her eyes pass over the factory floor below. What was once a brute was now a decaying beast, dribbling its way into extinction, the unmistakable reek of death all around. The natural death she'd always anticipated could take years, and she didn't have years to throw around. The time had come — and had she just reached this conclusion? — the time had come to put the thing down. To silence the noise

Webster had brought to the suburb all those years ago when the suburb was being born and the world, like the endless paddocks of thistle, was wide.

Oblivious of the still, silent figure in the chair, the activities on the factory floor continue as they always have: giant machines, dreadnoughts of a bygone industrial age, pressing scrap metal into parts, parts, parts. To become a whole object that, sooner more than later, will break, fall apart and become scrap metal all over again.

41.

An Unmarked Grave

Somewhere out there in the thistle country, just beyond the trestle bridge that spans the wide, ancient river valley, you'll find the old cemetery of the suburb. The one that did the job until the suburb grew and another one was needed. A thousand miles to the north, while Rita is contemplating the puzzle of Mrs Webster's confession, and not long after Mrs Webster quietly, almost casually decided to put the beast of Webster's Engineering down, Vic looks out of his kitchen window at the top of the hill. The lights of the town are popping on, the curve of the main road leading down into the town centre is illuminated, and the neons of the Twin Towns Services Club are already glowing in the twilight.

But Vic doesn't see the town. His eyes pass over the glitter of the Services Club and his gaze is fixed on the thistle country somewhere out there where the cemetery, its headstones at various angles, lies spread out under the same darkness that falls upon the town. Memory, a memory never so keen as it has been lately, takes him there. Trust it, says Vic, it will take you there. Walk through the old rusty gate, which is rusted beyond closing, noting the rows upon ragged rows of the dead, and continue walking, slowly and respectfully, until, eventually, you come to a bare open grassy section of this cemetery that sits on a low hill that gives the visitor a good view of the trains crossing the trestle bridge. The ground is uneven here. There are low mounds, some barely noticeable, others less worn down by the effects of wind and rain. These are the paupers' graves, unmarked, and barely recognisable as graves at all.

This is where they brought her, Mary Anne, to an unmarked grave in the thistle country at the edge of the suburb. Mary Anne, Ma, Mama, who kept her boy when everybody told her to farm him out, and whose voice now drifts on the wind towards him from the low, unmarked mound where her bones lie. Vic always meant to put up a gravestone, but marble doesn't come cheap and, somehow, the money just never turned up. And, as if she were noting the inconvenience of an old wood stove and no electric lights (as it was in that last house of hers in the country where she went to be near her boy, when Vic and Rita had fled the city drunks who called themselves mates to that broken town where even the river was called 'broken'), as if, indeed, it was a minor annoyance and hardly a matter of life and death, these bones of hers tell Vic that she can get by quite nicely without a gravestone. She knows where she is and she's not going anywhere. And if anybody walks over her grave, well, that's their look-out. There are more important things about dying than gravestones. And if strangers don't know where to find her, what does it matter? So don't go worrying yourself about gravestones and flowers; these bones that your mama once stood up in, and carried you in, and cradled you in, are well satisfied that they did their job when the job needed doing. And who cares for the stories that epitaphs tell? You and I know our story, and, if our story dies with us, so be it. And even when both us, you and I, have left them all to it, and there is no one left to remember it or tell it, our story will still be there, will still have happened, won't it? Because it *did*. It's a fact, and always will be. That we took them on, you and I, and came through and did what they all told us we couldn't do. And that's all that matters, not gravestones and flowers. The fact that we were *us*, and stayed us. These bones are well satisfied that they did their job when the job needed doing.

As the sub-tropical darkness flows in over the town, engulfing it in balmy, playful night, Vic leaves the thistle country and the bumpy, uneven ground of the paupers' section of the graveyard through the same old rusted gate he came in by, contemplating the club and the routine of his day that will soon take him to the glitter of clubland.

And it could just as easily be summer or winter, for this time of the day will always find him seated here in his kitchen. All days are the same day, and this will always be the hour that takes him back to the thistle country somewhere out there on the edge of the old suburb, where trains moan in the night and the bones of his mother sing to her boy over the paddocks of scotch thistle and over the years.

42.

The Farewell Party

There are no lights on in her house and he does not ring the bell. It is early in the evening. She will not be asleep. She will not be there. It is mid-week, the night of her farewell from work. Michael was invited, but he was invited in such a way that suggested it was more of a courtesy than a genuine invitation. It was a work farewell. He wouldn't know anybody. He wouldn't like it. He'd feel left out. These were the unspoken sentiments that came with the courtesy of an invitation. And because he agreed that he would feel left out, he had said no. But at some stage during the afternoon the no became a yes, and here he is.

With the house dark and everybody gone, he really ought to walk home and give it away. The evening would go on as it ought to, without him. But he scans the surrounding streets near the hospital, calculating where she might be, for the area containing the university and hospital is small. Somewhere out there, in that modest square of land they have shared for the last year, she and those with whom she works will be raising their glasses in celebration of her grand adventure. They'll be all cheers and smiles and jokes. Even those who never got on with her, for one reason or another. And Madeleine will have the eyes, the shining, bright eyes, of someone setting out on a journey. And perhaps that's why she doesn't want him there, because she doesn't want him to see those eyes. Because it would be in poor taste for her eyes to shine and her whole being to glow at the prospect of leaving, for this whole business of setting out implies an exciting, new beginning, and an ending. And, with every ending, some sadsack with that left-behind look written all over his face. And that's not the sort of face you want hanging about at a farewell when everybody's all cheers and smiles. He leaves her house, its windows black, and walks down towards the hospital and two small pubs he knows that she and her work friends go to, from time to time, for these sorts of farewell events.

He knows he has found them without even seeing Madeleine. He is staring in through the yellow glass of the pub at a group of people that gives every indication of having been brought together for a purpose. His eyes — as indifferent as a camera — rove over the gathered faces then come to rest on her. She is seated at the end of a trestle table, her sister on one side of her and the older married man whom he first saw at the ball in the summer (and who speaks with the same ease and eloquence on the mysteries of the kidney as he does on women and country fields) is on the other. The very sight of him should feel like a physical blow, but his indifference protects him. *Feel nothing*, a voice is saying. It is a voice from long ago, a child's voice, a wise one. A voice that learnt years before how to keep the world at bay, and how to feel nothing when feeling nothing was required. And because it is a wise voice he listens, and the blow that might well have fallen does not. It is a trick learnt young, and, once learnt, it never goes away. The child that learnt the trick when a trick was needed will always be there beside him, ready to take his hand when required, and whisper the right words at the right time. *Feel nothing*.

Her eyes sparkle, her face is radiant, she is glowing. Happy in a way that he never is when *she* is not there — happy in a way that some part of him is convinced she has no right to be. For it is an almost liberated happiness that she glows with. There is a liveliness to her manner that he is not aware of having noticed before: bright, flirtatious glances that he has no memory of seeing before, let alone receiving. Then again, he has never observed her at a distance before — and with this indifference. And the more he gazes upon this gathering, the more he becomes convinced that he is not destined to join them inside where there is noise and warmth and where Madeleine is happy in a way that he has not seen her happy before. It is, he concludes (as he steps back to take in the full panorama of the table and his eyes go click like a camera), a picture that is already complete, a group portrait, a *tableau* that stands as it is. One more and the balance would be lost, the harmony of the scene disturbed.

She has not seen him, but he has seen her. It is enough. The trick of feeling nothing was still good. The wisdom of the child he once was, still there and still valid. He could live with this, this departure. Feeling nothing was easy, if you learnt the trick early enough. Pain was a red, red ball, propelled through the air at speed to the other end of a cricket pitch, then propelled again and again. In the oblivion of the act of propelling it, throughout all those summers all those years before, he had learnt the art of feeling nothing. And like his father's walk — a winter walk in summer — it was a way of being that, once learnt, was never forgotten. Control the ball and you control everything else. A trick like that, once acquired, would forever stand its possessor in good stead.

Back in his room, he falls into his favourite armchair and is idly staring at the double windows that in summer open out onto the street. They are living a story. And this, logically, is how the story must end. Furthermore, it is the ending he wants. The gift of Madeleine was a kind of blessed ordinariness, a sense of being connected the way everybody else was, a confirmation of the belief that there really was someone out there after all, just for him. When she is gone, his consolation will be this, the consolation of the right ending at the right time. An aeroplane, a departure, the gesture of a final heartfelt letter. And, when this ending is finally upon them and everybody has gone their separate ways forever, he will be left with a deeply satisfying sadness that it had to happen. The way it does in stories where the longed-for moment is reached, hearts break on the printed page, and everybody steps out into the vast unwritten life that is left to them.

In the books that he reads, in the books that he studies and writes about, books in which lovers meet and destroy each other with their love or their lack of it, there is a common thread — that what happens happens because it could not have happened any other way. The moment, to use a fashionable student phrase of the day, is structured that way. A young woman called Madeleine meets a young man called Michael, one discovering love, the other gratitude. Then they part, because the mixture of love and gratitude can only sustain itself for so long. She weaves the sunlight in her hair and leaves with regret in her eyes, not because she is leaving but because she could find nothing more to offer. Nor does she wish there could have been more, because that something more wasn't in them to be discovered. Together they could only ever have amounted to what they became. And the regret is in her eyes, not because she wished for more but because she had always known that there was no more. Their story ends the way it was always going to. And with that ending he acquires — almost happily — the deeply thrilling sadness that tells him he has loved somebody. That he has known what it is to be connected and together they have known the days.

43.

The Mountain of Whitlam
Comes to Centenary Suburb

The mountain of Whitlam has been lowered into the back seat of a white Commonwealth car. He has been shipped to Melbourne, and is now being ferried to Centenary Suburb. This mountain, which seems to fill the entire car, has been travelling towards the suburb for much of the year. He is lowered into the back seat, the door is slammed, and the car draws away from the newly completed international airport.

Soon, the gleaming white car, bearing its monumental cargo, is speeding along the newly completed freeway, built to carry traffic from the airport (whose runways, hangars and lounges sit uneasily upon the old thistle country north of the suburb) to the city, with maximum ease. Everywhere the signs of Progress are in evidence, as the car bearing the mountain of Whitlam travels towards its destination.

The eyes of Whitlam move from side to side, roving over the open fields. He is impassive and looks out the window as a hiker might, stick in hand, surveying a landscape from a great height. As the car moves smoothly along the shining bitumen, the houses that mark the fringes of the city pop up into view, first one or two, then in the intensifying numbers of a massed army. And although he looks upon them with the rarefied eyes of the hiker, he also knows that these fringe suburbs are his territory. It is suburbs such as these that house or once housed Michael and his kind, and it is Michael and his kind who will one day soon push the mass of Whitlam to power. This mountainous statue on wheels will roll inexorably to power in just a couple of years, and it will be Michael and his kind who will provide the motive force, just as coal and water produce steam and provide motive force for an engine to pull carriages. So, even though his face betrays no emotion, this Whitlam is acknowledging deep in his core that all landscapes, especially those as flat as the pancake suburbs around him, require mountains. And he, the mountain of Whitlam, has come to this coastal plain of suburbs built on grass and thistle because plains cannot move, whereas mountains, housed on wheels, can.

As they leave the freeway, his eyes lower and scan the typed pages his speechwriter has just handed him. He has come to Centenary Suburb to officially open a sports ground. A minister in government might have been requested for the job, but the mayor of Centenary Suburb is a man who trades in politics, not believes in it, and he knows a mountain when he sees one, and knows that this mountain will soon command the eyes of the landscape. It is written into all of them — the mayor, Mrs Webster, Peter van Rijn, the rotting hulk of Bruchner, and Michael and his kind — that this Whitlam will one day rule. And, even though he can't know if the length of his rule will be short or long, the mayor is convinced that the country, and therefore the suburb, will never be the same again once the mountain prevails. And so, adhering to the age-old dictum that for things to stay the same things must change, the mayor has invited this Whitlam who moves with the unshakeable conviction that he *is* History, waiting to happen. The mayor is not about to dispute this. And so, when everything changes, the mayor will have the boast of having shaken Whitlam's hand before it did. And boasts such as that just might be enough to keep some things the same. By which the mayor means the chair in which he sits and the office he occupies. And the wide purple tie and the long greying sideburns that he now possesses as he waits for the arrival of the Great Whitlam, are, too, the concessions one makes to change and to Progress, so that things might stay the same.

When the white Commonwealth car pulls up at the sports ground, the mountain of Whitlam is lifted from the back seat and is wheeled to the welcoming party at the front of the cream-brick building. Even as he approaches, the mayor is enjoying a quiet smile as he remembers drawing up plans for the building and the architect informing him that the first thing the builders, planners and everybody else involved would want to do is work out where the bar goes.

As the shadow that prefigures the sheer mass of Whitlam looms closer, the quiet smile fades from the mayor's features and he is convinced that History is, in fact, rolling inexorably towards him and he is about to shake hands with it. And if Michael, who is standing just behind him, were to explain that cocktail of emotions that have overcome the mayor — and Harold Ford is an early-evening-martini man — he would, to the mayor's great surprise, use the word 'sublime'. He would tell him that what he is currently experiencing is that mixture of awe and terror that the great Romantic poets felt when they viewed, say, at close quarters, a snow-peaked mountain. For the mountain of Whitlam has this effect on the mayor, even if the word 'sublime' would be the last that he would draw upon to describe this strangely disturbing feeling.

And such is the kick of this particularly potent cocktail that when the mountain stretches out its hand, the hand of the mayor that reaches back is, for the first time in decades, betraying a hint of trembling.

They speak briefly and together note that the bar is in a good spot, then the wheels underneath the statue of Whitlam move down the line, greeting each of the welcoming party in turn. When he comes to the distinctly unmoved figure of Mrs Webster, he reminds her that they have met before, addresses her as Val (in a way that almost shocks the mayor, because nobody calls her Val) and indulges in the light chat of old friends catching up unexpectedly. But Mrs Webster remains unmoved, even distant. And, far from being flattered that he should remember her name, she is suspicious. She is wary of anybody with that kind of gift, if gift is what it is. And, as he moves further down the line, she shows no sign of emotional involvement, her pulse and the nerve endings of her being register no hint of sublimity.

Now, face to face with Michael — who (after having sat up in his armchair all night inwardly farewelling his Madeleine) is there, like the rest of the Centenary Committee — the shoulders of the mountain visibly relax. He knows he is shaking hands with the motive force that will propel him to power. For Michael, the lingering feeling (which will linger over the next few days, even weeks) will be an odd one. An odd feeling, in fact, that will accompany any future meetings with the 'Great' — that the 'Great' look so very human when you stand next to them.

After the tea and the biscuits, the mountain of Whitlam is wheeled back to the white Commonwealth car that carried him to Centenary Suburb, lowered into the back seat, and ferried back along the newly completed freeway to the newly completed international airport from which he came, all the way back his still, silent eyes roving over his domain and the change, everywhere in evidence, that signifies his time is upon him.

44.

The Moving Hand

The hand moves across the treated surface of the wall, sometimes slow, sometimes fast. But always moving. Mulligan, either reclining or standing on the scaffolding that he climbs each day up to his wall, seems to be both still and in a state of perpetual movement. As though he hasn't a minute to lose. As though the wall will crumble and fall before he is finished. And so the hand is always moving; even when pausing in mid-air, hovering over the surface of the wall, there is minute movement, thumb and forefinger slowly twisting the brush this way and that, as if the hand itself were thinking. At moments like these, the mind of Mulligan is emptied. He has (he fancifully imagines afterwards) no more thought for what is happening than a farm animal munching grass in a field. The moving hand is a thing unto itself.

The weeks, the months, the whole winter and spring have passed like this. In a trance. The jigsaw of faces and places on the wall all destined to come together into one whole picture, the nature of which only Mulligan knows. Only Mulligan has the studies of the public figures he is committing to the wall, only Mulligan has the sketches that reveal the full sweep of the picture. But even then, even to Mulligan, it seems that it is only this moving hand that really knows what is going on, and he, too, is a spectator, watching it, day by day, skimming across the treated surface of the wall, a thing unto itself, that seems to be moving, even when poised, thumb and forefinger slowly twisting the brush this way and that. Somewhere out there, on this mild spring morning, the Great Whitlam has come to Centenary Suburb. But this is of no concern to Mulligan and the hand that moves or does not move, according to its impulses.

Not that anybody actually sees either the hand or Mulligan at the end of it, for he works behind long drapes that fall from the top of the scaffolding to the floor. He arrives early in the morning and leaves late at night. Moreover, he barely emerges for lunch or breaks. Mulligan has found a world to which he can go each day. His own world. And he barely notices the one he shares with everybody else, or acknowledges anyone else's presence. Except when they come too close to his wall and his world, the one he will reveal to all of them when he chooses to let it go and open the drapes.

And those who walk past the shrouded wall, going in and out of the town hall offices — the mayor, the office clerks, Peter van Rijn and the various members of the Centenary Committee — have long since come to accept Mulligan's terms. He possesses an authority that was, at first, difficult to explain. But he had it. Then the mayor looked up to the wall in late winter and acknowledged that at some stage the wall had, in his eyes and those of everyone else, become Mulligan's wall. And the authority that they all accepted but found difficult to explain became recognisable as the kind of authority that someone has when they are speaking from their territory. Besides, in time, people had come to like the idea of a mystery in their midst. One that will reveal itself when the time comes. And the temptation to peek behind the wraps has been resisted, in the same way someone recognises but rejects the impulse to peek at the last page of a book.

What's more, it has also been recognised for some that this Mulligan is one of those who, more than likely, possess a short fuse. The eyes tell you that an explosion is never far away, and that he doesn't take kindly to people sticking their beaks into his business, opening their mouths to offer either comment or criticism. And so that world he is bringing into being spreads in silent majesty, day by day, across the wall for which Mulligan was destined and which is now accepted as his.

The moving hand of Mulligan moves on. Oblivious of the world around it. A thing unto itself. And Mulligan, either reclining or standing on the scaffolding, is a spectator to the designs and whims of the moving hand. But he also recognises that the time is approaching when he will part company with his wall, when it will no longer be his wall, and he will have to pull the drapes aside and give it back to the crowd. So he savours every day that he still has this world to step into each morning, for walls like this have a once-in-a-lifetime look and part of him is already contemplating how he will fill his days when the wall is gone from him.

45.

The Discovery of Speed (2)

'Take me with you.'

Mrs Webster is contemplating this run of ratty spring days and how they show no sign of blowing over. It has been a week since that Whitlam of theirs visited the suburb, and she puts this run of windy days (which sprang up the same day) down to him. It's all that hot air, she thinks. Then she eyes the sky and the estate gardens, stirred up by the winds, as if something more than just ratty weather were afoot. Rita's words, at first, are lost in the wind and the distant drone of a passing plane. Then, as quickly as it erupted, the wind drops. The small plane passes. A mid-week silence descends upon everything. Mrs Webster's eyes turn from the gardens and Rita's eyes are upon her, wide and expectant. The double doors of the garage are locked. She's closed those doors forever. She knows as much as she needs to know, as much as she'll ever know. But this woman's stare is fixed, even unrelenting, and although she has silently vowed that she never again needs to take that drive, she feels, somehow, obligated. She is wondering why she should feel this obligation, because Rita is not close enough to be called a friend, nor, Mrs Webster suspects, will she ever be. But she has, Mrs Webster silently confesses, implicated this woman, drawn her into her life. She has told her the kinds of private things that you would tell a friend, and, in the absence of just such a friend, she chose to tell Rita. Perhaps in the hope that the acquaintanceship would grow, or perhaps out of mere selfishness, out of the sheer need to speak. Whatever, there is a residual feeling of having used this woman, that having implicated her in her life, having drawn her into it, she cannot snub her. And, perhaps, this also explains Rita's long, direct stare. It is unapologetic. Uncompromising. As though, in some part of her, not consciously or deliberately reasoned, she has come to the conclusion that this much is owed her. This much is her due. For the service of having been the right ear at the right time, she has earned at least one request, and this is it.

Without a further word being spoken, without question or the need for explanation, Mrs Webster nods, simultaneously responding to the urgency and need in Rita's request, to a sense of doing what's right, and to a faint, niggling sense of quitting herself of a debt that she needn't have acquired.

With that, they stroll back to the house, quietly arranging the details of time and place, then part at the steps of the house as the wind springs up again, a sudden gust, a seasonal tantrum, scattering cloud across the sky and tossing fragments of the estate — leaves and buds — into the disturbed air.

The first thing Rita notices later that evening (a quiet Monday night, damp, cool and late enough for no one to be about) is the fit of the leather gloves on Mrs Webster's hands. They are skin tight — almost a second skin — and black and shiny like the car itself. She slips them onto her fingers with the unselfconscious expertise of a jet-fighter pilot or a burglar. Rita is not sure which. But she looks upon Mrs Webster now as if gazing upon a highly trained killer or a master thief, and a slight smile passes across her features. Rita knows her movies. She has known her movies since she was a teenager — in those distant days before the word 'teenager' was even invented. And because she knows her movies, because she spent her youth immersed in them (much to the disapproval of her mother, who forever told her that the movies were all right but they weren't life), she now feels as though she is in one, and the movies *are* life, feels as though she has been transformed into one of those ordinary types who find themselves lifted out of their humdrum houses and swept up into a world of drama and incident. And the darkness of the Webster estate and the silence of the surrounding suburb all add to the feeling of having entered a new dispensation — the world at night. That dark, quiet place that is governed by rules different from those that prevail during the day. She can feel the beating of her heart (something she rarely stops to even think about, let alone feel) and her palms are moist. At first she is not sure if it is fear or excitement that she's feeling, and then decides, noting that she has not felt the sharpness of fear or excitement for many years, that it is both. In short, she is alive. And, it seems at this moment, she could count the number of times in her life that she has felt this alive on one hand.

Mrs Webster's hand, that of the trained killer or the master thief, turns the key in the ignition and the car leaps into life. Immediately, it settles into an inaudible hum. The shiny black hands of Mrs Webster (who does not speak) turn the wheel with the lightest of touches and guide the car quietly down the gravel driveway of the estate, the way, no doubt, Webster would have guided the beast whenever it beckoned him. As they ease out into the suburb, the headlights part the night and they slowly, quietly, slip through the dark streets, down to one of the two main roads of the suburb, the same road that, apart from a slight dog-leg opposite St Matthew's Church, gave Webster his long, straight, uninterrupted stretch of bitumen.

And although the plan, the understanding, is to turn right at this point and drive to the new frontier out to the north of the suburb, where the excuse of a highway that runs through the thistle country can play host to speed the way the suburb once did, they don't. When they reach the intersection, the car pauses and Mrs Webster hesitates, her gloved, black fingers drumming the wheel. Rita stares at her, not sure why on earth they've stopped. Then, as Mrs Webster's head turns left, not right, she understands. And it is then that Mrs Webster glances at

Rita and says, quite simply and in a tone that suggests she'd rather not be disappointed:

'Well?'

Rita nods. And, as she does, she is not sure where the nod came from; whether she is deciding, or whether she has reached one of those points where events take over and you simply go with them. Mrs Webster acknowledges her response with the most minute arching of the eyebrow before turning her eyes back to the wheel, the windscreen and the intersection. And as the engine now rumbles with — it seems to Rita — unimaginable power, she lightly touches her seatbelt as if any second now they might indeed blast off, and that pale spring moon hovering above St Matthew's spire isn't so far off at all.

At first, speed is everything she imagined it might be. The sudden explosion of energy, the kind of propulsion she associates with rocket ships. And, even though she has never been on an aeroplane, there is a distinct feeling of being on the verge of taking off, of leaving behind the bitumen, the suburb and that part of the earth upon which it sits.

But, just when she fully expects this to happen, something quite odd comes over her. A strange sense of not moving at all. Or, at least, moving in slow motion. Can speed do this? Like those snap responses and actions — jumping out of the way of a passing car, falling from a bicycle. They are, looking back, over in less than a second, but at the time seem to go on forever — every detail, every constituent moment of that split second unfolding itself in slow motion to the most minute scrutiny. Can speed do that? Like film that is shot so fast that it becomes slow motion. Or the spokes of a wheel moving at high speed, yet looking like they're not moving at all. The noise of speed is all around her but at the centre it is silent. Mrs Webster is oblivious of her, lost utterly, given over exclusively to the task at hand. The cabin is still, the world at night glides by in easy frames as the film, the spool of her life, accelerates to the point where speed meets its opposite, where past and present clash, collide and cascade around her into a wondrous slowness. And soon, soon, she is seeing the suburb in which she has lived nearly all her grown-up life as she has never seen it before.

The bells of St Matthew's hang still and silent in the night. The party lights, blue and yellow, that permanently drape the cedar on the front lawn of the house opposite, dissolve into an emerald glow. In Rita's street, which runs parallel to them, over the rooftops and square houses, the young Bruchner once more beats his dog through Saturday afternoons that never end. Joy Bruchner's ashtray forever fills with the butts of her dreams, piling endlessly, as she reaches for a cigarette with her free, trembling hand even while extinguishing the previous one. She is both alive and long dead; stubbed her last butt, blown the last of her blue, filtered breath into the air. The dog is compost, yet forever howling. That was us, Rita murmurs. That was us.

A comet that never seems to be moving crawls across a long-lost summer sky at infinite speed, while Vic, Rita and Michael pause at a vacant paddock in the old street, in another life, before moving on. That was us. Mrs Barlow protests simultaneously to her husband and to the empty room she now occupies, alternatively screeching and sobbing, wretched with the same complaints she has always been wretched with: the house is too small, the street is all wrong, and the suburb is stuck out on the edge of the world. Why, why, why did he ever drag her here? That was us. So too the sound of Desmond Barlow hacking his lungs out into a bucket day after day, to the accompaniment of Michael's eternal bloody cricket ball ricocheting from fence post to fence post like a rifle shot. That, too, was us. And the house in which Rita lived out all these years (the house that they must surely now be passing) where everybody said things they never meant to say and heard things they were never meant to hear. That, too, was us. The house in which the married years, the mothering years, the working years, came and went, and which didn't seem much at the time, she now, in this wondrous, unfolding slowness, sees as 'us', all of us. That lost tribe. At once exotic, strange and utterly familiar. Gone. Wiped away by time and speed.

'Post-war' we were, although we didn't really know it at the time. And our children, our children who played and squabbled in these very streets barely days after the bulldozers had scraped them out of the sodden dirt and clay, our children became something called the 'baby boom' — you had to laugh at that one, all those booming babies — but we never knew that at the time. Things only get that neat afterwards. Things only get that neat when somebody who wasn't there looks back on your life and tells you what you were really doing, as apart from what you thought you were doing — just having a shot. Just having a shot at making things work and stuffing them up as usual. Just having a shot at being happy. Maybe not even happy, just happy enough. No, it wasn't neat. Things only look neat when you look back, or when you weren't there anyway, when you've got the distance (but not the days).

In the cabin of the car, in the midst of speed — Mrs Webster is utterly concentrated on the tasks at hand — Rita floats in slowness. Somewhere out there Vic is speaking words of love on a long-distant day. Wet kisses and wet words. And plans. Plans about the life they will live together, and which they have now lived — but which, in this wondrous slowness, is both done and waiting to be done again. As though, somewhere out there, this vast night of infinite possibility contains the chance of a miracle taking place — of finally getting it right. And what's been done is undone, and done again anew. Properly, this time. She smiles, a slow peaceful smile.

The golf course, all deep greens and fairways and bouncing white balls, floats by in a dream. The words of love all spoken, the wet kisses all spent, Vic once again stumbles from the golf-course gate to the home where Rita waits, through the years she calls her married years, which were always spent waiting, waiting for something she was always too tired to name. And Evie Doyle, opposite, even now, eyes it all through her venetians, although she's long since gone to heaven only knows where. That, that was us.

Houses rise and fall, at one moment gleaming with the promise of new paint, at another reverting to the vacant blocks, to the paddocks of thistle they were before the builders came along and the bare wooden frames that became houses were erected. And the bright tail of a comet that came to stay one summer, years ago, once again labours across the sky at the speed of light. And, though it doesn't seem to be moving at all, that inevitable evening strolling back from the station will always be there waiting for her when she will look up to the sky and discover that the comet is gone.

And it is then that the spell snaps and the world is rushing up to meet her. The end of the street is hurtling towards them. It occurs to her for the first time during the drive that it just might be dangerous. That their world is no longer wide, no longer young and can no longer accommodate this kind of speed. That the wrong car at the wrong time just might appear. Unluckily, in front of them. Anything could happen. They are, she concludes, being reckless. Simultaneous with this thought, a car, a bright yellow thing, appears out of nowhere, as if having dropped from the sky. Rita is, at the same time, aware of lurching forward in her seat. They *are* being reckless, and silly. The car's horn blares in the night, long and loud enough, it seems to Rita, to wake the whole neighbourhood. Mrs Webster's foot falls on the brake and the car majestically slides into the T-intersection at the bottom of the street. The speed goes out of the night. Soon they are idling by the side of the street. Trembling. Alive. Having just travelled Webster's road, where you could just as easily accelerate into death as into life.

Not long after, Mrs Webster pulls up at Rita's house. Inside the cabin it is silent. The hum of the engine is barely audible. And because there is either too much to say or nothing left to say, they say nothing. So that was speed?

The sudden sound of Mrs Webster moving in the driver's seat beside her brings Rita back. How long had she lingered with her thoughts? She has no idea. But, in Mrs Webster's restless shuffling movement, there is the distinct communication that they have lingered long enough. There is a brief nod from her. Nothing more. A nod. A duty dispatched. No smile, no grin. And Rita once again reads the unspoken thoughts of Mrs Webster. No more, the nod says. No more. Come no further into my life. We have been reckless enough. All of this Rita understands. They are too far apart, as separate from each other as that part of the suburb that lies beyond the boundary of the railway lines is from Rita's house. They have been a comfort, they have been a help. No more, no less. But for this alone Rita returns Mrs Webster's gesture, a slow, thoughtful nod of her own, with just enough gratitude in her eyes.

As Mrs Webster pulls out into the street, there is a sudden growl from beneath the hood, the briefest of ceremonial farewells, before disappearing into the night. Quite alone, on the still, smooth footpath, Rita turns to face the house that was once 'us'. The house that, simultaneously, will always be 'us' and yet not 'us' any more.

Rita is left with an overwhelming desire to be alone. Not to speak, not even to think. But to simply stand in her front yard and stare at the silvery rooftops, the paling fences, the trees and stars; feel the ground at relative rest beneath her feet but spinning madly towards the sun and whatever the day holds. My world, she marvels to herself. My world. From the golf course to the station, from the Webster estate back to the Old Wheat Road. A rectangle no more than a mile long and a half mile wide. Not much, but big enough to contain all their stories. And even as she stands, quietly marvelling at this vision of the street that fell upon her in wondrous slowness, even as she stands, drawing its many stories to her into one complete picture, there is also a vague sense of loss — both troubling and tantalising. A sense of having finally lost the thing she struggled against for so long.

They will all leave the suburb, and the place that was once theirs will become someone else's, the suburb itself someone else's suburb. But whoever they may be and however long they may stay, they will never have seen the thing born.

46.

The Art of the Engine Driver

The sub-tropical darkness falls suddenly. Out there, his little town is combing its hair, dousing itself in perfume and aftershave, and slipping into its dancing shoes. These are the cabaret hours, the hours to which the day was leading all along, that mark the conclusion of every day, and the Twin Town Services Club — nothing much to remark upon during the day — is now dressed in the glitter of its party clothes.

From his kitchen, while Rita waits to set out for Mrs Webster's estate and while Michael sits in his room contemplating that hour before meeting Madeleine for the last time, Vic has a clear view of the club and the lure of its lights. The beers from the pub at lunch and the beers that followed the conclusion of the day's golf are wearing off, no longer lift him, and there is a stale taste in his mouth that the fresh tea takes away. The club calls, the nightly dance of the cabaret hours, and the beers that will lift him once more. They'll all be there, the usual crowd.

Vic closes the door behind him and nods to the blinking eyes of the club. We have an appointment, you and I, the nod says. Every night we have an appointment. Your table, by one of the wide club windows overlooking the town, is waiting. Your chair. Your accustomed place that allows you a full view of everything that matters. Come, Vic, come to the cabaret.

As he walks down the hill, in short sleeves, for the night air is summer warm, there is music in his ears. Songs, the bits and pieces left over from all the other nights like this are playing in there, as if having gone into both ears and never quite come out, which is what happens to songs. And one of them in particular (which he heard that morning in his kitchen) won't go away, keeps nagging him, and he wonders why until he realises that the song (a light, sentimental thing like they always are) once moved him in the kitchen back in the suburb one bright morning long ago. And he now remembers the annoyance he felt then at being moved by a cliché. But cheap music does that. Takes you by surprise and gets under your guard. And he is annoyed once more, because some part of him is moved all over again. Only more so. And it is, he tells himself, because the song comes with baggage now. He is not simply being moved by a cliché any more, he is being moved by his memories of it, and the house which he left for which he now feels a sudden tenderness. The kitchen that he sat in then now appears to him, as he strolls down the hill to the club, in remarkable detail: the round green table, the smart new chairs, the servery looking through into the lounge room, the Laminex bench and the small plastic radio on it from which this song once issued (and he remembers telling Michael what a load of slop it was at the time) — this song that got under his guard one weekday morning years before for all the wrong reasons and became one of *those* tunes. The ones that come back at you with baggage when you least expect it and just when you thought you'd left your baggage behind.

Inside, it is the music he hears first. Each week it is a new singer — artists, they call them — and they all have names, but needn't have. They're all one. Male or female. It doesn't matter. They all say the same things, they all sing the same slop, and all manage to look the same. As Vic shows his membership card to the man at the door and watches other members signing guests in (as he himself did for Michael when he made his one and only trip up north to see the old man a few years before), he notes that this is the way it ought to be, after all. If each day is indistinguishable from the rest then so must each night.

In the main room he turns to where his table and his place will be waiting by the long, wide windows that overlook the town. And he can visualise them all, the same shifting crowd (retired bankers, teachers, builders and all the rest), without even clapping eyes on them. The same shifting crowd that comes together every night, the evolutionary history of which nobody remembers now. But it's distinctly possible that this crowd — albeit with different faces — has always sat at the same table. That the table has seen them all come and go. And it occurs to

Vic that if they were all assembled — all of them, from all the years — it is just possible that they all might bear a sort of family resemblance.

But even as he nears the table, he knows something is wrong. And he's not sure what it is. It's there all the same, though, and it's wrong. As he gets closer, he sees it. His seat. His spot is occupied. How? Everyone sits in their places. Everyone at the table knows to sit in any other place than his, the one with the unimpeded view across the town. It is, the table knows, a one-man seat. And nobody has ever made the mistake of sitting in it, until tonight. This stranger has slipped into his seat — and the table has allowed it to happen — while he was walking down to the club, contemplating cheap music and baggage. Of course it shouldn't matter, he tells himself. One chair is just as good as another. But these things can throw your whole night out, and it has.

The only seat available is against the window looking back towards the table and the whole roaring mass of the room with its piped music, laughter and poker machines. It is a view of the table and the room that he is unaccustomed to, but (once he was over his initial annoyance) it very quickly becomes an intriguing one. And, because the conversations around him are intensely animated and he can find no way into them, he is given a feeling of distance from the whole thing that he's never had before. Suddenly he is looking at the table and the room differently. More precisely, looking at his seat differently. The one that he would be sitting in right now if this stranger hadn't slipped into it while he wasn't here.

At first he resents this woman — whose name he is told upon sitting down but immediately forgets. And it isn't the fact that she is sitting in his seat; it is the way she is doing it. She is leaning forward talking to one of the usual crowd (a former banker's wife), in a flowery summer number with legs crossed, utterly oblivious of the casual manner in which she has done this thing which has never been done before. And, for a short while, this casual demeanour of hers is an affront — an insult.

Then something odd happens. The feeling of distance gives way to a feeling of invisibility. Which again, strangely, he likes. Vic is a big talker. He likes to talk, especially with a beer in his hand. And every night, at this table, in his usual chair, the talk and the beer flow in equal quantities. But not tonight. Tonight he is invisible. And the feeling is new, but good.

He watches their mouths open and close. At first he hears what they are saying as they drink their shandies, sparkling wine and beer and eat their — what do you call them? — pretzels. But at some stage, and it is quite early in the evening, he stops listening. He looks from one to another then settles on the woman in his chair. And soon he isn't even looking at her. He is looking at that anonymous steel chair, the padding of which, he imagines, has moulded itself over the years to accommodate his buttocks. And he falls into calculating the nights, the number of occasions he has dropped into it, but no one occasion stands out. A couple of evenings, good and bad, eventually surface. And it occurs to him that he could spend his life (or what's left of it) in that chair or one just like it and never really be able to distinguish one night from another, or one song or singer from another. That what's left of his life could pass in a routine blur until one night he either rises from the chair and never sits in it again, or sits in the chair and never rises from it again. People die in chairs as much as they die in their beds. And this chair of his, which until now had been acknowledged by the table as his and his alone, has the look of a chair in which someone could live a slow death. It is now that kind of chair. And he has never noticed before because he has never seen the table and the room from this angle and therefore never looked closely at his chair the way a stranger might. And he finds himself thanking the nameless woman who has so casually occupied his place and thereby given him this altered view.

And all the time a faint, nagging voice is saying — this isn't like you. This isn't Vic. Bloody Christ, look at yourself. Vic, the life of the cabaret hours, always the centre of things in your accustomed place, and here you are not even listening. On a hot spring night with your dancing shoes on and a glistening beer that mysteriously appeared before you — and you're not even drinking.

And it is then, while they are all engrossed, utterly lost in this talk of theirs to which Vic is not even listening, that he quietly departs, like a train giving the platform the slip. Before he knows it, he is out once more in the balmy night. Behind him, in the club, at his accustomed table, there is a space where had just sat. And at some stage the table will notice this space and ask each other if anybody saw Vic leave. And the space he has created will be an awkward one for a while, until somebody comes along. With that in mind, he ambles back up the road he strolled down only an hour or so before, and soon he is sitting on his doorstep, looking out over the town.

Then the breeze is upon him. He turns his cheek to it and he is driving again. The glow of a long-ago furnace illuminates the cabin and Vic has his head out the window, his freshly shaven cheek (shaved twice, even now, as he did every time before a shift) open and alive to the constant rush of air as the engine speeds through the night. His hair is blown back, his eyes aglitter. The beam of the headlight parts the night, the moon hovers over an open field, and, as he breathes it all in, the cinders, the cool air and the warm scent of freshly brewed tea, he is no longer Vic. He has simply become the moment as he always did when he drove from midnight into morning with the wind on his face.

Sitting on his doorstep, now oblivious of the view, he smiles upon the Vic that was. Was he ever so alive as he was then? And was his life ever so full of purpose as when he was doing, and utterly absorbed in, the thing he was born to do? Was he ever so complete as he was when he had it, this gift of the art of engine driving? For there was a time when he had it, a deeply privileged time when he had this thing to which he could go — in the mornings, evenings or whatever time the shift took him — and enter moments that were so complete he felt no need of any others.

And no matter where he goes, for all the grog and the way he stuffed everybody around, for all the bloody stupid drunken things he did just when things would be looking good, there is at least this to say of Vic in the end: that he once had it, this thing that enabled him to stand and stare up at the vast, indifferent heavens (as he does tonight) and not feel small. And it will always be a source of wonder to Vic that it was his job, his labour, that gave him this, and through which meaning entered his life. And as long as he can feel it all again as he does now, as long as he can summon it all up again, he can also remind himself that, once acquired, the art of engine driving is never lost or forgotten.

Out there, while Rita is discovering that at the heart of speed there is a wondrous slowness, the town has its dancing shoes on. But tonight it can dance without him. Tonight he is content with his memories, for they bring with them the reminder that he once had it. Something equal to the vast rolling eternity of this sub-tropical night, which the night itself acknowledges, and in recognition of which it now tips its hat.

47

The Last of Madeleine

They are careful. Both of them refraining from even the most oblique of hints that this is their last night together. He has lived the hour before meeting Madeleine for the last time. He has swirled the hot chocolate round and round in his blue, plastic mug for the last time. He has risen from his desk, upon which sits George Johnston (read, and waiting to be re-read and shared, but, oddly, not with Madeleine), the book that will give him a place to go when a place to go is needed in the hollow years afterwards, and has left the house to meet her for the last time, as though it were just another night together.

They talk in the same way as they always do, and their easy conversational manner is the manner of two people with all the time in the world before them. It is a quiet Monday night, not their usual night. Her plane leaves on Wednesday, their usual night. She is wearing new clothes — new jeans, flared jeans. Madeleine is not someone who wears jeans often, certainly not flared jeans. But tonight she is. She is wearing new clothes, new fashions, as if she were wearing a new self, the self she is taking away with her. And, already, this change is a hint of all the changes he will never see. That and all the other selves that she will wear and shed from now on, just as she will never know the various Michaels that he will put on and take off over the years. Or what this succession of selves — together — might have amounted to. They will never know any of this. They have known the days, and the days are almost over.

The evening passes in its usual manner (pizza, Italian soft drink) and soon they are sitting on the bed in his room, backs against the wall, holding hands and staring out through the French doors that open onto the balcony and look down over the street. It is a damp, cool start to spring and the windows are closed. They have, by now, given up talking altogether. It is enough to sit and hold hands, and contemplate the occasional passing headlights of a car or the street laughter of a world that goes on and will go on, indifferent to what is taking place in Michael's room.

He is, he knows, on the brink of something momentous. That longed-for ending, the only ending open to them, the one that has been waiting throughout the year, is at hand. Minutes away. And after the minutes come the seconds, and, beyond that, the margin that was before him will be behind him and the brink will have been traversed. And already he is reminding himself once again that pain, after all, is a red, red ball. And the trick of feeling nothing, when nothing is required, is still good, like the wise counsel of the child he once was who learnt the trick young, and, having learnt it young, never forgot it.

Soon they will each rise, leave his room, descend the stairs, close the front door behind them and meet their ending. And when they have, when they have enacted it and lived the last of the seconds they have left together, they will stroll right off the page of what has been lived and known and go their separate ways.

Michael has always been one of those who looks back on a moment even as he is living it. He closes the purple front door behind them and it is doors that he is contemplating: his, hers, and the length of doors that once opened and closed daily on his old street. The clear Nordic pine of Bruchner's front door, the dark rectangle of old man Malek's, George Bedser's that once opened to everyone in the street for his daughter's engagement party then clammed shut forever after. These doors, the doors of his life, they are all vivid. And he can, too, quite clearly, imagine himself at some distant point in time when this night is behind them, standing on the footpath some bright spring or winter's day, contemplating Madeleine's old front door, as it will be then, and the time they once shared. *How terribly strange to be seventy.* It is doors, the doors of his life that preoccupy him as they walk to the corner of his street (while Vic rediscovers the art of engine driving on his doorstep a thousand miles to the north of them, and Rita receives the gift of slowness), past Charlie's milk bar, closed and dark, then left to the bank corner where the taxis pass. They have pulled one door behind them, and are about to close another.

It is either late in the evening or early in the morning (neither of them is conscious of the time), the streets are deserted and a chilly wait in this cool, damp start to spring seems inevitable when the pale light of a taxi turns the corner. This is good. This is as it should be. No time to say all the things that ought to be said that are probably best left to silence.

It is upon them. They have used their allotted months, weeks, days and hours — and now they are drawing on the last of their seconds. This is how a year ends. The taxi pulls into the kerb outside the all-night petrol station. Michael knows it will take less than a minute for the whole thing to be over, that the presence of the cab, the only vehicle on the street, will hasten the process, hurry them when they might have lingered and said all the things that silence says better.

All night they have been on the brink of something momentous. They eye the cab, the dark figure of the driver inside, then return to each other, knowing without need of speech that this is as it ought to be — for the thing to be done quickly. From the moment she slips into the cab and closes the door, the dwindling of their time will cease and the whole process will begin again in reverse. For the momentousness of the situation is this: that it creates a before and an after. Old time gives way to new time. And in between they now each traverse this no-man's land in which they are simultaneously together and alone, two and one, the selves they have known and not known for the past year giving way to the selves they will never know.

They must have spoken, they must have said something to each other, they may or may not have embraced and kissed. He would assume they did, but, in the hours that will follow in his room, he will retrieve no memory of any such act. The only thing he knows for certain is that he is watching the last of Madeleine, her legs (clothed in the new jeans of her new self) disappear into the taxi as she slides across the back seat. The petrol-station attendant reads and smokes in his booth, the traffic lights change from red to green on a deserted intersection, and the taxi pulls swiftly out into the street. As it does, she quickly turns and glances back through the rear window and it is all as it should be, all written into their ending, this final glance. You'd have tired of me, it says. You'd have tired of my eyes, which you call green or blue, depending on how you choose to look at them, for their colour would become inconsequential. You'd have tired of my hair, which shines for you like gold in the morning sun now, but which you would cease to notice by evening. You'd have tired of my lips, and my kisses, and the whole of my body, which you have moved and troubled in ways that you shall never know, and which I would gladly have given you, if only for this — that you'd have tired of me when it was all done. Her face is sad and still, with that goodbye look in her eyes that she was always giving him and which she is now giving for the last time. And his head is shaking. Do you know me so little? But her stare is steady with sadness. You know you would, not now, but in that older, wiser heart that you carry with you and which will wake you one morning and tell you she was right, your Madeleine. In that older, wiser heart that will tell you that the boredom would have come, would have crept up on us day by day, until we became just like everybody else. And I couldn't have borne that because it's not our ending. I could never have borne watching us slowly turn into everybody else. I can with all the others that will follow — if they'll follow at all; maybe I'll live and die alone — but not with you. I could never watch *us* turn into *them*. *That* is their ending, not ours. Believe me, she knows what she knows, your Madeleine. I could have given it to you, the boredom of bedrooms that have given up, and given you their ending, not ours. But, look, I have given you so much more.

Her eyes remain upon him until the taxi disappears. The lights turn from green to red for nobody in particular, and when the taxi is gone he swings round to face the way he came and prepares to enter that part of his life that will be measured with such words as 'afterwards', 'since' and 'once'. It is done. He has lived a story. They have their ending.

48.

The Unveiling of the Crowning Event

The moving hand has ceased to move. The wall is done. The twain converged, and now their time is over. And only this thing, this product of their convergence, remains. This portrait of a suburb, currently shrouded in the same drapes that have covered it all winter and spring.

Mulligan, his job done, is not there for the unveiling. It is an early September evening and he is watching the spring sun slip down behind a line of trees in a city park. Nearby, a child is running from its shadow. Again and again. Trying to kick off these giant legs that dog its every move. But all Mulligan knows is that the wall is no longer his. Out there in the city the large march, this moratorium that swamped its streets, is over. The PA systems and the microphones have been switched off, the crackle of speeches is no longer in the air, the crowd has dispersed and disappeared into pubs, houses and parks. His wall will soon be passed back to the crowd and he has no desire to witness the exchange. Now he will have to find something else to fill his days, for the days will need filling. And if they can't be filled then he will have to decide what to do with them.

While he sits, and while the spring sun slips below the tree line of the park, the foyer of the town hall continues to fill. The mayor, wearing the suit in which he sat to be sketched; the sitting member; the entire council; Mrs Webster; religious leaders; shop owners — Peter van Rijn standing apart from the rest of the committee, a lemon squash in his hand; bankers; sporting figures; those the community deems as 'characters'; and the everyday faces of the suburb itself have all crammed the foyer for the unveiling of the wall.

It is their story and they have come to witness it. Their portrait. Now, and then. And the noise, it seems to Rita (who is standing back from the wall so as to see it better), is like Michael's descriptions of a cricket or football crowd just before a big game. And when the mayor and a number of nameless officials walk to the front of the hall where a lectern has been placed, the murmurs that accompany their movement are the same as the murmurs that follow the umpires out on to the field of play. Michael is not here. For, on this day, Michael and his kind have had their march. And this demonstration — a moratorium, they call it (whatever that is) — has shut the city down. The war, the war. Rita had barely heard of Vietnam before this war started, and now all she ever seems to hear is news of the war, and students like Michael, and demonstrations, like the one today, that stop the city. But that's always the way — you've never heard of a place until someone starts a war there, and then you hear of nothing else but that place.

So, as the hall settles down, Rita is thinking of other things, while Michael will no doubt be walking back from the city after this giant stunt of theirs with all those university types he calls friends. She doesn't even hear the introductory speakers, and only gradually becomes aware of the fact that the mayor is now speaking. And she is surprised, almost relieved, that he actually can talk in public. And the face of Mrs Webster, not far from her, has relief written over it too. For it is an occasion, an event, that demands ceremony. And as he talks, almost eloquently, Harold Ford, hand in his coat pocket where his pipe is, mayor of Centenary Suburb, eventually arrives at the subject of Progress. Here, Rita notes, Mrs Webster smiles. There is a line, he says, a straight line and a true one, that runs all the way from then until now. It is the thread that connects them all, generation upon generation, and which has produced the streets, shops, factories, schools, libraries and public buildings of a proud community. Proud enough to put this little number together. Proud, but not too proud. On and on he goes, transformed by his moment. For (to Mrs Webster, at least) it's almost as though it is not simply the mayor speaking any more, but all those portraits hanging in public buildings across the suburb, across all the suburbs, not so much portraits of people as portraits of the Age of

Progress. And for those people, the mayor continues (the collective voice of those portraits, the suburb and all the suburbs, the voice of the Age itself issuing from him), for those who might be tempted to smile at the very idea, to those young people not here today (and Rita cannot help thinking that he is referring specifically to Michael, who ought to have been here) let us pose them the question — was it so bad, this world we gave you? This world of trimmed lawns and modest gardens, of brick and timber block houses that have stood the test of time better than anybody thought, of paved streets and footpaths upon which you can stroll and survey this society that we — the Age — gave you. Was it so bad, after all? And was the single idea that fired our factories and lit our eyes with passion enough to bring this world into being really so amusing and so quaint?

And it is at this moment that Rita (noting that Mrs Webster is nodding in agreement) sees that the mayor has become what she can only call emotional, even sentimental. Which is odd, because she never picked him for the sentimental type. But there he is, his face quivering every time he utters the words 'Progress' and 'pride' and 'community'. And it occurs to her, possibly for the first time, that he just might believe it all, all this talk. And just as it has taken her by surprise, she suspects that it just might have taken him by surprise as well. That he had thought he simply trafficked in politics; never believed any of it. That he thought he would simply stand up, walk to the lectern, make a speech and sit down again. Just like all the other speeches. But something caught him out this time. A bit of emotion, an outbreak of humanity, the anarchy of which has ruffled his hair and tie.

As two council functionaries begin to pull the curtains back, the wall becomes a stage, the foyer a theatre, and a hush falls across the room as it does at the beginning of a performance. And it has power this thing, for the hush becomes a silence as a jigsaw of colour and form gradually begins to take shape. Soon the drapes have been pulled all the way back, and there, from one side of the wall to the other, is a grand tale. And as the crowd realises that this grand tale runs in a straight line from left to right, in much the same way as you would read a book, heads turn to the left and begin reading the images. From the very beginnings, open land, open country, just the way the leaders of the suburb imagine it all. But, not quite. For there are, in fact, figures on this landscape that Mulligan has created. And these figures, these earlier inhabitants, are hunting, fishing, painting, or simply standing still and looking over the valley out there in the old thistle country. People. Whole families. Just living. Just doing the ordinary and extraordinary things that everybody does. And the mayor is staring intently at the wall because this is not part of his grand story at all. Nor, it seems, is it part of Peter van Rijn's, because he is looking just as puzzled as the mayor. This is not History as most of those gathered in the foyer of the town hall understand it. No, History begins with an open field. Nobody in it. An open field, thinks Peter van Rijn, waiting to receive the footprints of settlers. Settlers who will carve something out of this open field, create a farm, then a community, and finally a shop. This is how History works. It begins with an untamed open country. Then people arrive. Not before.

But, as their eyes all move from left to right following the straight line of the story, these figures are no sooner in the picture than they are out of it. No longer there. Written out of the picture and written out of the grand story that it tells. The straight line of History is moving relentlessly from left to right. Settlers have arrived. Fences have gone up, farm houses where there was an open field. Then more fences, more settlers and houses. A community forms, is magically thrown onto the wall. And a shop appears. A fragile wooden affair that in Peter van Rijn's mind, at least, should have been where the story began, for a shop marks the beginning of settlement and the beginning of the suburb. The first of its hundred years. All the years that have led to this night. But it is there, nonetheless, this fragile wooden thing that heralds a community and brings to the community the gift of exchange.

And from the shop the narrative sprouts streets and houses and more shops. Progress is upon them. And Progress is rapid. For soon the flour mill rises from the ground, its twin silos like medieval keeps, dominating the land. And a railway, running in the same straight line as the story, appears on the wall. Stations and trains join houses and streets. And then the factory, low and wide like the cheap land it is built upon. Webster's Engineering. And Mrs Webster gazes in curious wonder as she notes that her life has been transformed into History. History as this painter sees it. And there is even a black Bentley on the wall, gliding through the streets of what is now undeniably a suburb, like royalty that has only just acquired its title. And it occurs to her that even though it will soon be torn down, Webster's Engineering will always be up there on this wall now. And that, at least, is something.

Soon, the streets are paved; tennis courts, the golf course, cricket fields and street after street of box houses, white, red, green and blue stretching out to the line of the horizon, all spring up. All filled with people, walking to or from the station and shops, serving and receiving in frozen motion on the tennis courts or forever chasing a red, red ball across a dusty cricket field when the time was theirs, before the time was taken from them. And standing at the end of it all a final frieze of figures: the mayor, Webster (drawn from his portrait), councillors, the sitting member and shop and factory owners (all of whom sat for immortality and now have it), all gathered at the end of the narrative, not so much individual figures as portraits of Progress. And all — it suddenly occurs to Mrs Webster, who did not sit — staring, not forward, not in the direction of the unwritten, out there off the wall, where Progress lies waiting to take whatever form it will. No, not looking forward, but backwards. While Michael, she reflects, while Michael and his friends have been out there in the streets of the city marching in this thing they call a moratorium, shouting and singing songs, the words of this Whitlam of theirs in their ears (this Whitlam, who talks to the whole country the way Michael and his kind talk to the rest of us), while they have been out there, this frieze of public figures has been revealed, upon this wall, to be looking not forward but backwards. Like — and the conclusion is inescapable — yesterday's men. And like yesterday's men they are forever now, upon this wall, facing the wrong direction.

And it's not just the direction they are facing. They don't look right. It's not striking. It's not dramatic. But it's there. In their faces, and their gestures. Something not quite right. A slight shift in the features, a wide-eyed countenance that borders on . . . what? After brief thought, the only word she can call upon to satisfactorily answer the question is 'silliness'. A wide-eyed countenance that borders on silliness. They have been made to look, and oh so subtly, just a little bit silly. Almost — and Mrs Webster seriously wonders if she is imagining this — possessing a hint of the inbred. And as she does, she notes the dark, gloomy eyes of the mayor, who is staring at Peter van Rijn (whose bright idea this whole business was) as if weighing the profit and loss of just one more brick through the shopkeeper's window. Mrs Webster turns back to the wall, the foyer now filling with sound, and eyes that final frieze of public figures, remembering those odd portraits of old European royalty that she has seen on her trips abroad (without Webster, who had no time for 'abroad' or its galleries) by painters whose only weapon was cunning, and who dared to leave behind portraits of kings and queens not looking quite right. And the same cunning, she is convinced, is up there on this wall. Barely there, but there all the same.

In the weeks that follow, this wall will, in fact, divide the suburb between those who dare to admire it and those who can't bear to look upon it. Between those who nod in quiet amazement that a thing such as this has entered their world, and those who, from the first, had formed such a distaste for the thing that they would happily see it erased. And as much as the mayor — and all the mayors that follow — will be called upon to wipe the thing off the wall and banish it from their midst, it will survive, and, in time, become known across the suburb simply as Mulligan's Wall. And eventually, even those who pronounced the thing an 'eyesore' will come to accept that the thing will stay, warts and all. For they'll know by then, the whole suburb, that they've got something no one else has. Mulligan's Wall.

Rita passes by Mrs Webster with a brief nod, the first time they have seen each other since their drive through the darkened streets of the suburb, and Mrs Webster nods quickly back. Rita leaves.

The foyer is now crackling with the sound of raised voices, laughter and squeals, the way railway stations crackle with sound. No, noise. And, unlike the noise that Webster brought to the suburb, it is an unwelcome noise. For, whereas Webster brought the noise of production, this is the noise of mere talk. Mrs Webster departs, leaving the jolly public face of the mayor behind her (wearing the best suit in which he sat for the portrait, and which is now up there on the wall), and, in the car park, passes a pensive Peter van Rijn, to whom she nods and who is pleased, even grateful, to receive her nod.

As she starts up the old black Bentley (now immortalised on the wall), and as she passes the thoughtful figure of Rita striding towards the railway station (although the walk is far, Mrs Webster does not stop), she is glad to be done with the whole place. Glad to be putting the ancient beast of Webster's Engineering down, glad to be selling up and moving on, without yet knowing where she is going. Glad to be looking forward and not back.

49.

The Sale of a Factory,
the Sale of a House

In the last, bright days of spring, when estate agents
pop to the surface like spring flowers, when 'For Sale'
signs and auction flags flourish in sunshine and sweet
showers, Mrs Webster watches one luminous Saturday
morning as the paperwork passes across the desk of the
mezzanine office and the factory passes from her hands
into those of a young lawyer representing a business
group from somewhere in Texas. This group own what
they call a chain of department stores. The suburb had
grown, its children had left home, the factory's workers
had aged with the factory and the suburb didn't need it
any more. In the brashness of its youth, the place had
required the noise of activity, the evidence of production,
of small and large parts being hammered into shape by
giant machines. Now it required department stores and
supermarkets. The factories had gone to the new

frontiers where the land was flat and cheap and the noise of Progress had followed them. Soon the acre of land on the corner of the two main streets of the suburb, that had been Webster's Engineering, would be cleared, the factory levelled as though it had never existed, and a department store with racks of cheap clothes, the wonder of drip-dry shirts, shoes, toys and all manner of knick-knacks that nobody realised they wanted but which they soon would, will take its place. It will be known simply as Walter's, and the new children of the suburb will grow up never knowing that it was once Webster's corner, where Webster's Engineering sat, as immoveable to the eyes of the young suburb as the pyramids. And when the new department store is built, the drapers by the post office, the clothing store by the station and the small shoe shop, all of which had survived until then, will disappear from the landscape one by one, and everybody will turn to the new department store for the things they both need and don't need.

As the papers pass hands in the mezzanine office, she hears Webster's noise die out there on the factory floor for the last time, and imagines the glazed eyes of the suburb strolling along rows of cheap suits, nylon shirts and the latest drip-dry trousers, and something inside her that was long in need of dying expires.

In the late summer, when construction on the store begins, one of the owners will descend upon the site, step onto it in the same wondrous way that the Great Arnold Palmer had once stepped out onto the fairways and greens of the golf course — a sun-tanned god come briefly to earth — and inspect (for the first and last time) the place they had bought. By then Mrs Webster will be gone, the noise that Webster brought to the suburb will have been silenced, and the beast of production that he had dragged into existence will have been put down, its machinists and staff either retired or gone elsewhere. And that portrait of Webster in his prime, hanging above the fireplace in the library, will become a portrait of yesterday's face.

The suburb noticed when Mrs Webster sold the factory, or, rather, that part of the suburb that had grown up with the factory. That part of the suburb that had grown up with its reassuring red-brick presence and cast-iron nameplate, a permanent centre to things, as permanent as Webster himself. An immoveable acre on a weatherboard landscape that drew strength from the brick-and-iron solidity of Webster's Engineering. Those who had grown up with all that noticed when Mrs Webster put the thing down; those who had been around long enough to assume that it — like themselves — would always be there noticed its passing as if a part of themselves had passed into local history with it. If Webster's factory could go then everything could — and there were no centres, after all, that could be trusted to last. The new residents of the suburb, those who had not grown up in the factory's shadow and shade, those who had barely noticed it in life, barely noticed its passing either.

The suburb didn't raise an eyebrow when Rita sold the house, but the street noticed. Even those who had only recently come to the street, those who never knew the history of the house the way the more permanent residents of the street did. And when people tramped through the place they, no doubt, pondered the secret life of the house. No doubt drew their conclusions. As though the private life of the place had been offered to the street, as on those hot summer nights years before when the house — like all the houses of the street — would turn itself inside out and furniture, lamps and televisions would tumble out onto the front lawn and the private life would be lived in public. Except back then, everybody's lives had tumbled out into public view together. The sale of the house had been different. It was just her house on display. And, as necessary as the sale was, it was still, above all, an intrusion: a final sufferance to be endured before she could finally quit the place altogether.

But with the house now sold, she tells herself, packing old clothes in boxes as she contemplates moving back to *her* city, the city on the other side of the river, it is the last time she will suffer the eyes of the street, the last time she will suffer them looking suspiciously upon her house and its French windows, which, like her dresses, were always just a bit too good for the street and which the street recognised and registered as an insult.

And there is a detachment in the way she goes about these preparations that Rita finds curious. For, the house that was once 'us' is no longer 'us'. She is packing up other people's lives. And those small objects — once-favoured tea cups — those things that ought to move her, and which would have moved her just a few years before, now leave her strangely untouched.

She's become, she notes, as distant from the whole business as Michael — or Vic, for that matter — and she never thought she would. One day, she'd tried to tell herself throughout those final years, one day this will all be a memory. One day she will look back on it all as the 'past'. And all the things that matter so much now won't matter then because they will be distant things. But as much as she wanted it all to fade into the past, there was always the nagging feeling that there was something, well, indecent, not right, about simply rising from your chair and walking out on it all.

When things end, you don't just get up and go. At least, Rita doesn't. Not that she knows what to call that interval between the ending and the leaving. Last respects, perhaps. Respect for what they were, and what they tried to do. She only knows she would not have it done any other way. Vic, Michael, they're the types that just get up and go. And while part of her admires that, part of her thinks they miss something. For in their haste to be rid of the past, they forget to say goodbye to it all. Or neglect to linger long enough for a proper goodbye to be said. Rita is one of those who cannot move on and leave that distant world of the past until she has lingered long enough to say goodbye properly. And perhaps this is what the last few years of waiting about the house have been for.

Now, the moment has arrived. She has said her goodbye in her own way, and in her own good time. The leaving can start and a beginning can be created out of an ending.

*

Not far away, Mrs Webster sits in the library of the estate, the books that Webster collected and never read, but which she did, are all around her. The portrait of Webster that was not really a portrait of Webster but a portrait of the Age hangs above the fireplace. That was our age, she muses. We *were* Progress, only we didn't know it then. But the world we made in our own likeness is changing around us and will soon be no longer recognisable as the world *we* made. Progress will wear drip-dry trousers from now on, light on the legs, cool in summer, and it will not stop and it will not look back in the way that we too neither stopped nor looked back.

It is late in the evening. That morning, the factory officially passed into the hands of the new dispensation, and she has gravitated towards this room to be alone with the portrait. She leans back in the swivel chair that was once Webster's and breathes them in, the last hours of Progress.

Not just now, and not during the dark hours of the night, but on the Monday morning, when the doors of the factory will remain closed, this world will have changed. Outside in the sleeping suburb, the machinists and staff who, for most of their working lives, drove and walked to Webster's Engineering, will not go to the factory any more. The clerks, accountants, and foremen will not go any more. Nor will Mrs Webster. And, within weeks, the red-brick monument to another age and its cast-iron nameplate will come tumbling down. She eyes the portrait. We dragged the Age into being with heat and molten metal and giant machines and tiny objects that meant nothing by themselves until they became part of a greater whole — we did that. We changed the world around us; now the world around us has changed and us with it. Made us the past and turned the faith that fired our factories into a set of quaint, old-fashioned beliefs.

You knew all this, and that's why you chose to go, to go while we could still call it our age. To go while those great machines of ours still pressed metal and tin and whatever came their way into the shape and face of our age. To go while we still had it in us to shape the times, before the times shaped us and gave the world a different face. That noise, that incessant hammering, those feet that marched to and from the factory floor, those hands that grasped the levers that crushed the scrap — that was us. But it's not us any more.

She rises from the chair, whisky in hand — her step betraying the slightest hint of unsteadiness — and paces slowly about the room. Already, it has the look and smell of rooms that belong to other times, old times. These trophies (tennis, from the days when she first laid eyes on Webster and saw in his eyes and his actions the utter, unquestioned conviction that his time was upon him), these books (which she has read, but which Webster, a browser not a reader, only ever flicked through), these framed photographs that captured their days, will soon have the dust of History upon them. And while there are those who are content, at a certain stage of life, to let the dust settle on their days, Mrs Webster is not one. And she never will be. As she finishes the whisky, she notes the unsettling thrill that comes of stepping out of your Age and into the uncertainty of a time that doesn't yet know what it is.

Part Five

Envoi

50.

The Time We Have Taken

T he time we have taken is no more or less than it takes for a dreamer to roll over in bed and wake from the dream. No more or less time than it takes for a suburb to be born and grow, for its streets and footpaths to be scooped out of the paddocks of old farms and wild thistle country. No more or less time than it takes for a factory to appear, flourish and fall into decline because time has moved on. No more or less time than it takes for a summer to come and go, or for a comet to pass across a suburban sky, looking as if it were standing still, frozen up there in the stars, when, in fact, it is moving at infinite speed. The time we have taken amounts to no more or less than that.

Michael is currently sleeping in his room; the street below is still and dark. He has gone to sleep with Madeleine on his mind, but in the moment before he wakes, in the first light of the summer's morning, he will once again be walking down the old street. Eleven or twelve, he will always be walking down the old street and wearing his best summer shirt with the button-down collars that he had forgotten all about until this dream retrieved it, his father just ahead with his ear turned to the sound of a distant engine, and his mother beside him in a floral dress that is just a bit too good for the old street. The sky will glow the colour of ripe peach and they will, all three, be pausing at a vacant paddock, staring at the gently swaying khaki grass. And they will stand like this forever after, because the dream will always hold them just so. It will take them in. And they will always stand like this, preserved in dream. No one will move or speak. And there will be no fates to be met because nobody is going anywhere, everybody safe and forever as they are inside the dream. It will be so clear and true that he will enter it and live it, as he did then when he walked the same street as a child and the suburb that he has now left was being born.

And while his son sleeps, travelling towards the luminescent moment of that dream, Vic sits, long into the night, on his doorstep overlooking the town, driving again, his freshly shaven, clean cheek turned to the sea breeze, at his most alert and alive, his most complete, wanting for nothing. Let us leave him exactly as he is now, seated on his doorstep, but in the cabin again of one of those dirty, filthy engines that he complained about all his life, without which he was lost. Let us leave him as he was, as he now is and will always be, an engine driver. His head leaning out of the cabin window, cheek to the wind, the engine's big wheels beneath him, turning, spinning through the night, its headlamp, like the light in his eyes, bright and strong enough to see clear into the next morning.

And Rita, unable to sleep, places the remnants of the old life into boxes. The remnants of that glorious shot at living — photographs, letters, and an old cigarette lighter that still flames — all packed away. Boxes that already have the look of boxes that will never be opened again. And while Rita sees this, there is also a Rita who registers the secret thrill of knowing that when the house is behind her and she steps out into the street for the last time, she will also be stepping into whatever it is that lies before her as well. And that very uncertainty will be a beginning, because the 'us' that lived there is now 'them'.

When everything is settled, when everyone has gone their separate ways and finally stop long enough one day to glance back, one day when slowness is upon us and time allows the view, the question we will ask is the question that will nag us again and again and again: did we hear the music of the years? Did we see the fiddler's hand, bowing it higher and higher through days emblazoned with wonder, or were we looking away?

The house, the yard on summer nights, the passionfruit vine where the spider indifferently spun its web, the street that started bare and filled overnight with weatherboard box houses and gardens that bloomed while you watched, the open farm land that hovered for a few years between town and country, the dances, the songs, the tennis, the cricket, the coming and going back from station, work, school and home, throughout the years that saw a suburb born — that, that exotic tribe, was us. And the time we have taken, our moment.

Acknowledgments

Many thanks to the following for their help during the writing of this novel:

The Australia Council for a New Work Grant (Established Writers) in 2005.

Shona Martyn, Linda Funnell, Jo Butler and Denise O'Dea at HarperCollins, and my agent Sonia Land (and all the gang at Sheil Land) for their support and enthusiasm.

Finally, my special thanks to Fiona Capp for her constant help, suggestions and advice during the writing of the book. And to Leo — the lion-hearted boy.

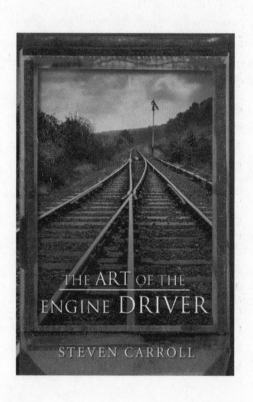

THE ART OF THE
ENGINE DRIVER

STEVEN CARROLL

THE ART OF THE ENGINE DRIVER
STEVEN CARROLL

Shortlisted for the 2002 Miles Franklin Award

On a hot summer's night, the old and the new, diesel and steam, town and country all collide — and nobody will be left unaffected.

As a passenger train leaves Spencer Street Station on its haul to Sydney, a family of three — Vic, Rita and their son Michael — are off to a party. George Bedser has invited the whole neighbourhood to celebrate the engagement of his daughter.

Vic is an engine driver, with dreams of being like his hero Paddy Ryan and becoming the master of the smooth ride.

As the neighbours walk to the party we are drawn into the lives of a bully, a drunk, a restless girl and a young boy forced to grow up before he is ready.

The Art of the Engine Driver is a luminous and evocative tale of ordinary suburban lives told with an extraordinary power and depth.

Praise for Steven Carroll

'Carroll endows ... the mundane with a curious convincing urgency.' Andrew Riemer, *The Age*

'Carroll writes with a powerful control that left me moved, shocked, even devastated.' John Hanrahan, *Overland*

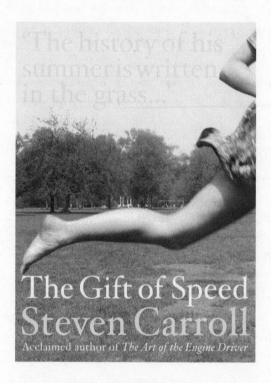

'The history of his summer is written in the grass...'

The Gift of Speed
Steven Carroll
Acclaimed author of *The Art of the Engine Driver*

THE GIFT OF SPEED
STEVEN CARROLL

Shortlisted for the 2005 Miles Franklin Award

In 1960 the West Indies arrive in Australia and Michael, who is sixteen, is enthralled. If, like his heroes, he has the gift of speed, he will move beyond his suburb into the great world ...

As his summer unfolds, Michael realises that there are other ways to live. When the calypso chorus accompanying Frank Worrell and his team fades, Michael has learnt many things ... about his parents, a girl called Kathleen Marsden, and about himself.

The Gift of Speed is a masterful blend of story-telling, memorable characters and a uniquely Australian sensibility by a novelist at the height of his powers.